A Novel

Time and chance happen to us all.

All the best,

LORI KNUTSON

Lori Knutson

© 2014 by Lori Knutson

All rights reserved. No part of this publication may be reproduced, stored in a retrieval system or transmitted, in any form or by any means, digital, mechanical, photocopying, recording or otherwise, without prior permission from the publisher and/or the author, except by a reviewer, who is permitted to quote brief passages in a review.

www.loriknutson.com

Cover art and interior design by Dean Pickup

Printed and bound in United States of America

ISBN 978-0-9866662-2-3

Library and Archives Canada Cataloguing in Publication

Knutson, Lori
Denby Jullsen, Hughenden / Lori Knutson.
ISBN 978-0-9866662-2-3 (pbk.)
I. Title.
PS8621.N88D46 2014   C813'.6   C2014-902087-2

This book is a work of fiction. Names, characters and incidents are products of the author's imagination. Some location names are real, but these locations are not depicted with historical accuracy. Any resemblance to actual persons, living or dead, is purely coincidental.

For Marci:

It was like you were with me the whole way through.

And, as always, for Doug

ACKNOWLEDGEMENTS

While I spent a lot of time alone while writing this book, it wasn't written in isolation. Ten years ago, Marci Copes-Genereux generously read through a not very coherent and only somewhat interesting first draft and lent me her insights. More recently, Ed and Mary Carson read through a much more polished version and told me, "Everyone in Hughenden had outhouses in 1935, Lori." I'd like to acknowledge the Hughenden Public Library and the Alberta Legislature Library for making available to me *The Hughenden Record*, Hughenden's weekly newspaper for so many years. I have Dean Pickup to thank for the cover work, the interior design of this novel and for the playful magpies that adorn it. My publisher, Tim Nordin of *birdfoot* Press, has been of help and support in countless ways, and he also understands the joys of rural life. Faith Farthing kindly agreed to have her staff take one last look at the manuscript before printing, and for that, I am grateful.

"Like fish taken in a cruel net, and like birds caught in a snare, so mortals are snared at a time of calamity, when it suddenly falls upon them."

~ Ecclesiastes 9:12

The Hughenden Record, November 27, 1935—Hardisty RCMP reported that the body of Denby Jullsen of Hughenden was discovered late on the afternoon of Sunday, November 24, in an abandoned vehicle south of Hughenden. The non-operational vehicle was located in a field off of Highway 13. The body was discovered by James W. Nillsen who had been hunting in the area. Mr. Nillsen became suspicious when he spotted several magpies flying in and out of the open windows of an abandoned car near where he was tracking deer.

Mr. Nillsen told *The Record*, "The birds caught my attention. When I walked toward the old car, I right away saw someone propped up in the backseat." The body of Denby Jullsen was identified by a slip of paper in his jacket pocket that read *Denby Jullsen, Hughenden*. There was no other identification found on the body…

— *Chapter 1* —

REMEMBERING

A mile and a bit from where he walked lay those train tracks that ran on parallel into the future until they just disappeared. Every morning since he'd come back home Cully Jullsen had heard that whistle call out in the distance, moaning low. Often it spoke to his brothers and to some of the other desperate young men who'd lost sight of the future. Only on that particular morning did it invite him. He resisted and veered away from the Siren sound, left the dirt of the driveway and crunched his way over the dry brown grass towards those hills to the west.

Cully walked up one gentle slope and then down another. At the top of the next treeless knoll, he sat facing northwest. The ice was gone from the lake and the water was low. This damn drought was just settling in the year he'd met her, a couple of years after King lost the election. Cully thought that with that election nothing had changed, that they might as well have voted in a scarecrow to take King's place. You could squeeze more money out of one than out of Bennett, Cully was sure of that.

He wasn't certain that he wanted to stay home when he returned in the spring of 1932, but thought he'd try to get some work where folks knew him. He'd wait out this slump they talked about then maybe buy some land after he'd saved up a bit. It was Ellie who finalized his decision to stay on.

He'd met her when he first arrived home and went to work for the Whitlocks. Before leaving the Hughenden area for the north he'd worked a bit for them—repairing fences and helping to harvest. When he returned, it made sense to approach Mr. Whitlock first about work. That was on a Saturday morning. He started work on the farm that same day. As Cully sat on the hillside, he remembered.

Cully rapped on the screen door through which he could hear bacon frying and the soft rattle of pots and pans. He was surprised when instead of Mrs. Whitlock a pretty young woman came to the door, wiping her hands on the faded apron she wore.

"Morning," he greeted her. "Mr. or Mrs. Whitlock around?"

At the sight of him, Ellie Pedersen froze and all the moisture left her mouth. For an instant not long enough to kill her, her heart stopped beating. Even in his work clothes, hat in hand and standing on the back stoop, Cully Jullsen was the most handsome man she'd ever seen. About six feet tall with sharp blue eyes and dark hair cut short, and for the moment, all his attention was on her. Held in place by shyness, Ellie felt the heat of his gaze and the warmth of his words.

"He's…he's out checking on the cows. They're calving." The words sounded stupid to her. Of course, Cully would know that. He's a farmhand, after all, but Cully just smiled and stood patiently on the other side of the closed screen door waiting to be invited in or sent out to the pasture to join Mr. Whitlock.

Finally Ellie pushed open the door and stepped back. "Where are my manners? Please, come in. Mr. Whitlock should be in any minute." Without asking, she reached out, took Cully's hat and hung it from a hook mounted on the wall by the door. She motioned to the set table and its four empty chairs. "Have a seat. Would you like some coffee?"

"Sure. That'd be good." Cully slid a chair out and sat down. His eyes stayed on her, slightly crinkled at the corners from sun and wind, and he continued to smile. "What's your name?"

Heavy steps on the back stoop made both Ellie and Cully turn. When Edward Whitlock spotted Cully Jullsen in his kitchen he greeted him with an extended hand and a hearty pat on the back. "Cully! How have you been?"

Cully stood up from his chair and shook Mr. Whitlock's hand, telling him, "I've been just fine, sir. Came back here looking for some work. Of course, I thought of you first."

Cully sat back down at the table and Edward Whitlock shrugged off his coat and hung it from a hook next to Cully's hat. At the table, he pulled out one of the heavy chairs and settled into it with a bit of a groan.

"My hips aren't what they used to be. Arthritis." Ellie set a mug down in front of him and he poured cream into his coffee, skipping the sugar, and stirred it slowly. He took a deep drink before setting his cup down and asking Cully, "You able to start today?"

"That's what I planned on doing." Cully went on to explain, "Just got back from working at a tie camp up north, pulling logs out of the bush for the CNR."

Edward Whitlock smiled appreciatively. "Hard work. How's your mom keeping? She still living in town? Sorry to hear about your dad. That was sudden." He shook his head and took another good drink of coffee. "It's been a bad year here. Birdie'll be glad to have you around."

As the two men drank their coffee, Whitlock organized things in his head and Ellie cracked eggs into a hot cast iron skillet. As Ellie slid two eggs onto each of their plates, Edward Whitlock spoke. "There're two things I need done right off. I want you to come with me and check on the cows out in the pasture, see if any are close to calving. Seems they're all coming at once this spring. And then I'll need you to feed the ones I already got in the corral and barn. Most in there are calved-out and the rest are mighty close so check on that first, before feeding."

Ellie set a bowl of fried potatoes and a plate of bacon on the table between them. "Will Mrs. Whitlock be joining us for breakfast?" she asked.

"She's got a headache this morning, Ellie. She'll be down in a while," answered Mr. Whitlock. He looked at Cully and added, "You can see the missus at lunchtime. She'll be glad to lay eyes on you again."

"It'll be good to see her, too." During breakfast, Cully thought about how he wanted to get to know the cattle he'd be working with right off. Cully wanted to get a feel for the girls, their breed, their temperament, whether they were easy or tough calvers. But he thought more about how he wanted to get to know this Ellie girl.

After breakfast the two men walked out into the pasture. About thirty cows stood in the dust and straw outside, eight more in the barn stalls. Mr. Whitlock was over a quarter ways through calving out his herd of a hundred and fifty. He had Herefords and that was fine by Cully. He'd worked a lot with Herefords. Not the easiest calvers but for sure not the worst, either.

The grass crunched beneath their boots as they walked under a cloud-free sky. The wind had finally let up that day, and it felt good to be out. Something in wind sucks the energy right out of prairie people. That was one thing Cully hadn't minded about working in the bush. There was no wind. It was dark, lonely and cold, but still, no air running past your ears to nowhere, drying out the land and making you edgy.

"Dry," Cully commented.

"Yep. Sure is."

While they walked, Cully glanced over at the hills to the north covered in scrawny, struggling trees but bright green with new growth. He wondered what the tent caterpillars would be like this year? It wasn't unusual for them to strip the branches bare by June. "You been on this land a long time, haven't you?" Cully asked Mr. Whitlock. He knew, but Cully liked the way Edward Whitlock told the story and so he listened again.

"This place belonged to my father. He bought it in 1900 and moved up from Idaho in oh-two to farm it." Mr. Whitlock chuckled disbelievingly. "That's more'n thirty years ago already. Hard to believe. Seems like only yesterday that I helped him plow that first field. I was young so it felt like an adventure. But it didn't to my father. He would've been forty-five or so years old then. Helluva time in your life to consider building up another farm in another country." Edward Whitlock took off his hat and wiped his brow with his sleeve. To Cully the morning air still felt cool.

"Ellie worked here for a while?" Cully already knew the answer to this, as well. She'd told him back at the house, but it seemed like a good question to get the conversation steered in the girl's direction.

"You know her from before? She's from Hughenden," Mr. Whitlock told him.

"No. Just met her today for the first time." The young farmhand stooped down to pick a long, dry piece of grass and broke it apart as they walked, letting the pieces fall onto the ground.

"Nice girl," Edward Whitlock added. "Yeah, she's been with us for almost two years now, I think. Pedersen family. Good people. Came up from Idaho, too."

"She's probably spoken for?" Cully felt really obvious

asking this question, but it was what he really wanted to know. The older man didn't seem to think anything of the question and simply answered it.

"Nope. Free as a bird, far's I know." Mr. Whitlock shielded his eyes from the sun and pointed straight ahead to the herd of red and white cows, indicating one on the very edge off by herself. "See that one. I think she'll be next. The wife and me call her Dora. Real gentle and a good mother. We'll bring her in as soon as we're done checking."

Right then and there, Cully knew he was going to ask that Ellie girl out—the sooner the better. She had good legs and a soft voice, and there was something about her that was different. Refined, perhaps, but not quite there yet. Ellie would be. She seemed to want something better for herself. So different than the girls Cully Jullsen had known both up north and down south in those camps and towns along the way, girls with dirty fingernails and rough talk. They were easy to get and hard to keep—not that Cully had intentions of keeping any. They were company, that's all. Mostly just a beer-blurred jumble of strong perfume, skin and that kind of loving that feels only a bit better than lonely and that makes the lonely sharper when it's done. Except for Darlene. Now her Cully remembered.

Darlene Sinclair worked in the tie camp just outside of Hinton where Cully had spent two winters—the years he was twenty-one and twenty-two. Her dad was a foreman in a different camp, one a little further east and north. That's how she got on cooking in that creaky shack for the crew of teamsters, sometimes a dozen, sometimes six. The work was cold and hard, and lots of guys didn't last.

They were mostly young, fifteen or sixteen years old, most of them strong as horses themselves but lacking staying power. Always looking for easier work, better pay. Cully was that way at first but he quickly learned that there isn't such a thing. Most times, work was what you made it. You put your back into it and the days went faster and the work got easier. If you were lucky, more money would come from the work you put in but not usually. Not in those days, anyway.

    The first time Cully met her was a day late in February, warmer than the rest of the month had been—including January. The guy who had been cooking for the crew got burned badly. Bare-handed, he'd grabbed the handle of an iron skillet that had been in the hot oven. Maybe he was in a hurry, or just not thinking. It was Roy who heard him scream, and it was Roy who smeared a glob of lard over that blistering skin, wrapping the cook's right hand tight in a clean tea towel. That cook had some kind of a French name. Cully had only been in the camp a couple of weeks before the cook's accident—the accident that brought Darlene Sinclair into the camp.

    She was a little out of place in that rough camp. When Cully first saw her, Darlene wore pants, like a man, a heavy plaid jacket and boots, and she was chopping wood. Her hair and skin reflected the sunlight in a gentle sort of way as she swung that axe. The blade struck the log she'd set upright dead in its centre. The log split into two neat halves, each falling into the deep snow on either side of the chopping block. Right then, Cully's heart should've known its own fate.

"Good aim."

Darlene Sinclair turned to look at Cully, still holding the axe in her left hand, fresh snow from the night before up past her boots. The cook's replacement smiled, eyebrows arching. "Thanks. You get good with practice."

"Stan brought you in?" Cully asked her.

She kept on smiling. "Yeah, this morning. He's my dad, did you know that?"

Cully nodded. Roy said Stan was going to ask his daughter if she could fill in. She laid her axe over top the wide stump she used as her chopping block and held out her hand.

"I'm Darlene."

The skin on her face looked smooth and young, feminine, but her hand was like Cully's: rough and calloused. Strong, too.

"Cully," he told her. "Good to meet you. We were getting hungry out here in the woods. What's for supper?"

"Bread dough's rising now—thought we'd have beef stew. Not many vegetables besides potatoes and onions. Got a few carrots. Should be all right."

"All right? Frenchy never made bread and we ate more'n our fill of bacon and eggs for breakfast and supper. Sometimes fried egg sandwiches for lunch, too. I'd just about marry you for a thick piece of bread spread with butter and jam," Cully teased her.

She laughed softly, like the snow falling down from high in the treetops. Like that. Cully could barely hear it, but he thought it was the prettiest sound.

Darlene did up the top two buttons on her coat and

told him, "I gotta go see if that bread's risen." She gave him a sideways look and grinned, "Especially if it might mean a marriage proposal." And off she trudged back down where the path, now obscured by the latest snowfall, still lay tramped down and out of view beneath the snow. Between the woodpile and the cook shack, her feet left two sets of prints, one coming, one going, both shadowy blue in the tumbling sun's glow. Cully's eyes stayed focused on her until she reached the shack. Then he looked at Darlene's axe lying there across the stump and thought about her perfect aim.

They used to do it in back of the cookhouse sometimes, Cully Jullsen and Darlene Sinclair, when Cully could sneak away and Darlene wasn't busy preparing meals. He'd unbutton her pants and she'd kick off one boot so that she could get a leg free. Cully would sit her on the countertop between two piles of dishes, one washed, one dirty, and she'd hang on tight around his neck, so tight that when she got close, his air was cut off for a moment. He thought it was worth it, though. If Cully was going to die, her choking him and moaning deep in her throat was a good way to go. The thought of getting caught never crossed their minds. Probably, they didn't care. Why would they? They were just kids.

One afternoon, when they'd just finished making love and with Darlene still sitting on the counter and Cully still standing between her knees, he asked her, "You like this tough work? These tough guys? Doesn't really seem to suit you." Cully lifted his hand to brush away the hair that was stuck there on her flushed cheek.

"Could be worse. I like being outside and Stan...Dad can always get me jobs. So I never have to look for one myself, which is nice." She smiled and Cully felt warmth fill him.

"What does your mom think of you being all the way out here in the bush like this? She must worry that someone will take advantage of you. Someone like me." Cully teased her and stepped in closer, nudging the bare insides of her thighs with his own. She looked away.

"Mom died." Darlene swallowed hard so that Cully could see a lump of emotion move down the length of her throat.

"Sorry to hear..."

She cut him off and he could tell immediately that she didn't want his sympathy. Cully thought that sympathy seemed to sting her almost worse than grief. Darlene told him, "Stan takes care of me and so I take care of him. I owe him that much."

"I don't know that you owe anyone anything. Especially your parent for taking care of you," Cully said.

"Without him, I'd die."

Tired of Darlene not looking at him, Cully reached out and cupped her jaw. He turned her face to his and repeated slowly, "You don't owe him anything." As soon as Cully dropped his hand from her face, Darlene looked away again. Just like that, she was gone from him.

Cully wasn't the only one who'd been involved with Darlene Sinclair. Cully felt he should've known this by their conversation that day. Unfortunately, he didn't understand until he caught them himself. Cully was not a man who regretted many decisions or actions, but remembering this, he tasted the copper flavour of self-loathing fill his mouth. Each time he remembered, he thought about how he still hated himself for failing her. Cully assumed that even if he couldn't have saved her, he'd feel a lot better now if he'd at least tried then.

Darlene and Cully hadn't planned to meet that day. Neither of them thought they'd have time. The crew was supposed to head up to the road with a load of logs and they were all ready to spend overnight at the top if necessary. The crew members had tied their bedrolls to the sweaty backs of the draft horses and Darlene had packed them plenty of food to take along—sandwiches, oatmeal cake and cold tea. The men would be well-fed. There was a cabin up top, built by the CNR just for the tie gang, for when they needed shelter for the night, which happened often enough.

At first, things were going so smoothly that Roy thought the guys might not even have to stay overnight, that they might make it back down to sleep, but Cully knew that was pushing it. It could be the easiest haul ever but that didn't change the fact that it was a mighty long one.

They trudged along through wet snow clear up to their knees still, and it was already April. The land of Eternal Winter. Cully led Shank that day. He was a good work horse but a mean one. He'd nip your thigh soon as look at you. You could tell he liked to pull, though, like he needed the work, like it gave him a reason to be. Cully had met a few horses like that since him, but Shank was by far the most determined. Down through the years,

Cully thought he had met more lazy horses than hardworking ones. He considered that horses were kind of like people that way. Some were really ambitious with an aim in life, and most just did what they needed to in order to survive.

The group was moving toward the steepest hill when Cully heard from somewhere behind him the unmistakable shattering, splintering crack of a runner splitting then breaking apart followed by "Oh, shit!"

"Whoa, Shank! Whoa." Cully planted his palm in the middle of Shank's chest and planted his feet, too, before the horse would stop. "What's going on? Runner gone?" Cully yelled to the back toward the origin of the racket.

Roy yelled back from the rear. "Damned if we didn't lose 'em both—nearly. But the right one's gone for sure. Left's cracked pretty good, but it might hold together! Shit!"

Cully stood there pressing hard against Shank, now with his shoulder, running the risk that Shank may succeed in somehow biting the top of Cully's head. The horse didn't, but Cully sensed clear as anything that he wanted to, felt Shank's impatient breath coming in hot bursts against his ear. Finally, Roy told the men what they needed to do. Cully knew already, but it was Roy's job to tell the crew, a job Cully judged he did well.

"Well, boys, guess we'd better unload the whole damn lot." Then, one more time, for good measure, "Shit!"

They arrived back at camp late that afternoon having eaten Darlene's oatmeal cake on the return trip. The men had left Roy with the sleigh while they headed on up the hill to let someone know that the load had been lost, that they'd bring it up maybe tomorrow but probably not until the next day.

Back at the camp when the other guys invited Cully for a pre-supper game of cards in the bunkhouse, he told them "later" and made his way to the cookhouse. He half-expected to hear Darlene chopping wood but, as Cully got closer, he didn't hear her axe cutting the air or splitting wood. He strode around to the front of the kitchen and pushed open the door, looking forward to the expression on her face when she saw him, back early and unexpected.

Darlene was surprised all right, and so was Stan. He pulled himself out of his daughter from where she was bent over the countertop and jerked back quick, tripping over the big bucket of melted snow water behind him. Darlene didn't look at Cully. Instead, the girl just buried her face in her hands, and the water sloshed out of that bucket, spreading slow across the floor. Cully turned around as if he hadn't seen a thing.

So it was that Cully joined the bunkhouse card game after all, skipped breakfast and lunch the next day, and helped to repair the sled's runners, working fast so that they were able to head back out by one o'clock that afternoon. The crew stayed that night at the top. For Cully, the night was sleepless, made restless by the cold weight of his guilt and anger. Cully didn't return to the camp with the rest of the crew. On the prairies, spring was setting in and he knew he could find work on a farm some place a little farther south, a little closer to home.

It was for sure Ellie's softness that caused Cully to like

her right off. Both her face *and* hands were so soft. He wouldn't know how soft the rest of her was until their wedding night, like it should be. It wasn't just her skin, either, but also the way she talked and moved that seemed so gentle. Cully remembered wanting to move into that soft gentleness, settle in, sink in, and never come out.

It wasn't hard for Cully to ask Ellie out. He succeeded in doing this just one week after they'd met. She was leaving work, walking down the driveway and he was just coming in from the field.

"Hey, Ellie." Cully sped his pace to catch up to her. "Going home?"

She nodded and squinted at him against the bright sunlight that her hat brim didn't quite block.

"Mind if I walk you part way?"

"You'll be late for supper." Was she trying to get rid of him? He persisted anyway.

"Doesn't matter this once." Her cheeks were flushed and her eyes were bright.

"It's up to you." He could read people pretty well and it seemed that Ellie wanted his company but didn't want to seem too eager. Cully trusted his instincts.

"Then I will. Can I take that for you?" He gestured to the cotton sack she carried that held her good shoes, and Ellie willingly handed it over to him.

"Thanks."

"Hot out again, eh?"

"It wasn't bad in the house. You're dusty." She pointed beneath her own nose to show him where the dust was under his. Cully swiped at it with the back of his hand.

He'd been snorting dust all day long cultivating that desert. Tomorrow, he'd suggest to Whitlock that he let the rest of that field go to grass.

Cully grinned at her, eyes flashing blue. "I'm going into town this Saturday night. If you're not busy, would you want to come along?"

She looked at him and then at the ground before replying, "Can I let you know Friday?"

"Sure can," he told her amiably. "I'm going either way, but I'd like to have your company."

When each Monday arrived, he'd ask her again and she'd put him off until Friday and then say "yes." It was a game she played and he didn't mind because he picked Ellie up every Saturday night that year in Whitlock's wagon. (Except that week in February she was down with that bout of the flu, but they were engaged by then anyway.) By the time spring rolled around, he was staying for supper at her mom and dad's each Saturday evening before going into town, and sometimes he'd get invited to Sunday dinner, too.

Cully sat there amid the rustling grasses and in the increasing wind thinking about those nights spent sipping Coke floats at the drugstore and walking up and down those boards, looking into the shop windows. He was always careful to be a gentleman, understood that Ellie needed him to be that. Near the beginning of August he'd tried holding her hand in the wagon on the way home and she'd let him. It was a triumph, that kind of closeness.

He'd watched his mom for years yearn for that kind of respect from her husband, the kind that Cully was now intentionally giving to Ellie. He'd seen that treating women better made them better women. Not that there was anything wrong with his mom, Birdie. Ask anybody and they'd tell you that she was kind and generous. She gave to her church and to her neighbours and friends.

But when Cully was a kid, he'd heard her tears too many times late into the night and seen too often the black rings of worry and sleeplessness under her eyes. She'd made it work, his mother, held that family together with every fibre of her being and despite the antics of her husband which threatened to rip them apart. The life they had wasn't what his father wanted, and it wasn't something he could manage, a wife and a family. So he didn't even try. Instead, he left Birdie to somehow pull them all through.

He went out and drank all the time when they were kids. They didn't know anything different. Lots of times, his late evenings allowed them late evenings, too. With Birdie busy and their father gone, often the three boys would head outside to the backyard or venture even further. Sometimes they'd go down to the slough on the outskirts of town where they'd launch their homemade raft long after their schoolmates were tucked in and sound asleep.

The night Cully recalled now, their father had come home very late—well after they'd all gone to bed. Sometimes he didn't come home at all and sometimes he passed out quietly. Then it wasn't so bad. But that night, Norrie Jullsen did come home and did not tumble into a safe, drunken sleep. Instead, he raged. It was probably a whiskey drunk. They heard harsh words between he and their mother, voices breaking like glass, sharp edges piercing, slashing at the thin membrane of peace that surrounded the house in which they lived one block west of Main Street.

Alice dove under her bed, a cot in the corner of the room farthest from the double bed shared by her three brothers. The boys didn't hide, didn't even pull the covers up over their heads, but all three pretended to be sleeping, slowing their breathing and closing their eyes. When Norrie Jullsen flung the door open, that's how he'd found them. He didn't seem to notice that Alice wasn't in her bed.

"Wake up, you little bastards!" He tore back the covers leaving the boys lying exposed in the pajamas Birdie had sewn for them the Christmas before. "Your old man wants to talk to you!" He plopped down onto the edge of the bed. "Must be nice to have someone lookin' after you all the time without havin' to do nothin'. I coulda done so much with my life if it weren't for you and your mother. Coulda been anythin'. Stead, I'm tied to here." He jabbed his finger at the mattress. "Y'know, you wouldn't have any place to live if it wasn't for me. You wouldn't have this bed or food on the table. You'd have nothin'. You'd be nothin'." Norrie Jullsen shoved that same tobacco-yellowed finger into Cully's face. "You *are* nothin'."

Norward sat up from where he lay between his older brothers and stated angrily, "That ain't true. Cully *is* something."

Norrie Jullsen's burning eyes focused on his youngest son, the one named after him. "You talkin' back?" Without warning, the back of his large hand caught Norward across the bridge of his nose and droplets of his blood spattered across the front of Denby's pajama top. Leaping up from the bed, Norrie Jullsen clenched his fists and screamed at them all, "Don't you talk back to your provider—ever!"

The next day, while her husband slept it off, Birdie walked Norward to Doctor Stromquist's office, telling him that her youngest son had taken a fall from a tree. Harold Stromquist, decked out in his white coat, pushed the bone painfully back into place, taped up Norward's nose and pretended to believe Birdie's story. The middle-aged Harold Stromquist thought he saw the truth in the little boy's eyes, dull in the purple-black rings that surrounded them but the doctor didn't say so. Instead, he gave the five-year-old a lollipop that swirled with colour. The previous spring, the doctor's own brother had gotten two ribs broken in a tousle with Norrie Jullsen. The fight was most likely as much his brother's fault as Norrie's, but the doctor thought that Jullsen did have an unreasonable temper.

As he sat, Cully's ears began to ache from the unrelenting wind on that low hill, and he considered the possibility that his younger brother may have really hit that grain elevator operator with a baseball bat. Did Norward have it in him to murder someone? Next, Cully wondered how much kids were like their parents, how many parental traits offspring could escape and how many were unavoidable. He felt that he'd outrun his father's legacy or at least had inherited some of his more positive attributes. For example, Norrie Jullsen had an unaccountable patience with animals that he clearly lacked with people. Perhaps it was because animals couldn't talk back, as Norward had done all those years ago. Norrie Jullsen had been an excellent stockman, and folks would often hire him to help effectively and gently break their horses. Cully had that same talent.

Cully's father had also been good with his hands and could build nearly anything out of wood. That tiny house in Hughenden had only one bedroom when he'd purchased it in 1919, and right away, he'd built the second bedroom, the one his kids shared. It was horse breaking and those temporary carpentry jobs that helped to keep Norrie Jullsen's family's head above water—if barely. Some of Cully's abilities resembled his father's, and every day he hoped to God that that was where the comparison ended.

— *Chapter 2* —

THEN COMES MARRIAGE

Cully had waited for this a long time. It gave him a reason to scrounge up enough money, save what he could as quick as he could, so that they could get married. Once, and only once, had he tried to have her. He remembered that now. Cully and Ellie had been on a picnic a few of months after the two had met. He'd brought her to Czar Lake, and after they'd eaten the sandwiches and pie she'd packed, they'd lain in the hot September sun beneath the spreading, drooping dust-grey branches of the poplar trees.

Ellie lay with her eyes closed, her wide hat resting across her chest, her ankles crossed. Where the sunlight came through the quivering leaves, it dappled her face, her bare arms. She looked so welcoming that he'd bent to kiss her lips. And she'd let him, received him with some measure of willingness that Cully misread as full consent. He ran a hand, rough from work and sun, down her rounded thigh and then up her dress. She shrieked her outrage and sat up fast, the floppy hat tumbling into her lap.

"Get your hands off me, mister! Who do you think I am? What'd you bring me out here for? I thought you liked me!"

He sat up fast, too, immediately hating himself for his misjudgment. "I do *like* you, Ellie. I'm sorry. I really am. I don't know what got into me. Don't cry. Please. I'm sorry. Don't go, Ellie. Please. Talk to me. Where're you going?"

"I'm walking home. You stay away from me." Her hat was back on her head, and she strode away from him, leaving the picnic basket and blanket there in the shade. Cully saw her lift her hand to brush a tear away, and he ran to catch up with her. Desperate to halt her retreat, he gently grabbed her wrist. With full force, Ellie yanked her arm out of his grip and whirled around to face him.

"Don't touch me!" she screamed at him.

Cully didn't know what else to do. He fell on both knees and told her, "Ellie, I don't want to live without you. I love you. I really love you."

He wasn't sure until that moment, but as soon as the words were out, he knew they were true. "I love you. Will you marry me?"

There they stood on the soggy lawn outside of the United Church manse and on the edge of a new life they could only imagine. Avoiding the large patches of half-melted snow, the couple, he in black, she in white, posed for long minutes in front of the car borrowed from the Whitlock's. The photographer, all the way from Killam, fiddled with his camera until he had it perfect, but by the time he did, their smiles were false and forced. Years later, their grandchildren would see that picture and mistake their grandparents' stiff looks for uncertainty.

Ellie felt her white satin heels sinking slowly into the earth beneath last summer's grass and felt his large hand resting comfortably on her hip. Against her thigh, she clutched the tiny white purse that her sister, Stella, lent to her because it matched her shoes so well. And her dress, the ruffled hem about three inches above her ankles, showed off these pumps that had cost as much as the wedding gown itself. As soon as the picture was taken, Ellie would put on her sweater as the late afternoon chill was freezing her bare arms.

"All righty, folks. I got it now." Timothy Regent said cheerfully, "Say 'Cheese!'" Neither of them said anything, but they both smiled. With a blinding flash, Ellie and Cully's April wedding day was frozen in black and white time. As with everything, time would gradually fade the photograph.

Ellie turned to look at her new husband. She'd always have the picture, but she wanted to remember him this way, too. His dark hair slicked back and up from his forehead, cut drastically short and way above his ears on the sides. Cully had let Stella to cut it just that morning. She said it was the latest style for men. Stella would know.

If she could've seen into the future, Ellie would've known that the newlyweds wouldn't have clothes this new on their backs for another eight years. But as it was, the future gleamed, and she felt happy.

Back inside the manse, a slightly flustered Mrs. Andersen cut a large slice of cake for each of the four young people left at the house and set it before them. Spice cake with brown sugar icing. Cully lifted his little dessert fork, glanced around the table and, seeing that neither Reverend Andersen or the others were digging in, set it back down. Ellie sat with her hands folded in her lap, the little white purse tucked beneath her chair by her feet.

"Everybody want coffee?" Mrs. Andersen asked them, a constant smile between her ruddy cheeks. When coffee was served and cream and sugar had been added, the Reverend finally lifted his fork. He smiled a tight smile at the newlywed couple before taking a bite. As he swallowed, Daniel Andersen asked them, "You two have a place lined-up?"

Ellie looked at Cully and, again, he set down his fork. "Yes, sir. We talked to Royland Johnson, and we're going to stay in that house he's got for rent out by Hughenden Lake. It'll do for now."

Reverend Andersen followed his bite of cake with a swig of coffee from a flowery cup that nearly disappeared in his large grasp. He said, "There's not much around right now. And what there is isn't much, it seems. Got some work for yourself? That's another thing that's hard to come by."

Cully felt the hairs on the back of his neck rise along with his irritation. He cleared his throat and answered, aware of the strain in his voice, "Well, guess I've been lucky, Reverend. Been on at the Whitlock's for the last couple years." Hadn't he mentioned that just prior to the ceremony? That he had work? He'd also talked to Andersen on those occasions when he met up with him in town and at church. He knows where Cully works and knows he works hard, too. So why the questions? Was the Reverend trying to make the groom look bad in front of his new bride?

"Cully and Ellie met when he went to work for the Whitlock's. Did you know that?" Stella piped up, setting her coffee cup down, her fork poised in the air above her cake. Mrs. Andersen lifted her eyebrows and looked at the others over the rim of her own cup, full, red lips ready to sip. "Is that right? So you two've been courting for two years?" She waved a plump hand in Ellie's direction indicating that Ellie should be the one to answer.

"Almost exactly." Ellie's cheeks turned pink, and she took a hurried sip of her coffee, dabbing at her lipstick with her napkin.

"That's a nice length of time." Mrs. Andersen solidly patted her husband's thigh beneath the table and with an air of exaggerated confidentiality, leaned in towards the two young couples. "Daniel and I were engaged for six years before he finally had his schooling out of the way and could find the time to marry me." Everyone at the table laughed politely at this, everyone, that is, except the Reverend Andersen. He shifted in his chair and crossed his arms tightly while his wife went on, "I always say, he needed to marry the church before he could commit to me."

"That's enough, Helen." The Reverend's voice was stern, his eyes hard, and when he returned his attention to his guests, his eyes barely softened. "You were fortunate to have such good weather for your big day. There was talk of a crow snow. Henry." Reverend Andersen riveted his eyes on the big, quiet man seated beside Stella, who, until then, had managed to escape notice. "Are you still working with your father?"

"That's right." Henry, Stella's boyfriend, made steady eye contact with the Reverend Andersen, challenging him, until the clergyman's eyes shifted to Stella. Henry had won. He wouldn't let the good Reverend shake him today. Having been stared down by Henry, Daniel Andersen continued, "Pretty soon it'll be your turn. Why don't you set a date today, since you're here anyway?"

"Well, I don't know...we..." Stella looked at her boyfriend and then back to Reverend Andersen, but Henry interjected sharply.

"Not today, Dan," heavily emphasizing the preacher's first name. "We're not getting married for a while. Thanks, anyway."

It was Cully who broke the hollow silence that followed this exchange between Henry and Reverend Andersen. "Well, this has been great." He stood up and extended his hand over the table to the Reverend Daniel Andersen. "Kind of you to have us in, but we've got to get to Mom's. They'll be expecting us shortly." At Cully's lead, everyone else stood, thanking Mrs. Andersen for her hospitality and shaking her hand which caused her upper arm to wobble back and forth. The four young people nearly tripped over one another as they rushed to make their way to the front door through the cluttered living room. None of them wanted to appear rude, but all of them wanted to get out of that house.

Mrs. Andersen replied, "Oh, you're welcome, kids. Any time really. We always like it when young people drop by so don't be shy. Take care, now." She stood alone on the step, waving and smiling as they piled into the Whitlock's car. Mrs. Andersen breathed in the air outside of the manse and watched the black Packard drive the three blocks up the hill until it turned the corner towards Birdie Jullsen's. On the step, the Reverend's wife sadly reviewed her own life's course. She breathed in deeply, freely one last breath before turning back inside and letting the door close resolutely behind her.

Driving down the muddy road to his mother's house, Cully leaned over Ellie, whose head lay on his shoulder, and kissed her on the mouth. "How're you doing?"

Ellie smiled up at him. "I'm fine," she said, snuggling in closer. The two in the backseat, giggled and tickled each other on the drive, the wind picking up and tousling their hair.

The rice that wasn't allowed in the manse was tossed generously when the bride and groom burst in through Birdie Jullsen's front door. Every available chair in the house and others brought along by family members lined the living room walls wherever space allowed. Unnecessary furniture such as plant stands and end tables had been temporarily stowed in Alice's bedroom. A mountainous collage of coats and sweaters had appeared on Birdie Jullsen's double bed and would remain for the evening.

Birdie took her new daughter-in-law into her expansive embrace and held her until Cully said, "All right, all right Mom," laughing. "Don't smother my bride. That's my job." When Birdie pulled away, holding Ellie at arm's length, there were tear streaks down her face. She grabbed one of Ellie's hands and one of her son's. "I love you both," then squeezing tighter, added, "So *much*."

The air was warm with the aroma of roasting beef, baked bread and strong, strong coffee. There were countless more hugs to come, and congratulations and best wishes peppered the air. The newlyweds were not used to this much attention and sometimes caught themselves looking at the floor or at the ceiling, trying to escape for a moment the feeling of being on display. Still, they couldn't deny friends and family the happiness of an occasion to celebrate. It was their gift to the people who loved them.

When the evening had wrapped up, Ellie and Cully stayed to help with the dishes ignoring Birdie's protests. When most of the mess was cleared away, they accepted a final cup of coffee and a second plate of the wedding cake. Ellie's mom had made the cake and now the five of them, three in-laws and the new husband and wife, ate tiredly and contently at the kitchen table. After the last of the hugs and congratulations, Ellie and Cully were finally met outside the door by the freezing night air.

The groom opened Whitlock's car door for her, and Ellie got in gingerly, careful not to dirty the hem of her dress on the Packard's running board. Cully went around to the other side and got behind the wheel while Ellie adjusted her dress and toyed with the bobby pins that barely held her hair in place.

"Well," he said, grasping Ellie's left hand and giving it a matter-of-fact squeeze maybe a bit too hard, perhaps a bit too nervously. Cully smiled. She smiled back at him and moved in closer, sliding across the seat. "Well, yourself."

"Sleepy?" he asked as she laid her head on his shoulder.

"Mmm-hmm. You?"

"Yep. Beat."

They both fell silent for a bit, then she softened against her husband and Cully wrapped his arm around her, pulling Ellie even closer. Clouds had obscured the moon and stars, and the road was swathed in blackness. The car's narrow tires broke the wafer-thin layers of ice that covered the puddles that formed in the deeper ruts of the dirt roads. This caused a series of musical splashings to bounce up from under the car and out into the night. The municipal government hadn't the money again last year to put down any gravel and probably wouldn't for the upcoming year, either, so those ruts were bound to get deeper still.

They pulled up in front of the house, and Ellie got out on the driver's side. She let Cully close the car door. Hand in hand, they walked to the house slowly, breathing in the night air, gulping it down as if they hadn't breathed for long minutes before. Doing her best to dodge the puddles she couldn't see that dotted the under-used driveway, Ellie still managed to step into depressions deep enough to fill her shoes. She held tight to Cully's hand and thought that she'd wasted money on silk stockings, chose between them and a veil. Chose wrong.

"Oops, watch yourself there. Lots of water. Hard to see, isn't it?" Cully let go of her hand and guided Ellie by the elbow up onto the boards and bricks that served as the front stoop. He opened it for her as a gentleman should, but they walked across the threshold.

"Hang on," Cully said. She stood there blindly while he disappeared into the dark of the living room and, with the strike of a match, instantly reappeared in the soft yellow glow from a candle. "I haven't had much of a chance to clean the place up. Better leave your shoes on. Want some water?" he asked.

"Please." *Hadn't had a chance? No kidding.* To Ellie, the place didn't look any different than it had on that muddy Saturday a week ago when Royland Johnson had given them the grand tour. As her eyes adjusted to the dim, she noted that the same beer bottle poked its neck out from under the same worn bench in the corner and that cigarette butts still littered the soiled floor. Ellie sighed.

"What's that for?" Cully handed her a clean jelly jar of water, same as the one in which the candle stood.

"Pardon?"

He pressed, "The big sigh? It's about the mess, right? I haven't had any time, El. I told you I didn't think I would."

"No, it's not that." It was the first of many lies married people tell each other so that they can stay married. The roof of Ellie's mouth was dry. She took a deep swallow of the water and tried not to look around, focusing on him instead. "I'm just tired. Besides, you're right. Neither of us has had a chance." She forced a smile and reminded him, "Now we've got all the time in the world."

Ellie started to hand the jar back to him but instead of taking it from her, her new husband touched the back of her hand lightly, suggesting, "Why don't you bring that into the bedroom in case you get thirsty in the night?"

Before she could agree or disagree, he surprised her by snuffing out the candle, scooping her up into his arms, and carrying her like a child through the living room and the kitchen, and up those dark stairs to the bedroom. She wasn't sure if it was because of the fluttering in her stomach or the picture that remained in her imagination of the crushed butts there on the floor from the first time they'd been shown the bedroom, but Ellie felt sick. Holding on tight to her water jar, she pressed her eyes shut with her free hand. Cully saw her hand over her eyes and thought she was playing coy. He took the jar from her.

"That's right. Cover your eyes, missy, and keep 'em closed till I say you can look." She shuddered when Cully laid her on that narrow bed, remembering the bare, rusty wire and unstable frame that Royland Johnson had showed them. At least now there was a mattress. Ellie could feel it under her shoulder blades. She heard him strike the match, smelled the sulfur, saw the soft yellow light seep in between her fingers to touch her eyes.

"All right. Go ahead and open them." Ellie took her hands away. Cully stood at the foot of the bed pulling off her shoes in the lantern light. "Your pretty stockings are all dirty. I probably should've carried you. Sorry, honey." He sounded so sincere, disappointed in his judgment. "I wasn't thinking." Without removing the silk stockings, Cully began to massage the bottoms of his wife's feet. This was the first time that anyone had touched Ellie's feet like this. It made her feel uncomfortable. This was to be a night of firsts.

"Wow," Ellie said when she propped herself up on her elbows and looked around the room with its one window and sloped ceiling. "What happened here?"

He chuckled. "I paid Kathleen to come in and clean our honeymoon suite and to make a few things. You know, to spruce it up a bit so we could spend the first night being comfortable. You like it?" Cully placed his hands on his hips and scanned the room critically. He was pleased with the work his mom's teenaged neighbour had done. The kid had really made the place cozy.

Ellie ran her hand over the quilt. Not new, but it was clean and patched where it needed to be. She pressed her hand flat.

"Where'd you get the mattress?"

"It's not a real mattress—just a straw tick I got cheap. Kathleen made this cover for it," Cully confessed.

"You bought fabric for her?" Sounding impressed.

"No, but I gave her the money to pick out what she needed. She's young, but she's already good at sewing."

"I can see that." Ellie looked at the bedroom window, narrow and tall, the bottom pane built to slide up and over the top one in order to open. There was no screen. In the window hung white sheer curtains tied loosely back with broad yellow ribbon. "Did she make those curtains?"

Cully shook his head and explained, "Got them from Mom. They're old. Kathleen had to re-sew them to make them fit the window. Got the ribbon from Mom, too. Nice, isn't it?"

"Yes. It's a really nice touch," she assured her husband. "I like that lamp, too."

Ellie touched the base of the kerosene lamp on the nightstand by their bed. It had come from the Whitlock's attic, an early housewarming gift from them; it was the first of many essentials they would give or lend to the young couple in the years to come. The nightstand was the same simple apple crate that Cully'd had beside his own narrow bed at the Whitlock's. One of Ellie's mom's old tablecloths, once sharp white, now lightly ivoried by time, was draped over it. Cully lifted the corner of the cloth.

"Look here, Ellie," he said to draw her attention to the inside of the crate. There, lined up tidily as if on a shelf, she saw seven or eight hard cover books. "If you've got books you want to read at night, you can keep them here with mine," he offered her, sounding conspiratorial, like the books would be their secret.

She smiled up at him from where she lay on her side, propped up now on one elbow. "Thanks. Maybe I will," Ellie told him. And for the first two years they were in that house, the couple kept the crate as their nightstand, and Ellie's childhood Bible stayed beneath it all that time, sharing space with her husband's cowboy novels and history books.

Ellie reached up to remove the bobby pins that were jabbing into her scalp. She set them on the nightstand and that's when she noticed the pillowcases. "Hey, how'd these get here?"

Cully smiled. "You can thank your sister for those. When I told her that Kathleen was cleaning our place, Stella said she'd steal anything out of your hope chest that we needed. Kathleen asked her for pillowcases, and she got pillowcases. Got this too." With his chin, Cully pointed down at the floor. Ellie peeked over the edge of the bed to see that her husband was standing on the colourful rag rug she'd made that winter two years ago when the temperature had dropped to forty below zero for nearly three weeks. She remembered the rug as the project that kept her from going stir-crazy those long, oppressive evenings.

Ellie conceded, "I like it here by the bed. It's bright. Cheery." Even in the lamplight, Ellie could see that this room looked substantially more livable than the rest of the house. From where she lay, the new bride could see that Kathleen had swept and washed the floor, scrubbed down the walls and cleaned the windowpane and sill. On the wall by the door hung a picture that Cully admitted had come from the church bazaar, a pastoral print of sheep grazing on a nearly emerald green hillside. Birdie had found it.

Cully stretched his arms out above his head and yawned. He told Ellie, "I'm going to make a trip to the outhouse. There're some slippers and a nightgown in the closet there for you. From Stella—again." He cleared his throat and rubbed the back of his neck. "There's a pot under the bed." With that, the groom was gone, leaving behind the kerosene lamp for her. He'd make his way outside in the dark.

Ellie sat up and swung her feet over the edge of the bed onto the rag rug. It was cold. Any heat that had risen over the course of the day into that little upstairs room was dispersing rapidly. She walked over to the closet and peeked inside. Sure enough, there hung her warmest, newest flannel nightgown. In that moment, she didn't know which was more important: new or warm. Both, she supposed, on her chilly honeymoon night. On the floor were her crocheted slippers, a gift from her grandma back in Idaho. Perfect.

By the time Cully re-entered the room, her clothes were neatly folded on the paint-chipped chair and Ellie was safely under the covers.

He said, "Hi. I made it back. You under there somewhere?" he teased her, pulling off his shoes just inside the doorway. Cully walked over to the closet and placed his shoes beside hers. From beneath the covers, Ellie giggled and to her own ears, it didn't sound like her. She never giggled. Stella was the giggler. From the closet's top shelf, Cully brought down his own pajamas and changed right in front of her.

"Move over, cutie." He looked down at her, her face illuminated by the lamplight. "You're beautiful." Cully smiled. "Cold?"

Ellie shook her head. A nervous heat that she would not tell him about flooded her body and brain. "Not now." Ellie flipped back the quilt, wool blanket and sheet to invite him in. The bed frame creaked under the weight of them both. They cuddled up close to each other. The old bed didn't allow for anything but closeness, and their bodies quickly warmed the space beneath the covers.

Cully stroked her hair, moving it away from her face then kissing her hard. The taste of her reminded him for an instant of time spent with Darlene in that northern CNR camp—only he didn't believe he and Ellie would do it anywhere but in their bed. He hoped he was wrong. He'd imagined taking her in the back of the Whitlock's car, bent over a corral rail or in the fresh hay in the dim, dusty light of the barn. But for now, this was enough. For now, it was all he'd ever wanted.

When it was over, Ellie thought that it hadn't been as bad as her mother's preparation talk had made it out to be. She'd do it again without hesitation. Ellie kissed him on the mouth, slipping her tongue between his teeth as he'd done with her earlier and then stroked his back and bottom with her fingertips, under his pajamas. There were fine hairs there, on his lower back and on his backside, and she liked the feel of them, the newness of it all.

"Culvar? Are you all right?" Ellie asked from beneath him, her question muffled against his shoulder, salty and smooth. He hadn't moved for a while, and she was beginning to notice his weight on her.

He lifted his head to look at her, surprised, and laughed. "I'm fine—really great. Really, really great." Cully rolled off Ellie, stroked her hair and kissed her forehead. "I love you, Mrs. Jullsen."

"I love you, too, Mr. Jullsen." Then she whispered, "Good night," but her husband didn't hear her. He'd already drifted too far into sleep.

— *Chapter 3* —

IMPRESSIONS

They got up late the next morning, and Cully made coffee while Ellie stripped the bed, wrapping the sheets in such a way that the bloodstains weren't visible. On the top shelf of the closet, she discovered a set of sheets that also belonged to her hope chest and shook her head at Stella's sneakiness that somehow both pleased and annoyed her. Ellie put on the pink blouse and skirt that she'd found on that same shelf. Her good shoes were there, too. Stella had thought of everything while she was sneaking around behind Ellie's back.

Carefully, Ellie smoothed the bottom sheet over the lumpy straw tick then added the top sheet, giving it the same treatment. The coffee smell drifted up the stairs, and she heard the scuff of a corn broom moving over the bare kitchen floor.

Cully called up to her, "Ellie? You coming down? Coffee's ready."

She called back, "I'm just making up the bed—I'm almost done." Finally, she spread the thin quilt and wool blanket over the bed. Both nearly touched the floor on either side, and she imagined this little bed with a metal headboard, painted clean white. It was an improvement that could be made later. Ellie plumped up the pillows, not bothering to change the cases. They were still fresh and a lovely reminder of the fact that Ellie was now Mrs. Culvar Jullsen. A shaft of light drifted through the sheer curtains and across their bed. In the daylight, the new bride thought the room looked especially pretty.

"Maybe we should go for a walk before we go to Mom's," Ellie suggested, coming down the stairs into the kitchen. There, Cully sat on one of the three wooden benches, the broom leaning against the wall next to him. Ellie started toward the stove, but he stopped her.

He told her, "Here. You sit down." He brought Ellie a tin cup that matched his own, a light green enamel one with a black rim and handle. "Your coffee will have to be black. We'll get some cream and stuff tomorrow. Yeah, a walk might be good. We can check out the place. Then we'll go get you some more clothes and anything else you'll need from your folks'."

His new bride took a sip of the coffee he'd made and smiled. "Mmm. Good. I'm finding out that you're a talented man, Mr. Jullsen." Then with her slipper, Ellie nudged the pile of debris he'd swept up. "This place is a disaster. That Royland Johnson didn't touch it after we looked at it, did he? At least it doesn't look like there's been anymore parties. Those kids of his are such riff raff."

"Yeah, it'll be a bit of work, all right, but it'll be fine." Cully was aware of the defensive edge to his voice and tried to soften it.

"A bit of work? It's going to take me forever to get this kitchen to the point where I can work in it," Ellie complained.

Cully sighed hard and said, "Look, you know as well as me that it's all that was available, all right?"

"Fine." The air thickened between them. Staring straight ahead, Ellie and Cully both took deep draws from their cups. They both noticed the palpable physical distance between their bodies on that little blue bench.

Cully finished his coffee first and set his empty cup down on the bench between he and his wife, a hollow sound. "Want to go for that walk?" he asked.

"I guess we may as well. The sun's shining." Ellie picked up his cup and set it with hers by the white enamel basin with red trim. It was encrusted with dried vomit, and she dreaded the chore of chipping it off, but she'd think about that later. Maybe she'd just find another basin. Right now, they'd go out and explore their new home. There would be plenty of time to consider vomit-chipping during the long spring and summer days to come.

Outside, the bright sun was melting what was left of the snow. Cully reached for Ellie's hand and she placed her hand in his. The couple headed out behind the house.

The outhouse was there. It was a rough little building but far better than no outhouse at all. There was also the barn and a couple outbuildings, one useable, the other beyond repair.

Cully said of the salvageable building, "Maybe we could make a coop out of this one, get some chickens." As Cully planned out loud, he could picture the buildings straightened and painted.

"I hate chickens," Ellie told him flatly.

"But you like eggs? And roasted chicken and potatoes, don't you?"

Ellie had to laugh and agree, "Yes. Yes, I do."

"Well, then." Cully squeezed her hand as they walked. "Maybe someday, down the road."

"I suppose. Maybe someday. Would be nice to have our own eggs. Milk, too," she conceded and laughed again.

"You used to milk that skinny Jersey of Whitlock's, didn't you?" he asked her.

The day-old bride nodded her head and, looking across the back pasture, noticed that most of the ice was gone from the shallow lake. She'd like to see it filled with rain this summer.

"Would you ever want to milk again?" he pressed, squeezing her hand again, trying to extract an answer.

Ellie shrugged. "I don't really know. I suppose if it meant fresh milk every day."

He explained, "But that's the thing, El. It would be every day. I'd like for us to have a milk cow, soon as we can afford one, but I'd need your help. I have to warn you that there'd be days, lot of times, when I wouldn't be in soon enough to take care of the milking. I think you could handle it, no problem. I just don't want to put you in the position of doing something you don't want to do."

"Well, to be honest, I can't say I'm looking forward to getting to know the cow, but I sure am looking forward to having the milk." She looked at him out of the corner of her eye and smiled warmly. "You buy that cow soon as you can, dear, and I'll get to know her. I promise."

"All right. If you say so." Cully gave her hand another friendly squeeze and looked down at her raised face. "You still tired after all the excitement?"

"Maybe a little."

"You want to go back to bed for a bit before we have to leave?"

"Let's go." She said it shyly but sincerely, and as they turned back toward the house, they were both smiling.

* * *

"So, what's it like?" Stella looked at Ellie sideways. Ellie was used to this look, one that Stella thought was cute but her older sister found annoying.

"What?" They were sorting donated clothes in the church basement. When they'd finished folding them, they laid them all out neatly on two long rows of tables so that people could come by that night and take what they needed. The sisters folded baby clothes first as they were the least worn of the all the donated things. Those tiny tops and bottoms would go quickly—there were lots of new babies around that summer.

"You know!" Stella leaned into Ellie, nudging her sister's shoulder with her own. "What's it like sleeping with someone every night? What's Cully, you know, *like*?" She looked at Ellie hard, trying to get her to look back. Instead, the new bride concentrated hard on folding those little buttoned sleepers into tight rectangles. Most of them were white or else the pattern was badly faded from repeated bleaching.

"Oh, Stella. Really. That's not something you ask," Ellie responded irritably.

Her sister protested, saying, "Not even my sister? Come on! If not you, who then? Who should I ask? You know firsthand. And I waited awhile. You've been married a few months now. It's not like I asked you the next day!" Stella laughed out loud, too loud, with her head thrown back. Ellie folded a tall stack of baby clothes while Stella talked on. The younger sister sat on the edge of the table, swinging her legs and holding a bonnet in her lap.

Ellie sighed. "Come on. Let's get these things sorted so we can leave before the others start to show up."

The "others" Ellie referred to were the older, bossy women who were responsible for organizing the clothing swap, which wasn't actually a swap at all. Instead, those who had gave what they could while those who had nothing, came and took what they needed. And although Ellie wouldn't admit it as loudly as her sister would, she was happy for an excuse to skip out on the swap that evening. A Saturday evening in June should be spent downtown with friends, not biding time in a grey church basement.

Mrs. Andersen, the minister's wife, suggested that tables be set out on the lawn, but all the hens got together and cackled her idea down, claiming that they feared rain. Rain! It hasn't rained for three years! Certainly, God wouldn't open up the clouds to soak clothing for the poor when He denied this spring's crops the moisture they required to grow.

Stella paused, watched Ellie closely and then pouted. "You're not going to tell me anything, are you?"

Ellie finished folding the last of the baby clothes and pushed the little piles together, grouping them: socks, receiving blankets, bonnets, sleepers, tiny dresses, tiny pants. "No, I'm not. What about these dresses? Do you think we should hang them up or just lay them on a table?"

Stella shrugged and continued to swing her legs back and forth. "I don't care what we do with them." Then she reconsidered. "Well, maybe hang them up so they don't fall off onto this dusty floor." She hopped off the table and dumped the dresses onto its surface from the burlap feed sack that sat stuffed on the concrete floor. "I'm just going to keep right on bugging you until you get so sick of it that you'll give me some information. You know how I am! I don't give up, Ellie," Stella warned her sister.

Instead of answering, the eldest sister pulled one garment from the tangle Stella had put on the tabletop for them to sort. "Why do people bother bringing in stuff like this? Cut it up and make patches or rags, for goodness sake." Ellie held a dress up to the paltry light that made its way into the basement through the grimy windows sitting just above ground level. The fabric was translucent.

In fact, Ellie could easily make out Stella's facial features through it. Later on that fall, Ellie was to see Betsy Neillson's girl walking to school, holding her little sister's hand and wearing that very same dress.

Stella asked, "Do we have hangers?"

"There're lots in the cloakroom. Let's just use those and if we need more, Mrs. Andersen said she's got some at the house. There's that rack in the furnace room. Want to help me with it?" Ellie asked.

"How do you figure she ended up with that toad, oh newly married sister of mine?" said Stella.

"Who?" Struggling with the flimsy metal coat rack, the one dragged out for every Christmas Eve service and all the community suppers, they finally got it set up by the tables.

"Mrs. Andersen. Helen." Stella spoke in a confidential tone. "He's such a jerk. How'd he get to be a preacher?"

Ellie reminded her seriously, "All types of folks get to be preachers, Stella. And just because you or I don't like them, that doesn't mean God didn't call them." Ellie paused to consider before confirming, "But you're right. He is a jerk."

Stella giggled then did her best imitation of the Reverend, which wasn't half-bad. She lowered her voice, squared her shoulders and lifted her chin so that she was literally looking down her nose at Ellie. "Not much for work right now, Culvar. How do you plan on supporting that pretty little wife of yours?"

Now Stella whirled around and tilting her chin upward, she changed her voice. Higher, but still deep for a woman's voice, and said, "Well, sir, to be honest, we'll have much more important things on our minds. I don't foresee that we'll be thinking a whole lot about money," Stella gave her sister an exaggerated wink, still playing Culvar. "If you know what I mean."

Next, Stella reclaimed the Reverend's stance, looking down at the very spot upon which she'd just stood as Ellie's husband. Her Reverend's face looked blank, maybe a little puzzled, as he responded to Culvar's innuendo. "No, Mr. Jullsen. I'm not sure that I do."

Ellie laughed and thought *Stella can be a real cut up when she wants to be*. The hollow sound of the Reverend clearing his throat echoed through the basement of the Hughenden United Church. After a deathly still moment, he said dully, "Bravo, Miss Pedersen. I'm glad I was here for your interpretation of me. It's always interesting to see yourself as others see you."

He stood straight in the doorway, his balding head almost brushing the top of the frame. That afternoon, he wasn't wearing his collar and the top two buttons of his shirt were undone. How long had he been there? He'd obviously seen Stella's entire performance. Had he also heard Ellie call him a jerk?

"Oh...I..." was all Stella managed, her usually animated hands now hanging limply at her sides, her face flushing scarlet. Daniel Andersen paused for what seemed like minutes there in that doorway then, finally, he turned and made his way back up the stairs without saying another word.

Later on that evening, the four of them sat on the

bench out in front of Bryton's Ladies Wear, the sun still as hot as it'd been at three o'clock that afternoon.

"I could've died! We turned around, and there he was standing in the doorway listening and watching. How can I ever go back to church?" Stella cried, retelling the story of what had happened in the church basement earlier that day.

"He caught you doing your Andersen imitation?" Henry laughed and slapped his big thigh. "Good for him. He's an arrogant bastard."

Stella wailed, "Yeah, but what about me! I can't show my face! I'm so embarrassed! It was stupid to do it right there in the church. I was just *asking* to get caught." She buried her face in her hands and shook her head back and forth in dismay.

Then Culvar spoke up. "What about him? What'd he do?"

Stella sniffled. She had started to cry for real. "He…he…just stood there and stared. Said he was glad he caught me!"

"Glad?" Henry repeated. "What did he mean 'glad'?"

Stella wiped the tears away with the back of her hand, and Ellie handed her a handkerchief from her little black purse. "I think he meant he was glad I felt stupid!"

"Wouldn't surprise me," Henry said.

"I don't know if he'd be glad to see you embarrassed, Stell." Culvar looked at his wife. "How do you think he felt?"

Ellie lifted her shoulders. "I think he was angry. Probably embarrassed, too. Who wouldn't be?"

Stella countered, "I'd rather be made fun of than be caught making fun of someone, that's for sure!" Stella handed back Ellie's handkerchief. Her nose was a little red, but besides that, it was hard to tell that Stella had been crying.

"Really, Stella?" Henry pried, poking her gently in the ribs. Then, he grabbed her hat and plopped it on over his own. He puckered up his lips and held out his left hand, letting the wrist go limp. "Hey everyone! Let's go shopping! Oh look, I've found the *cutest* fabric! Let's all make a dress!"

Stella whacked him hard on the arm. "Oh, be quiet, Henry!" But she was laughing. "That's how I feel today, that's all I'm saying. I just feel *so* dumb!"

Henry plunked the floppy hat back down on Stella's head. She straightened it and sniffled one more time. Then she and Henry stood up, walking in the direction of the drugstore. As she watched them, Ellie couldn't help but think that at times like these, it seemed those two were made for each other. But other times Ellie had her doubts—not so much about Henry, who was clearly smitten, but about Stella. It was obvious that Henry thought the sun rose and set on Stella. As soon as Henry can afford to move from his parents' house, Ellie was sure he'd ask Stella to marry him.

She liked this idea, this picture of the future because Ellie was concerned about her sister. Now and then, not often, Stella would say things that gave Ellie a real jolt, things that made her wonder if she even really knew her sister at all. One of these times, the sisters were working together in Muriel Pedersen's kitchen. It was during the summer before Ellie and Cully got married.

*   *   *

Ellie and Stella were canning saskatoons and rhubarb for their mom and making dilled carrot pickles. Because they wanted to get their work done while the day was still decently cool, they'd got up early while the dew was still on the grass and the clouds were fringed with a rosy hue. Their parents took a ride to visit friends who had also come up from Idaho to start a new life. Muriel had plans to do some berry picking and visiting while there, and Benson had plans to play some cards. They'd stayed overnight and would be home that evening—maybe even in time for supper. But that was a long way off. Ellie had just begun slicing rhubarb, and Stella was washing Gem jars, her bleached hair mostly hidden by the red and white scarf she'd knotted around her head.

"Hey, El?" Stella's hands were red and soapy as she brought the steaming jars out of the basin.

"Hmm?"

"Y'know Daisie Williamson?" Stella asked.

Ellie answered, "That girl Horace married and brought all the way out here?"

"Yeah, that's the one. You think she's pretty?"

"I suppose. She's very tall." The kitchen was already beginning to heat up, the humidity from the boiling canner making them feel like they would suffocate. "I sometimes wonder if she's bored here, coming all the way from a city like Montreal." Inwardly, Ellie considered the woman's loneliness.

"I know I would be." Ellie's little sister sighed. "I kinda feel sorry for Daisie. What a change! Coming from there to Horace's old frame house on the edge of town. You've gotta wonder if she knew that he works in a lumberyard before she came all the way out here? What did he say to lure her?"

"Are you suggesting he lied to her to get her to leave Montreal?" Ellie asked pointedly.

Stella shrugged. "Well, maybe not exactly *lied*, but he may've exaggerated the truth a little. Horace has been known to do that from time to time."

It was true. Horace Williamson was a storyteller and a nice enough man, if not that much to look at. Ellie wiped her hands on her apron. She'd already sliced up a couple of quarts of rhubarb. Not too bad. "What did Daisie do in Montreal?" Ellie wanted to know.

Stella replied, "I'm not sure. Thought I heard she'd worked as a store clerk or something. I'll ask her sometime, if I see her around."

The rhubarb seemed tough, but then Ellie realized that her knife could use a good sharpening. She thought she could work faster if she didn't have to saw through each stalk individually. Ellie made a mental note to mention that dull knife to her father when her folks got back. The knives in the house were usually very sharp. Ellie and Stella's dad was particular that way. "She doesn't come to church much," the older sister pointed this out about Daisie.

Stella said, "No, but you do see her downtown, just

looking in the shop windows on Saturday evenings. Sometimes she's with Horace's mom but most of the time, she's alone."

"Waiting for him to finish up at the lumberyard, I suppose. Not wanting to sit at home." Ellie forced her knife through a new rhubarb stalk. "Can't blame her for that, I suppose."

"If I was a man, I'd want to kiss her." Stella blurted.

Ellie set the knife down. "Pardon me?" She turned her head sharply to look at her sister. Stella seemed to be concentrating hard on her task, hands buried in suds, jars knocking hollowly against one another. "What do you mean by that?"

"Nothing, really. Just that I think men would go crazy for her, that's all." Again, Stella shrugged. "She's very attractive, she's interesting, probably has a ton of stories to tell about where she came from. Why wouldn't someone —anyone—want to kiss her?" Stella kept her focus on the basin while speaking. Finally, she looked up from her work to find Ellie staring at her. "Do you think this will be enough jars to start?" she asked, beginning to silently count the steaming jars lined up on a tea towel.

Ellie blinked. "Yes...yes, that'll be fine. That canner's been boiling for a while so we might as well get some of them in."

Stella didn't bring up Daisie Williamson again that day, and Ellie sure didn't ask for more details. The older sister knew when to leave well enough alone.

— Chapter 4 —

ELLIE NEVER NAMED A COW DORA

Ellie never named a cow Dora or had a pet cat—although she liked to feed the birds in winter. It would seem that viewing wildlife was more interesting to Mrs. Jullsen than working with farm animals. There's evidence that in fact Ellie *hated* working with livestock. When Cully saw her fly off the handle the very first time, it was because of a cow. Specifically, a milk cow.

He had been heading out that morning to go to work. Cully had promised Edward Whitlock that he'd bring his axe that day. They'd need more than one to get all the wood chopped from the trees they'd felled the day before on the north side of Whitlock's property.

As Cully walked toward the barn to fetch that axe, he heard a mighty ruckus that stopped him dead in his tracks.

"You lousy cow! Damn, damn, damn you to hell! Damn you! Goddamn you all the way to hell, you damn cow!" It sounded to her husband, as he stood there disbelieving, that the only source of curse words for Ellie was the Holy Bible. This proved there are better, more varied sources for profane language. Cully heard what he guessed correctly to be the echo of a rubber boot meeting a tin milk pail. Somewhat alarmed, he began to jog the rest of the way, coming into the barn just in time to see his sweet wife, wooden milk stool held high above her head like she was very seriously considering bashing Bossie with it. Down the back of Ellie's chore coat, one of Cully's old coats, and along one sleeve, ran a goopy brown stream, shiny in the glare of the lantern hanging above the stall where she'd been milking.

He halted in the open door and Ellie turned her head to look at him, milk stool still suspended above her. Cully couldn't help himself. He started to laugh. Hard. Trying to stifle it just made it worse, made it come out in kind of a snort. Whether he liked it or not, the laughter was moving down from his throat right into his belly, and he was forced to brace his hands on his knees to keep from collapsing with mirth.

Her new husband tried to tell Ellie, "I'm so...so...sorrrry...It's just...you...I..." He looked up, wanting to see if his wife was listening, if Ellie was now madder at Cully than the cow. Still, she stood there, holding that stool a little lower now, and it seemed to Cully that Bossie looked less worried. Ellie stared at Cully, her eyes fixed and narrowing. He saw it coming, but the debilitating spasms of laughter wouldn't let him move quick enough.

Finally, Ellie spoke to him. "You be quiet, you!" Then, she dropped the stool and charged Cully. In his weakened state, he was barely able to make it out the barn door before she caught him round the waist and hauled him to the frosty ground in their barnyard.

That really got him going, laughing silently, finding it hard to get enough oxygen. The sight of his wife flying through the air at him doubled him over, set Cully to gasping like a fish out of water. That's when Ellie rolled over and got on top of Cully, holding his wrists. From there, their eyes locked.

It started as easy twitching at the corners of her mouth, that quickly became a smile that let go into a laughing fit neither of them had seen since they were teenagers. That soft woman collapsed beside her husband, holding his hand and clutching her own stomach. The newlywed couple lay there until the laughter stopped, their bodies melting some of snow and frost that thinly covered the late-April ground.

When Ellie and Cully finally made it to their feet, she hugged him tightly and said, "I hate that darn cow." Then, she disappeared into the barn. Cully followed, still needing the axe that he'd gone in there for in the first place. Walking behind her, he noticed that most of the shit had rubbed off Ellie's coat onto the frozen grey grass.

* * *

Ellie wept and blisters had started to form on her right hand. With the rust-spotted trowel, she chiseled away at the hardened bubble gum that was stuck in the corners of the kitchen walls and pressed down hard along the bottoms of the baseboards. The shapeless pink blobs were petrified and, at first, she wondered how long they'd been there. Soon, though, she didn't care. Ellie just wanted it all gone. This was just the kitchen—she hadn't even touched the living room yet. She couldn't think about it. Instead, she focused on the picture in her mind of how it would all someday look as bits of ancient chewing gum crumbled off the walls and onto the floor. A numbingly slow erosion.

Her knees cracked as she got up from where she knelt on a sheet of newspaper, the black ink from it forming patches on the front of her threadbare housedress in the places her knees had rested on the paper. The headline read: DROUGHT CONTINUES. NO HELP FROM BENNETT FOR PRAIRIE FARMERS. Ellie took the corn broom from where it stood at an angle against the wall and deftly swept into a neat pile all the hard, dried chunks of gum, along with the day's newest accumulation of dust. Next, her eyes searched the room for the dustpan. Why wasn't it on the bench? She was sure that's where she'd left it yesterday afternoon. Not on the countertop. Not on the staircase. Not in the back porch or in the living room. So where was it? Ellie's hands tightened around the broom handle as if she wanted to strangle it, and she began to gnaw at her bottom lip.

Bright and early that morning, her new husband had, on his way through the kitchen, spotted the battered dustpan and recognized it immediately as the ideal tool for cleaning the deep dust piles from the corners of Whitlock's granaries. Without a second thought, Cully scooped it up and carried it out the door. If she had known, perhaps Ellie would've been wishing the grip she had on the broom was instead firmly about her husband's throat.

She flung the corn broom to the floor, its handle not breaking yet hitting with force hard enough to cause a cracking sound to reverberate off the walls. "I hate this GD house!" she yelled to herself, to no one, and gave the nearest bench a mighty kick. Ellie told Cully later that she'd broken her toe when she misjudged her step and stubbed it painfully on the staircase.

The young wife slumped down on the bench she'd kicked and allowed herself to cry hard, face in hands, and sobbing so that her shoulders heaved. Then she limped over to the counter, noticing now the pain in her foot, and began to scrub the potatoes soaking in the basin lent to them by her mom. Ellie couldn't bring herself to wash dishes or prepare food in the basin that had been there on the counter when they'd moved in. She'd cleaned the vomit from it and then set it out in the porch. It would be useful one day—just not in the kitchen.

When Cully entered the back porch he steadied the stolen dustpan against the wall and took off his boots. By the time he called out to her, the potatoes were boiling on the stove, and she'd swept up the dry gum and dust onto an old newspaper.

"Ellie!"

She peeked around the corner into the porch. "Hello."

"Oh, sorry. I thought you might've been upstairs. What're you doing?" Cully stepped into the kitchen. "Smells good," he commented. He kissed her cheek and touched her arm. Then, Ellie's husband noticed that her eyes looked puffy, a little red around the rims.

She told him, "It'll be potatoes, beans and bread tonight. And which bench would you like to dine upon tonight, sir?"

"You mean, I gotta *eat* one? No, really, the potatoes'll be fine." She didn't chuckle along with him. Didn't even smile. He knew what Ellie was getting at and said, "Look, I'll check with my brother about picking up that table from the Morrison place. I'll talk to Denby tomorrow, and we'll get it figured out." Cully sighed in exasperation and added, "I know you don't like it, but the benches are fine for now."

Ellie let out a sigh, too—an apologetic one. "I'm sorry. I'm just used to having a table to eat at. It's not your fault. I know that."

"Aw, El. It'll get easier. It's always hard when you're first settling in. Ask anybody."

Ellie smiled a bit sheepishly. "I know that, too. I'm just tired. Like you." Now it was her turn to touch him. She rested her hand on Cully's shirt, feeling the grit that was embedded in its cotton threads and the heart that beat beneath them. This time he kissed her lightly on the lips. Then deeper.

While they continued to kiss, Cully reached over and moved their supper from the stovetop to the counter. Ellie forgot her hunger and happily shut her eyes as Cully gathered her up in his arms and carried her up that treacherously steep staircase. He set her down gently in the bedroom's doorway, kissing her neck now. He leaned there against the battered doorframe, kissing his wife while she began to undo the buttons of his thin shirt. Ellie ran her hand inside his shirt, next to his skin, thinking about how much she enjoyed the feel of the hair on his chest.

They undressed quickly there in the doorway and left their clothes in a heap on the bedroom floor. Cully held her hand and led Ellie over to their bed. On her way past the closet, Ellie grabbed her pink robe, the one Stella had bought for her. As Cully drew back the covers and hopped in, Ellie wrapped the robe around her nakedness, feeling a little like Eve under the gaze of God.

"You don't need that on. Come here." Cully invited her softly into the bed, and when she took one small step forward and stopped, he asked, "What's wrong?"

She stood there blushing in the evening warmth of the room. He laughed but not unkindly. "Are you shy, my wife?" Cully lightly touched the back of her right hand, the hand that clutched at the pink fabric. He moved over, making room for her to slide in next to him.

Instead, Ellie sat down on the edge of the bed, hands now folded in her lap, the robe falling open. "I'm sorry."

"Don't be. Here. Lie down. No. Just leave your robe on for now. I want you relaxed and comfortable." He lifted the blankets so she could join him beneath them. "There." And then, "This is where you belong." He kissed the top of her head.

She snuggled in beside him. "I love you, Culvar Jullsen."

This time, he kissed her forehead. "I love you, too," he assured her, hiding his frustration at her hesitancy. He would need to be patient with this process. Slowly, deliberately, he moved his kisses to her mouth and his hands to the front of her robe. Ellie brought her arms up and clung around her husband's neck. He read it as permission to proceed and so opened her robe. To ease the tension, Cully teased her. He poked a finger into her belly, sending her into a ticklish spasm, and she retaliated, aiming her fingertips at his exposed rib cage. To stop her, Cully brought his arms tightly around his wife and placed his knee between her thighs. This time it was she who kissed him.

By the time they got back downstairs, the potatoes and beans had grown cold. This seemed funnier to them both than Cully's earlier joke about eating the bench. The days were lengthening steadily, and they ate in the early evening light sitting on the combination of boards and bricks that made up their front step. From there they watched the sun retreat from the sky as the full, low moon moved in at the same time. He thanked God on behalf of them both for the food then Cully took a long drink of water from his jelly jar. It reminded him of something Whitlock had told him earlier on that day. "Johnson's well is going dry. Or they think so, anyways."

"Why do they think that?" She drank, too, tasting the sweet cool on her tongue. They'd been lucky with the well on this place.

"The water's real murky. Sandy. Pretty much undrinkable." Cully took a bite of the food he'd mixed together, mashed potatoes and green beans, and lifted it to his mouth on a thick slice of bread. "They'll probably come here for water. There're closer water sources at other people's places, but this is their land so it makes sense."

"Can't they dig a new well?" Ellie asked.

He shrugged. "I don't know. Maybe they'll try. Yeah, most likely they'll try. Lots of work, and could cost them money unless old Royland can call in another favour from someone."

She asked him, "We won't run out of water, will we? Our well is really good—isn't it?" The prospect of being waterless made Ellie nervous.

Cully touched her cheek. "We'll be all right. We're a lot higher here and close to the lake. It'll be fine." It was then she noticed for the first time the lines around his eyes from worry and weather. *I love this man so much.*

The next day, the sun shone brightly again and seemed higher in the sky. Ellie opened up all the windows in the early part of the day while the air still held some of the night's cool. It felt to her that too much time had been wasted that last week, running from chore to chore. There was so much to do. It was easy to become frantic, to clean the walls one minute, scrub the countertop and potatoes another, to wash out cupboards and wipe off shelves, and then to start on some laundry. During the first week the Jullsen's lived there, Ellie had darted from one task to another, like a worker bee, overwhelmed by the sheer abundance of pollen in a meadow of flowers. She never completed one job before she noticed another that took immediate precedence. The new bride was run off her feet, but when she looked about her, she felt that she hadn't completed even one thing fully.

Right off the bat, Ellie realized that the work around their starter home was so much harder than most of what she'd done as a domestic. Ellie would polish one pane of glass, scrub and wring one sheet, peel potatoes, varnish one stair, wire-brush the flaking paint from one window sill. It was going to drive her crazy. Something had to change.

The second week in the house on Hughenden Lake brought the need for order and routine paired with the new idea that she was her own boss. That's when Ellie sat down and made her first list on the back of a paper bag. Perched on the edge of the worn bench nearest the counter, she wrote neatly with a dull pencil she'd found in the recesses of one of the kitchen drawers:

1. clean out cabinet under sink
2. put cleaning supplies in cabinet—make rags
3. dust top shelves
4. line shelves with paper
5. plates to the left of sink; cups to the right
6. pots and pans beneath
7. put extra plates in box—take to the church Sunday
8. sweep kitchen area
9. mix bread—let rise while mending pants
10. bring in wood
11. sweep
12. bake bread
13. cook supper—stew
14. do dishes
15. read Psalm 148

When she was done, the housewife promised herself that she'd stick to it. Nothing on a day's list would be done out of order, and she wouldn't even consider doing anything not on the list. She'd begin by cleaning out that cabinet under the kitchen counter. It was good. It was control. Finally.

While cutting the vegetables for supper, Ellie started to sob. "Father God, when will this end?" She laid the knife down and slumped over the counter, her tears splashing down on the blue countertop, slashed and scarred repeatedly by knives that existed here long before her. It was strangely comforting, the thought of those other people preparing food in this rundown place maybe even in a time when it wasn't so ramshackle. Through the tears in her eyes, Ellie pictured a bachelor, tired and lonely, cutting open a tin of ham for his solitary supper. He'd eat it standing up.

Ellie's face was still wet with tears when she heard Cully's footfall at the back door. She pressed her face into the cool, damp tea towel. She put a hand to her hair and smoothed the front of her housedress, the once cheery pattern now mostly washed away.

"Hey there." Her husband greeted her with a kiss on the cheek and a jar of cream from his mother. "I talked to Denby. We'll get the table from the Morrison's the day after tomorrow," Cully told her.

Ellie replied, careful to sound steady, reasonable. "That's good news. Thanks, honey. Is it just a table or are there chairs, too?"

"Just the table, but I was thinking maybe we could clean up these benches a bit and use a couple of them." Cully noticed disappointment flash across her face. It passed as quickly as it had appeared, and he chose not to comment on it. He noticed, also, that his wife looked beaten down. Cully came and stood close to her as she made that night's stew. From the tin pail on the counter, he ladled himself a drink of well water, soft and a little rusty looking, but cool on the throat.

"Culvar, please don't drink out of the ladle," Ellie reminded him.

"I forgot." He reached up and brought a jelly jar down from one of the shelves mounted alongside the window. "You smell good. Like you did on our wedding night." Cully sniffed the air appreciatively. "Are you wearing the same stuff?"

Ellie blushed her pleasure. "Yes, I am." She set down her knife and leaned into him, her cheek resting against his chest. "I'm glad you noticed." He put both arms around her and Ellie returned his hug, her arms around his waist.

"I'm exhausted tonight," he shared. "How 'bout you?"

She didn't let go of him. Not yet. "A little. I'm fine, though. How was work?" Ellie looked up into his face. Along his jaw line there was already a shadow. He could stand to shave twice a day.

Cully shrugged. "Work was the same. Fencing today again, but by next week might do a little seeding. I don't know if it's worth it, though. Pretty dry. We'll need some rain if anything's going to grow this year." He kissed the top of her head and let her go, returning to filling the jelly jar. "You want some?"

"No. I'll just finish this up and get it on the stove." She asked him, "You feel like making some coffee?"

Cully swatted Ellie's backside and told her, "Sure, if

you think you can handle my strong coffee, little lady." She smiled at him and raised her eyebrows at the challenge. "If I can handle you, I can handle your coffee." "That's probably true." Cully laughed, pulling the lid from the tin canister labeled "sugar." There was another one that didn't match it also labeled "sugar" that contained sugar. Brown sugar and not much of it.

While the stew bubbled, they took their coffee and walked outside. Cully watched the sky for rainclouds and Ellie examined the ground for traces of new green life. Neither found what they were looking for. The sky remained a sharp blue while the soil along the south side of the house from which tulips might emerge was bone dry. They strolled out back, talking about what they'd do when they found money and time.

"I can't use this clothesline the way it is. I need a step, some way to reach the reel," Ellie stated.

Cully laid a hand on the weathered pole. It had a bad lean to it and so did the one opposite, the one that held the other reel. When he pushed it, it gave. "Must be rotten. I'll have to replace the whole thing, but it should be easy enough. I'll build you a step, too. I'll get it done before fall, I promise." He pulled down the tin syrup pail that hung from a spike driven into the dry wood of the slanted pole. It was rusted through on the bottom. "I'll get you a new pail for your pins, too. This one's had it." Cully held up the old syrup pail and peered out through the bottom of it at her. "Land ahoy, mateys!" he called out, his pirate impression winning only a small smile from his wife. Ellie remained focused on solving the laundry problem long term.

She told him, "I can hang things inside for now, anyway. I won't mind that for a while, but once we get the house set up, I'd like to hang the laundry out."

"Yeah, I'd like that, too. Makes the sheets smell nice." Cully pointed and commented, "This garden plot is in the right place, I think."

They'd stopped at the edge of a rectangular patch of dirt, some shriveled remnants of gardens before lying in a brown tangle across its uneven surface, but mostly it had gone to weeds. In its far corner closest to the road and despite the drought, thrived a rhubarb plant.

"Needs work, though. Mom's got a rake we can have. Next time we're out there, let's remember to ask her," Ellie mentioned this before swallowing the last of her coffee. She looked at him and asked, "Know what I like best about this yard?"

"Nope." Cully turned toward her.

"This tree." They had made their way around the yard to the other side of the house. Now they were outside of the kitchen window where they stood under a willow tree, ten or eleven feet tall. "It's beautiful."

Cully didn't say anything to Ellie about it, but he had an idea. Right then and there, he knew what gift he would give her.

Ellie grabbed his hand and swung it gently back and forth, telling him "Let's go in and eat our supper."

— *Chapter 5* —

THE FISHING TRIP

The heat was oppressive already that early August morning, the wind flattening the dry grasses absent of both dew and resiliency. Cully was shaded by the spreading branches of the willow tree near their rented house on the edge of Hughenden Lake. He was digging a hole, two or three feet deep with a circumference of less than a foot. Beside him on the crispy-baked lawn lay a sturdy clothesline pole. Whitlock and he had made a trip into Hughenden on Thursday afternoon for some feed and to see if Ollie Lowen was able to repair that old harness one more time.

"Cully, you want to stop in and talk to Horace, see about getting a couple of poles for Ellie's clothesline?" Edward Whitlock guided his wagon up to the post in front of Hughenden General Store. They were good about keeping a water trough full up for the visiting horses, and the shade provided by the wide awning was much appreciated.

"Yeah, sure. Thanks." Whitlock always thought about other people.

"Why don't you go see what they've got, and I'll bring the wagon down there as soon as I'm finished here. All right?" Edward Whitlock said.

"All right."

While Whitlock went in to get a few groceries to tide his wife over until the weekend, Cully walked down the block to the lumberyard, the grit in the air sticking to his teeth. Horace Williamson helped him select two sturdy poles, and the two men visited while Whitlock finished up at the store.

Upon their return to the Hughenden Lake place, Ellie was happy to see Whitlock's wagon pull into the yard, the ends of two poles sticking out of its box. She came out the front door and waved.

"Hi! Hot day. You two have time to come in for a glass of lemonade?" She leaned in the doorframe, the hot sun picking up the gold strands in her dark hair.

"Thank you, Mrs. Jullsen. That'd be great." Every time Whitlock saw her after she and Cully had gotten married, he formally called her "Mrs. Jullsen." Ellie loved it.

"How're you doing, my wife?" Cully came across the lawn and kissed her warm cheek.

Ellie asked him, "What's that in the wagon, Culvar? You didn't happen by any chance to get poles for my clothesline, did you?" The question was light and teasing.

Her husband of five months laughed and Whitlock, who'd stepped up beside him, answered, "Needed to go into town anyway. Thought it'd be a good time to get those for you. Kill two birds with one stone." Then he addressed Cully, "Should we unload those now or wait till we've had our lemonade?"

Cully thought for a moment then said, "Might as well do it now, if you don't mind. Get it out of the way."

"Good idea. It's not getting any cooler out here, either."

Ellie slipped her gumboots on by the back door, left her apron on and met them around the side of the house. The men hauled the poles from the wagon and laid them so that they were parallel with the garden patch Ellie had successfully spent part of her time taming.

"Looks like your garden's coming along." Whitlock walked along the seam where the grass ended and soil began. "Your carrots look good. Not much for peas this year, is there? Lots of pods with nothing in them. Same with our garden." Whitlock, who must've loved peas, shook his head sadly. Ellie noticed that his walk seemed to be getting stiffer. She thought that he had to be nearing sixty years old.

She agreed with him, "No, my peas aren't doing very well at all. I've been hauling water up from the lake. I hate to use the good well water on the vegetables."

Whitlock took off his hat and scratched his head. "Can't blame you for that. You're in a pretty good area, but others around here, further east and south sure are having trouble with their wells," he said.

Cully had been deciding on the best place to put the new poles. Should he leave them where the old ones had been or dig new holes? The old ones had been a bit too close to the house, so he thought he'd probably move them. It'd mean some digging, but then it'd be done right and they wouldn't have to worry about those poles being improperly placed or wobbly. Cully came and stood by his wife at the edge of the garden.

"Yeah, I thought Royland Johnson might be around to get water, seeing this is his place and his own well's dry," Cully commented. "But we haven't seen him. They must've dug a new well or maybe they're getting water from somewhere closer than here."

Whitlock put his hat back on, a little straighter than before. "Glad we've got good water. Never been a problem. It's a blessing, really."

"Amen," Ellie agreed and asked, "Ready for that lemonade?"

Whitlock smiled with crinkly eyes, telling her, "Sure am, Mrs. Jullsen."

* * *

So now, months after first discussing it with Ellie, Cully had time to get that clothesline up. He'd almost got that first hole dug and was thinking that once he put that pole in, it wasn't going anywhere for a long, long time. Just then, on the wind and above the whisper of the leaves, the twitter of birds and the hum of insects, Cully heard voices,

voices he recognized although it'd been a while since he'd had the pleasure of hearing them. His brothers! Cully tossed the dull spade to the ground, its weathered handle landing with a soft thud on the withered grass. He walked around to the front of the house to see Norward and Denby bouncing up in that old wagon belonging to Gunnar Olmstead, Norward's friend more than Cully's or Denby's.

"Hey!" Cully called out to them. "That wagon's gonna bust apart. Slow down!" He met them part way down that rutted drive and patted the bay's neck. "Drive it over here. We'll get a drink of water for this big fella." Cully stroked the horse's moist neck.

"Hotter n the belly of hell, ain't it?" Norward jumped unsteadily down from the moving wagon, and a quart sealer of some clear liquid fell out of his pants pocket onto the ground. "Oops! Better not let the little wifey catch me with that!" He stooped to pick it up and stumbled. Denby laughed and Cully, guiding the horse along by its halter, shook his head.

"Don't breathe in too deep when he talks right at you, Cull," Denby warned him. "The fumes could give you permanent lung damage."

At the well, Cully filled a tin chop bucket with cool water which the gelding snorted up thirstily. Denby got down from the driver's seat and joined Norward sitting in the shade of a lilac bush.

"Wonderin' if you could get away for a bit? Come fishin' down to Greene's Pond?"

"When'd you two get back?" Cully's brothers had been

out working for the CPR, loading and unloading grain and freight in the yard at Wetaskiwin for most of the summer. He'd asked Denby because Norward was already lying down, his crumpled hat tilted over his face.

"Just yesterday. Spent some of the day with Mom, some of it downtown." Denby glanced around. "Place looks good. You've done a lot of work since I was out here in the spring helping you move that table. You like it all right?"

Cully told him, "It's all right for now. Ellie's got the inside nice, too. Want to come in and take a look, say hello?"

"Sure." Denby nudged his sleeping brother's leg. "Norward. We're going in. You wanna come?" There came a grunt from under the hat—a negative response. It was probably a wise decision on Norward's part. Ellie likely wouldn't appreciate the condition he was in. The remaining two brothers, after refilling his water bucket and securing the horse's reins to a tree by the old granary, headed into the house.

"Hey, Ellie! Did you see Norward and Denby're here?" Cully called from the back porch. His wife appeared in the doorway.

"Hi, Denby." Ellie reached out and laid her hand on his lower arm. "How've you been, brother-in-law?"

"Better for seeing you, sister-in-law." He placed his hand over hers.

"Come on in," she invited the two men. "I've got coffee cake. How's the clothesline coming along, Culvar?" Ellie asked over her shoulder as the brothers followed her into the kitchen. Then, before her husband could answer, she asked, "Where's Norward? I thought I saw you both come in on the wagon."

Denby chuckled. "Ah, well, let's just say he's off the wagon now—so he chose to stay outside."

Cully moved quickly to get the topic of conversation off Norward and his state and onto anything else. "Yeah, the clothesline. I've got one hole dug and the other started. Good sturdy poles. Those aren't going to rot and lean again any time soon."

Ellie turned to Denby and gestured to the table. "Go ahead. Sit down. You want coffee? It's made."

"Yeah, that'd be good, thanks." Denby's quick glance took in the length of Ellie and then the length of the room and returned to Ellie once more. "So my brother's building you a clothesline, is he? About time. What've you been doin' with your laundry?"

Ellie lifted a hand to touch her hair. There was a pale smudge of flour on her cheek. "Oh, hanging it up inside, just any old place."

"That works for a while," Cully told them both. "But you can't beat the smell of laundry that's been hanging outside, fresh and crisp. When you crawl into bed, it's that same fresh outdoor smell." While his brother spoke, Denby watched Ellie and although she didn't look at him, she felt his eyes on her. When Ellie reached for her cup, she missed catching the handle and nearly knocked the mug over.

The three visited for an hour or so, Denby doing most of the talking, his voice and hands equally animated, while Cully and Ellie sat back in their seats content to listen.

Norward stayed outside, and no one at the kitchen table mentioned his snoozing presence just beyond the back porch door under the lilac bush. Eventually, after they'd all caught up on the news, Denby resurrected the idea of an afternoon fishing trip, bringing it back out into the light of day.

"So, Ellie, I know you've waited a long while for that clothesline of yours, but we were just on our way to the fishing hole and were wondering if you could spare your husband for the rest of the afternoon? We'll bring him back safe and sound sometime after supper. I promise." Denby laid his right hand over his heart to demonstrate that he would keep his word.

Ellie smiled, her lips thin, pressed together. "Where are you going to fish?"

"They were thinking Greene's Pond and it sounds good to me." Cully stood up, signaling his intention to go whether or not he'd finished the clothesline. He kissed his wife's cheek and she didn't move, holding tightly onto her cup, the little coffee left in the bottom having grown cold. "We won't be gone long. I'll finish up that clothesline first thing tomorrow morning."

Still looking into her cup at the half-inch of wasted coffee, Ellie said icily, "On the Sabbath?"

Denby had stood up as well and was already making his way toward the back door.

"Right. I forgot." Cully forced a sigh. "It'll get done, El. I haven't seen these guys in weeks." He waited for her reply, but Ellie refused to meet his eyes. Finally, he shrugged and turned to follow Denby.

Outside, the two brothers rousted the remaining brother from where he was sleeping soundly on the patchy grass. "C'mon, Norward. Let's go," Denby ordered him as Cully began to unwind the horse's reins from the tree trunk.

"There you go, big fella. Feel better?" Cully spoke softly to the bay and the horse nuzzled the palm of his hand. "I'll bring some carrots from the wife's garden. You can have them at the lake. My treat."

"What the...? Oh. You guys done with your visit?" Norward sat up, his crumpled hat falling into his lap. Denby extended his hand and his brother accepted the tug up to his feet. "Whoa, I needed that sleep. You comin', Cully? She gonna let you outta the yard?"

"Norward. Shut up. You're drunk and stupid," Denby reprimanded him, his tone serious.

Cully spoke up. "You want me to come along? Then shut up about my wife."

"All right, all right. No pickin' on little Miss Ellie. I got it. Now can we get the hell outta here?" Norward walked stiff-leggedly to the back of the wagon and miraculously hoisted himself over the side of the box, muttering under his breath as he did. "Jesus, so fuckin' proper, can't say a goddamned thing round 'em."

Behind his back, the other two brothers exchanged annoyed glances, and Denby rolled his eyes.

"I'm going to grab some carrots." Cully shot a look at the bay and handed his brother the reins. "I promised." On his way back to the wagon with a handful of gnarled carrots, Cully watched the kitchen window out of the corner of his eye. He saw Ellie's outline against a curtain move away as he walked by.

"You wanna drive?" Denby asked when Cully returned from the garden and eased himself into the wagon, a bunch of wilting green tops protruding from his shirt's front pocket.

"Yeah, sure." Cully sat down on the rough wooden bench and clucked his tongue. The horse's ears flicked, and he began to move. Norward sat silently propped up against the back of the wagon box along with the fishing rods, a bucket of dirt writhing with earthworms and the jar he'd bought from Gunnar's uncle.

"You been out this year?" Denby meant fishing.

Cully answered him, "Nope. Too busy. You guys?"

"Nope. Same thing. Just too damn busy." Denby paused. "Liked the work though. I'd do it again. Hard but predictable, y'know? I like that in a job."

"Why're you back then?" Cully wanted to know.

"Fired. Both of us and two other guys." Denby shook his head. "He had to let us go. Crop production *and* prices is way down. You know that."

Denby decided he'd save the rest of the story for later, after he'd had a chance to think about the best way to tell it.

"I know. I thought it'd be better by now. It's been nearly four years." Cully squinted against the midday sun and tugged his hat brim lower. Both men rode in thoughtful silence for a bit and, from the rear of the wagon, they could hear liquor slosh as Norward tipped up the jar. Softly, he began to hum an unrecognizable tune.

After a while, Denby spoke up again, looking straight ahead at the deserted road. "Yeah, one of the guys fired—he'd rode the rails up from southern Saskatchewan, Estevan, I think—he came back to the elevators that night, roaring drunk and carrying a baseball bat. That's what they say, anyway. I guess old Morris opened the door and—crack!—he caught it right across the head. Found the bat in the neighbour's front yard in the morning."

Cully switched his gaze from the road to Denby and asked, "He all right?"

Then from the back: "'Course he's not all right. Just got cracked 'cross the head with a goddamned bat! Son of a bitch's dead."

In answer to Cully's questioning expression, arched eyebrows and wide eyes, Denby nodded gravely and told Norward, "Pass that jar up here."

For the next couple of miles, the three rode in silence, the quart jar moving steadily between them, Cully accepting about one drink to their four. There were many still places along the way where trees lined the roadway or at those places where the wagon moved down into a coulee, really just a dip more than a valley. These low spots had been wet, nearly impassable in springs past, but in recent memory, they'd been as dry as the hilltops. Over the prairie, gophers skittered between holes and a hawk circled low and silent, waiting for an opportunity, her shadow sliding across the land like a dark ghost. With a warning scream, she plunged, wings back, talons poised. Within seconds, a rodent spine was cracked in two places and the hawk, flying with its prey dangling, headed toward a nearby stand of trees.

Norward had stretched out on his back and was beginning to snore loudly.

"He like this a lot?" Cully glanced over his right shoulder at his brother passed out on the rough planks, surrounded by fishing gear and jackets.

"More and more. Not at work, though, but usually when he finishes up a job somewhere. Then he goes on a tear—sometimes for as long as a week."

"Hmm. Too bad." He looked at Denby and then back at the road. "How about you? You been drinking?" Cully asked him.

"Not enough to keep up with him, if that's what you're asking." A thin layer of frost covered his words. "Don't worry. I take care of me."

Cully instantly caught the edge to his brother's voice. "I didn't mean you can't. I just meant it's a hard life. I've done it. Drinking will make life seem worth living, then it'll kill you. I've seen it or I wouldn't say anything."

"Thanks, preacher man." Denby flashed a grin that melted the cold. "I'll keep it in mind. Should we wake him up and let him know the good news? That the booze'll kill him? Bet he's dying to hear it."

"Shut up." Cully told him, but he smiled and clucked his tongue again to the horse who had slowed his pace, not realizing that they'd nearly reached their destination and that the time for carrots was drawing nigh. Denby was right not to worry about the booze killing him. It wasn't alcohol that would.

On the five mile or so drive out to the shallow prairie

lake, the men never met another vehicle or anyone on foot, for that matter. Outside Benson schoolhouse, there were a couple of old cars and a wagon, but no sign of their owners. The fields were deserted, too, with just the occasional washboard-ribbed cow or horse munching on what sparse green they could find poking up out of the brown and dust. Denby and Cully talked, soft-spoken at first and then, as the jar made more and more trips between them, they got to laughing and laughter's volume increased with each swig. The wagon rocked back and forth gently in the ruts that had been worked down into smooth hollows over the course of the rainless spring and on into the summer months. Norward's slack body shifted ever so slightly over the wagon box's floorboards as it swayed.

Denby asked, "How's married life treating you anyway? You haven't said too much about it." He added a touch of sweetness, compensating for Norward's obvious bitterness. "That Ellie's a nice girl."

"Yeah, she is. She's great." Cully meant it, and his tone said so. He gave a little shrug before he continued, "It's a change, that's for sure. If I'da known that the economy would still be slumping so low, I don't know. It's tough. Our place isn't the best. Sometimes I think she might be better off with her folks, living with them still and working for the Whitlock's."

Denby looked thoughtful while his brother spoke. He answered quickly when Cully was done. "Ellie had the choice. She knows what she wants, Cull. If she didn't wanna marry you, she'd be home now and working over at the Whitlock's, like you said. And she's sure dolled-up that place of yours. Lots of girls couldn't do that, wouldn't do that. Hard worker but classy, too. Wish I'd…" This last idea fell off the edge of verbalization with an empty thud, not one they could hear, but it sure was felt. Denby took a long drink from the quart sealer then explained self-consciously, "Sure am thirsty."

Cully glanced irritably at his brother and told him, "I hate it when you trail off like that. Dad used to do that and it'd drive Mom crazy. I can see why. Say it or don't. You wish you'd what? Finish your thought," he commanded.

Denby rubbed his cheek, felt that his face had grown numb and his limbs heavy from the moonshine. The stuff was like gasoline. Made his tongue too loose and tried to strangle his good judgment. "Wish I'd found someone like Ellie." There. He'd said it.

Cully shot Denby another look, felt his heart speed with anger. He looked away over the horse's back and breathed in deeply the hot air that dried his taste buds. "You keep your hands off my wife." Cully kept his eyes fixed on the road ahead, didn't hear but instead felt his brother's silent consent. After a bit, after the blood had ceased pounding the walls of his skull, Cully asked, "Where's that shortcut through the meadow?" The two of them stared hard up ahead, each trying to spot it himself, each wanting something on which to concentrate. It was easy to miss, not even a road. Not really.

"See that black stump? Just past it." Denby turned around. "Hey. Hey!" He shook his other brother's limp boot. "Wake up. We're here."

Norward sat up and Denby passed him the jar, and a wide smile pasted itself on the drunk's face. "Good sleep?"

"Yup. Catchin' up. Feels good to just relax. Have time to myself again." He drank deeply and belched a sour belch.

There were two paths running parallel through the woods. It would've been generous to describe this trail down to the lake as a road, or even to call that shallow body of water a lake. But it was more of a lake than Hughenden Lake, and in wetter years, it was the nearest fishing hole, a peaceful place, relatively bug-free and shady.

When Greene's Pond came into view through the drooping leaves, holey from the voracious caterpillars that inched their troops through the bush, Cully pulled back gently on the reins, telling the horse, "Whoa, boy." Denby hopped out first, and Norward passed him the rods and tackle out of the wagon box. After, he jumped out himself, clutching the bait pail in one hand and the jar in the other. Another nap had perked him up.

"Lake don't look too bad for it bein' so dry," Norward commented, standing on the few rotting boards at the water's edge and looking out toward the opposite shore. The lumber could've been the remnants of an old dock or some boys' unfinished raft. He bounced on his toes on the old wood planks. "Remember that raft we made?" Norward asked his brothers.

Denby stepped up beside him, the boards beneath his boots sinking slightly. "Yeah, we coulda drown. Geez, we were stupid kids." They all laughed, and then Denby tacked on, "But at least I got over it."

At this Cully gave Denby a little shove that made him step off the boards into the thick, green sludge at the water's edge.

While his brothers got their fishing gear organized, untangled line and baited hooks, Cully unhitched the tired bay and ran a length of rope through his halter shank, tying it to a nearby tree. "Here you go, big fella." He stroked the horse's nose with its crooked, white streak and pulled the bunch of carrots from his pocket. The gelding snorted his anticipation, lifting his head so that Cully's hand slid off his long nose. Cully held the carrots out and the horse munched contently. Cully patted the bay's neck, brushing away a mosquito. "Thanks for the ride," he whispered to the horse.

Cully turned to see his brothers settled in about fifteen feet apart and beginning to cast their lines. "Hey! Starting without me?" He picked up the jar that was sitting alone about halfway in between the two fishermen. Cully took a drink, set the quart sealer in the shade and set to fishing.

— *Chapter 6* —

BAD NEWS

They'd left the lake just as the sun was going down, and they wouldn't have been so late if it hadn't been for the music that danced out into the middle of the road, inviting them with its jilting rhythms.

Cully interrupted his brothers' conversation, saying, "Hey, shut up a minute. You guys hear that?"

"Hear what? Whoa." Cully stopped the wagon and sure enough, the voices of fiddles and guitars moved through the dusk, faint by the time they reached the three men on the evening breeze. Faint but enticing.

Denby said, "Must be coming from the Benson schoolhouse." He craned his neck, trying to bring the music closer. "Yep. Bet it is."

As the wagon drew nearer the whitewashed building with its wide porch and hitching posts out front and back, the catches of notes grew into recognizable tunes and now talking could be heard weaving clumsily in and out between those notes. Male and female tones mingling inside and outside of the building, converging and then moving apart. Coyotes howled along in the night, remaining under cover but drawn nearer civilization, both charmed and soothed by the melodies. The brothers, with the first jar long emptied and rolling around in the wagon box, and with the second sealer now making its rounds, were no more immune to the music than those other creatures. Only less cautious.

When Cully guided the wagon into the schoolyard, his brothers leapt out before he halted the horse. The bay headed for the water trough that had been set up in the yard and Cully allowed him to drink awhile before tethering him to one of the rails. With the horse taken care of, the middle Jullsen brother stood up straight and took a look around him. There were quite a few cars, all of them older, their bodies dull with dust and age, and two of them rigged up as Bennett buggies. But mostly, in this rural place, there were wagons like the one lent to them by Norward's friend, Gunnar. They were parked haphazardly both in front of the school and behind by the barn and the privies.

Men of all ages sat on bumpers and perched on the edge of wagon boxes, the half-moon every so often capturing the flash of a silver flask. Liquor wasn't allowed inside, and outside it was kept discreet although discretion tended to wane as the moon rose and filled out. Women came out to use the outhouse and to scold the men.

"Bjorn Orudson! I haven't seen you all night! Why'd you even bring me out here if I'm expected to sit in there all by myself?" a short blonde woman called as she stormed out of the schoolhouse to stand on the step.

"Cuz you wouldn't let me come if I didn't bring you!" the man hollered back.

His unhappy lady friend responded with, "I'm going home with my brother. You can stay here till you rot for all I care!"

"It'll be a quicker death than the one you got planned for me!" was his reply.

Cully shook his head and grinned like an elementary school co-conspirator as he passed the man identified as Bjorn Orudson by his enraged wife who had already headed back inside, presumably to search for her brother. Cully commented to Bjorn Orudson who was leaning with two others alongside a wagon box, "That's gonna be a tough one to fix up in the morning."

"You're tellin' me. Shoulda thought that one through." Bjorn Orudson held a small flask out to Cully, which he accepted, tilting the vessel up but blocking its searing contents with his tongue. He was full. He was having trouble feeling his feet and didn't want it to get worse.

"Thanks" Cully said.

"Hey," a tall, lanky fellow there with Mr. Orudson addressed him. "You Cully Jullsen? I thought I recognized you when you guys first drove in." The man slurred his words and leaned heavily against the wagon box behind him. Cully was certain that the solid presence of the wagon box was solely responsible for keeping the familiar man mostly vertical. "Remember me? We worked in the tie camp together—out by Hinton. Remember? Alan Forsbie."

"Oh yeah! That was a few years ago now. Good memory." Cully exclaimed, recognition lighting his face. "Alan. How've you been?" The two men shook hands. "Small world. What're you doing now?" Cully asked him.

Alan shrugged and took a swig from the flask that had made its way to him, passing it back while he answered, "Same as a lotta guys. Not much. Little farm work here and there. Was workin' pretty steady for the CNR, but it's got pretty tight. Gotta be related to the boss to get on anymore." Then a bolt of memory lighted up his face. "Speakin' of bosses, it's lucky you left when you did or Stan woulda killed ya with his bare hands! Swore he'd chop off your nuts if he ever caught ya. I'll tell ya when he…"

Cully interrupted. "*Who?*" The liquor he'd consumed all that afternoon now made his head swim. He struggled to press through the fog in an effort to understand the details being tossed out at him by this drunk he barely knew.

Alan Forsbie filled in the details, "Y'know. *Stan Sinclair?* You were doin' his daughter, the hot little cook shack gal?"

Despite the alcohol that weighed down his limbs, Cully straightened up. Bjorn Orudson again offered him the flask, but Cully just looked at it hard and then back at Alan. Bjorn Orudson responded with a shrug and a, "Suit yourself." The tension heating up between Cully and Alan didn't seem to bother him.

Cully stared at Alan Forsbie, telling him, "Darlene.

Her name is Darlene. What about her?"

Alan Forsbie might have been unaware of the searing tension, too, as he kept right on talking, digging himself a deeper hole. "Knocked up, that's what. You knew, didn't you? Thought that's why you took off in such a hellfire hurry. That's what we all thought. Good for you. Get out while the gettin's good. Stan was fuckin' *choked*, but the resta us was rootin' for ya. She woulda turned out that way with the helpa your dick or someone else's. Didn't matter. That's the kinda girl she was. Good lookin', though."

His friends must've become aware of the danger as Alan's words sloshed out because each had taken a step or two backward, over towards the front of the wagon and out of the way. Alan Forsbie himself was too drunk to see it coming. Cully Jullsen had never hit anyone in his life—not in earnest, anyway—and this wasn't something he'd decided to do now. It was as if the fury in his heart pumped that hot, rage-fueled blood into his arm and down on into his fist. It was out of his control: his fist flying, connecting with Alan's jaw, and Alan hitting the ground heavy as a sack of feed. Cully felt like an onlooker, a casual observer of his own actions and somehow detached from their consequences.

Hours later, when Cully drove into the yard, Norward singing beside him, still playing the spoons he'd picked up at the dance, and Denby sleeping in the back, it was a little after two o'clock in the morning. That half-moon was high now, pretty much directly above the frame house where even as she slept, Ellie listened with one ear for the creak of wagon wheels on the driveway. When she finally heard it, it was accompanied by Norward's caterwauling—she'd heard that often enough to recognize it now—and Ellie knew which racket she preferred. She got up, put on her slippers and robe, and made her way to the bedroom window not bothering with the bedside lantern. Moving aside the sheer curtain, Ellie could easily make out the black shape of the wagon against the background of lighter shadows and, as her eyes adjusted, of its passengers, as well. The freshly painted window frame was propped open with a brick, and although the summer night air that drifted in smelled delicious, it did nothing to improve her mood. The breeze felt warm and soft, but the men's chatter broke up the stillness into small, useless pieces. Ellie whirled away from her upstairs lookout and headed down to the kitchen where she'd wait in the dark.

"Norward! Put those things away and quiet down now. We're going to wake Ellie," Cully told his brother in a hoarse whisper, his throat dry and rough as sandpaper. Norward obediently tucked the spoons into his shirt pocket with a final clink.

Norward said, "I was gettin' sick of playin' anyway." And then, "Hey, you wanna get out here and let me drive back out so you can sneak up kinda quiet-like?"

Cully answered, "Nope. I want you to stay."

Cully saw that Norward looked shocked and maybe a little afraid. Norward stammered, "Stay? Stay where? Sleep in the wagon? I was gonna…"

Cully explained, "I got something to do and I need your help. Both of you." Instead of pulling the wagon up alongside of the house, Cully directed the bay through the front yard and over toward the garden. In the moonlight, Cully could see those heavy poles lying in the grass, could see one hole dug and one not yet finished. The clothesline reels lay there on the lawn catching just enough light from the moon to make their round edges glow.

Denby woke up on his own with the slowing of the wagon. He sat up, ran his sleepy fingers through his hair and put on his hat.

"Morning," Cully greeted his groggy brother over his shoulder and stopped the wagon. He got out, tied the horse's reins to the willow tree and walked over to the garden patch for one more installment of carrots. Cully told Norward, "Go get a bucket of water and a handful of chop for this fella. He's worked hard today. Now it's our turn."

"We're not gonna set that thing up tonight, are we?" Norward asked.

"Sure are."

Without speaking, Denby lumbered out of the wagon, located the spade Cully had left lying beneath the tree, and began work where his brother had left off earlier that day. When Cully was done feeding carrots to the gelding, Denby asked him, "How deep?"

Cully walked up and peered into the dark hole. "It's getting close. Should be a couple feet." He clapped Denby on the shoulder and grinned as Norward strode up with a bucket that he set down at the horse's nose.

"Now what?" Norward wanted to know.

Cully told him, "Now we need to get that other pole up."

Looking through the kitchen window, a disbelieving

Ellie leaned over the scrubbed-clean counter and watched. After a few minutes, she opened the door of the black stove and gently set two logs into the ashes along with a little kindling and half a page of her mom's spring of '28 Eaton's catalogue. As the fire came to life, Ellie ladled fresh water from the kitchen bucket into the coffeepot and lit the lantern that sat on the centre of the table.

"Uh, oh," Norward said and steadied the post as Cully filled in the hole around it with dirt. "Guess who's up."

Cully lifted his head from his task and saw the light from the kitchen. "Must've heard us drive in. No wonder, with your wailing and bad spoon playing."

"So whatta we do?" Norward asked.

Cully told him, "Just keep working. It's gotta get done. I told her and myself it would."

"It don't gotta get done. She's been hangin' clothes inside for months..." Norward began.

Denby had been listening in. "Norward, Cully started a job and now he wants it finished. How many times has that little girl in there cooked for you or given you a cup of coffee? Count 'em and then get back to work. This won't take long with the three of us at it." Then to Cully, "It's actually a real nice night to be out. I thought it might take a week for the bad moonshine to wear off, but I think I'm soberin' up already."

"Yeah. No wind for a change. Still. I miss that, the quiet, no howling wind sucking the life out of everything, out of everyone. Wasn't bad down by the lake, either," said Cully.

"Nope, it wasn't. Good day for fishin' even if we didn't

catch anything," Denby agreed congenially.

"Speak for yourself," Norward spoke up. "I got a coupla bites."

"Mosquito bites don't count, little brother," Denby joked and Norward had to smile. "Besides, by not catching anything we saved Ellie the chore of cleanin' fish," Denby pointed out.

"I wouldn't have cleaned them anyway. They're your fish." There she stood, having just come around the side of the house, flannel nightgown and robe not quite hiding the fact that she wore her gumboots. Ellie carried the coffeepot and three tin cups stacked crookedly within one another. "I thought some coffee might make the work go easier. Here."

Cully took the cups and coffeepot and set them down on the wagon bench. Ellie and Cully's eyes met for a moment during this exchange and he looked away first.

"Thanks for doing this, boys. I appreciate it." His wife brushed her hand against Cully's upper arm as she walked away, and he knew it was all right.

"Who wants some of this?" Cully offered his brothers, already pouring himself a cup. Both men came over to the wagon and let him pour their coffee.

"Ahhh. That's good." Denby sighed at the flavour, deep and rich, clearing his mind and restoring strength to his booze-sogged limbs.

Norward leaned against the wagon box and looked out over the horizon. The azure line that traced the rise and fall of the earth was becoming lighter. "Sun's comin' up already." he commented. "Most nights I'm up to see the sunrise, I ain't buildin' no clotheslines…and I ain't usually in such fine company. Cheers." Norward lifted his coffee cup to his brothers and downed what was left in it.

Ellie heard the soft clank of the spade outside the open kitchen window as she brought the eggs out of the icebox. *It's too early*, she thought, *to be Sunday yet*. Like the men, she'd get her work done before the day fully dawned and that would be just fine in the Lord's eyes. And so it was with a new, straight clothesline in the yard that the four of them ate eggs, fried potatoes, and toast with saskatoon jelly as the sun broke over the hilltops, flooding the kitchen with light.

Cully leaned back on his bench balancing it on two legs and Ellie, occupied with listening to the men's stories, overlooked mentioning this to him. She herself had her elbows on the table, holding her coffee cup with both hands and laughing over it at the brothers' tales.

"And so we pried open those crates and, sure enough, there was room for me to squeeze in 'longside that radio they'd packed in there. It was tight, but it was better than a whack over the head with a billy club. I've had lotsa those since they've been patrollin' more." As he spoke, Norward tapped his skull for emphasis.

Denby jumped in here, adding, "Remember, I was hiding in that crate, the one with the chesterfield in it? That wasn't as bad as your radio box, but I was pretty worried that they'd notice the top was loose, flip it up, and see me stretched out there, like I was relaxing on a Sunday afternoon."

Cully said, "Or they could've nailed it shut, Denby.

Then you would've ended up in somebody's parlour."

Denby laughed. "Might not be so bad if it went to some good looking widow's house. I'd hop outta that crate and tell her, 'Merry Christmas, darlin'! Look what Santa Claus brought you!'"

Ellie laughed and said, "And the poor woman would be wondering what horrible sin she'd committed to receive you on Christmas morning! It's worse than getting a lump of coal, that's for sure!" They all laughed at this.

Cully threw in, "Yeah, Denby eats more than a lump of coal."

Norward snorted, "Farts more, too!"

Norward continued with his story. "Anyway, you could hear 'em walkin' around the crates, talkin' and keepin' an eye out. We was never alone in there. Sometimes there was as many as three or four together, pacin' back and forth. The CNR hired those guys to make sure fellas weren't ridin' for free. I knew one guy—you weren't with me that time, Den—he was layin' on top a boxcar, flat and holdin' on for dear life. It was terrible windy, of course, and the wind blew him right off the car, right down into the river valley. Not into the water, neither. Nope. He landed on the slate banks. Lived for a day or two more, but wished he hadn't."

"That's just awful!" Ellie exclaimed.

Norward shrugged. "That's the way it goes."

At seven-thirty, there was a loud knock on the front door. Ellie moved from the kitchen counter to look out toward the front of the house. "Who could that be?"

"Don't know," Cully righted his bench and got up, the

legs scraping against the floor as he pushed out from the table to answer the door. "But they're up early." There, on the boards and bricks that the Jullsens called their front step stood Stewart Ames, hat in hand. He told Cully, "I got a call from Wetaskiwin. Is Norward here?" From behind her husband Ellie asked, "What's going on?" She clutched a tea towel, soap suds encircling her wrists like delicate bracelets.

"I've got to talk to Norward, Ellie. This doesn't concern you," Stewart Ames stated flatly.

"Whatever you gotta say to me can be said in fronta these folks." Norward said as he and Denby entered the living room.

"Morning, Norward. Morning, Denby. Look, I got a call from Wetaskiwin." The RCMP officer looked directly at Norward. "You been charged with the murder of Morris Randell, grain elevator operator. You'd better come with me."

— *Chapter 7* —

NORWARD AND DENBY

After Norward had left with Stewart Ames, the remaining three Jullsens sat around the table in stunned silence for a moment. Finally, Cully spoke up, "Can you tell us what's going on, brother? Is this about the guy that got cracked over the head with a bat? I thought some guy from Estevan did it."

Ellie leaned forward, listening more intently, waiting for Denby's answer.

"Apparently." Denby said, taking another drink of coffee from his tin cup. "Apparently they think Norward done it."

"Did what?" Ellie wanted to know.

Cully made a long story short, the abridged version of what Denby had told him earlier. "The grain elevator operator these two worked for last was murdered. They're accusing Norward."

"Murdered someone with a baseball bat?" Ellie said it like a question, disbelievingly. "That's ridiculous," she pronounced. "Your brother has many unsavoury attributes, but he's no murderer!" And then she started to cry while the men sat helplessly by.

After a bit, Cully stood up. "You want more coffee, Denby? I'll make some."

"Sure. That'd be good." Denby cleared his throat. "Make it a good, full pot, Cull. I'll tell you two everything I know, right down to the last detail. Might stop your wife from crying—probably not, though. What difference does it make now?"

"It would make a lot of difference to me," Ellie uncovered her face, bringing her hands down to rest listlessly on the tabletop. "To know the details. So I can sort it out for myself."

Denby smiled at her. "I hope it works out that way for you, Ellie. Truth is, I know all the details and I ain't got it sorted out yet."

Cully sat back down with a resigned sigh. "Well, tell us then, brother. What all happened?"

* * *

The young couple sat and listened while Denby drank the fresh coffee and related the story as he remembered it:

"It all started this one time in the dead of winter when the two of us, Norward and me, were standing on the edge of some prairie town—Veteran, it was—waiting to jump a ride.

I told him, 'Maybe we ought to head back into town, break in somewhere warm to sleep. A barn or something. Even that shed out behind the hotel.' I recall rubbing my bare hands together to get the circulation going then stuffing them back into my coat pockets. We were both freezing, but Norward had his own reasons for not wanting to stick around.

'You kiddin'? Curly catch me there, he'd kill me!' He had a point.

Before I'd joined him in that grey town, our brother'd already got a day's work out of the hotel owner, a burly Irishman by the name of McInnis with a head of flarin' red hair and a temper to match. Norward had washed the dishes, wiped the tables, swept the floors then stole two loaves of bread and a bowl of beans from the kitchen. That wouldn't have impressed the old Irishman too much.

So I asked Norward, 'Do you at least know when the train's supposed to come through here tonight?'

Our brother stamped his feet and held his hands over his ears, his flat cap pretty much useless against that cold, cutting wind. He said, 'Maybe half an hour. Could be less.'

I stated the obvious, 'Could be more, in this weather.'

'You wanna walk back up Main Street, see if we can find anythin'?' Norward suggested.

'Might as well,' I told him. 'Keep our feet from freezing. But if we're gonna wander away, we'd better keep our ears open for that whistle blow.' As if we'd miss it, that brittle air carrying every little sound miles and miles across the desolate flatness in that middle-of-nowhere place.

Shivering too much to talk a lot, we headed back into town circling through the alleys, searching for something, anything, warmer and safer than a boxcar. Norward knew the town better'n me and had some ideas. There was a stable behind that big house in the centre of town. We tried that, but it was locked up tight, of course. If we wanted in we'd actually have to break in, and that just wasn't real smart. Norward knew a lady who worked in the café at the hotel. We knocked on her back door, but she already had company. A teenage boy was sleepin' on her chesterfield, his dad in her bed and another guy in the kitchen curled up in front of the stove without a blanket or nothing.

Heading back outta town we heard that whistle voice calling us loud and clear through the cold-crystalled air, and we sped up.

'Here. Let's wait right here.' Norward told me when we'd got to the closest patch of willows. He'd ridden from that point on the line a lot of times, so I trusted his judgment. We rested on our haunches as the light appeared and sliced through the icy dark straight up the tracks.

Norward muttered, 'I'm gonna freeze to death by the time the goddamned engine goes by.'

'Yeah,' I answered. 'The engineer's slowin' her down—but that's gonna help us jump on in a minute or so.'

'You got that old newspaper still?' Our brother had found a couple of newspapers in a trash barrel back in town behind the dentist's office. He picked them out and stuffed one of them into his coat and handed me the other. 'Grab any of these ya see lying around. They might save ya later,' he told me. In a lot of ways, Norward is a pretty smart guy.

It wasn't long before the engine light was blinding us. Good thing, too, because my backside was going numb sittin' there like that, the circulation cut off and my thighs colder'n hell—pardon the expression, Ellie. After what seemed like forever and a day, those cars began passing by us nice and slow, creakin' and rockin'. I like that sound. Even when I'm not riding and I've got a little work somewhere, whether I'm in a town or out in the country, I'm likely to find those tracks and just sit alongside listenin' to that whistle and to the sound of those steel wheels on the rails. It's the sound of moving that proves you're not trapped. Not any place, not ever.

'This one comin' up looks good. You ready?' Our brother was pointing to an open boxcar maybe six or seven cars away. Hard to see in the dark, but he knows how to spot them.

'Go!' Norward shouted and sprung up and out like a cat running for its life. I'm the tall one, but you know, he's always been real wiry, strong and flexible. Me, I'm more bulky and not half as quick. From the floor of the car, he held out his hand to me. 'C'mon, goddamnit!' he hissed impatiently. I grabbed that hand I could barely see against the night, swallowed hard, and leapt. That boxcar had been open for a while. I could tell because the floorboards were white with frost and it made them slick. My boots shot out from under me as soon as my feet hit those frosty boards. Norward laughed. I do believe it made him feel good bein' better than me at somethin' for a change, so I didn't begrudge him this rare opportunity.

On one end of the car were stacked wooden crates from the Hudson's Bay Company, Simpson Sears and some others stamped in black with the words flour, sugar, coffee, tea. Along the other end of the car was a stack of barley bundles, tied snug with twine and piled high. Norward had chose our hiding place good.

He was all business. 'Let's get our feet looked after first.' Norward took off his left boot and began wrapping his foot in layers of that newspaper he'd found in town. This was the other side of our little brother, so serious, so concerned about our survival. Most times, he seemed to be daring death to come and sweep him up into the sky. That was the side I think we're more used to.

There was this one time, as a joke, he'd pretended to be passed out on the train tracks out across the street from the tavern in Fairview, up north a ways in the Peace River country. He'd waited till the train was coming, and then waited a little longer to see if I'd seen him. I did. I spotted him from across the street. 'Norward!' He was pretty full when he'd staggered outta the bar twenty minutes before. I learned later on that he was just looking for a peaceful place to puke up most of what he'd drank that Saturday evening. Waste of money, if you ask me. Anyway, I sprinted out into the street that ran between me and the train tracks and those elevators, painted that bluish green, strong shapes on a smeared dark blue-black background.

A rusty truck swerved around me, its horn honking, the guy on the passenger side yelling at me, 'What're you doin', you stupid son of a bitch! Get off the road!'

By the time he finished jawing, I was off the road and getting close to the tracks, that engine light still a ways away but close enough to be terrifying when your drunk brother is sleeping sprawled 'cross the tracks. 'Norward!' He didn't move from where he laid. I pictured that engine rolling right over him, glinting wheels sliding through neck muscles, cutting his head right off and taking his legs right under the knee.

'Jesus Christ! Wake up!' Sorry again, Ellie. The whistle screeched. It was really close now. I screamed at Norward, 'Get up! The train's comin'! Get up!' Sure enough, by the time I'd finished my yelling, Norward's loose limbs began to glow as that yellow headlight moved nearer and nearer. Still, he just laid there. I was screaming in my head asking myself, *How come he can't hear that whistle?* Of course he could, the dunce. It was like I was having one of those nightmares. You know the ones, when your feet feel made of lead and you wanna yell, but the noise gets stuck in your throat like a walnut you tried to swallow whole, hurting and choking you. That's how it felt.

I tried to stop the train, to get the engineer to see me. Frantically, I flailed my arms, hopping up and down, jumping high as I could, sweat pouring down my back. Must've looked like a crazy man. Thought I'd finally heard the screeching of brakes too late. That train wasn't twenty feet away when our brother shot off those tracks and into my outstretched arms, bowling me over and laughing like a hyena. I slugged him hard, but he just kept on laughing. What an idiot.

And yet he could be so sensible. Once we had our feet wrapped up in newspaper, he told me, 'C'mon. Get down inta this hay.'

I didn't argue. Carrying my boots, my feet wrapped round with the news of the day and tied with a bit of string, I worked my way into that barley stack so that nothing of me was showing. Norward did the same, and pretty soon we were both sound asleep. I'd heard about guys fallin' asleep in real cold weather like it'd been for that past week, and losing their fingers and toes as a result. But those guys weren't sleeping in a barley stack or with their feet bundled snug in newspaper.

I don't know how long we slept there in that stack, burrowed in safe between those sheaves that were being shipped to someone rich enough to transport the stuff. It was the train slowing, then finally stopping altogether, that woke us both up at the same time.

'Shit. You hear that?' Norward whispered closer than I thought he was, maybe less than a foot away.

'Yeah.' I'd heard it, all right. Outside the open car in the bleak of dawn, our brother and I could hear the crunching of boots on gravel and a couple of fellas in discussion.

'Yeah. We gotta check 'em all,' One guy said.

Then another answered him, 'C'mon. It's five o clock in the morning. It's forty below. Nobody's gonna be on this train.'

'Probably not, but it's our job. We got nothin' else to do, right?'

'Go inside and have coffee, that's what we got to do.'

'Tell you what,' the first guy bargained with the second. 'Let's make a check of every second car—and any car that looks like it'd be easy to jump. Sound all right?'

Norward spoke up in a hoarse whisper close to my ear, 'Sounds like goddamned trouble is what it sounds like.'

We could hear the two of them climbing into the car, their work boots slipping on those frosty planks. Like an electric shock moving through me, I remembered my boots! I'd taken them off and hadn't pulled them into the stack after me. Just left them sitting out there in plain view! Damn it all! Stupid.

'Hey. There.' This was Guy Number Two talking.

'Somebody took his boots off,' the deeper, older-sounding voice of the two commented, then said, 'If that guy's still on board, he'd better get the hell outta that stack before I fetch a fork and start stabbin'.' He didn't sound like the type of fella to be bluffing. I felt Norward shift beside me, felt the space where he'd been fill up with dust and cold, cold air.

'Norward Jullsen!' exclaimed the deep voice. 'Well, I'll be good and goddamned! How ya been, pal?'

'Better now, I'll tell ya. Good to see ya, buddy.' I heard the two men clasp hands and assumed it was safe to poke my head out.

'Hey, who's this?'

'Sam, this here's my big brother, Denby. And those,' he said, thrusting his chin in the direction of my frost-covered boots, 'Belong to him. He's about as sneaky as he is good lookin'.'

The deep-voiced guy called Sam laughed at this and

said, 'You fellas want some coffee? James and me were just heading in for some.'

'That'd be just fine. Thank you, sir.' Norward took off his hat and gave a little bow to Sam and nodded at James. Both guys grinned. That's our brother for you. What a charmer.

Long story, I know, but that's how we got on at the elevator in Wetaskiwin. As it turned out, Sam's uncle Elwood knew the guy that ran it. Morris Randell was his name. He was the guy that got killed after we'd been fired. Anyway, Sam managed to get us on there for a few months—right through till pretty much now. Funny how sometimes things work out. I liked the job all right. Long hours, hard work, but you got up in the mornin' knowing what you were going to be doing.

Norward worked hard at the elevators, too, loading and unloading freight, cleanin' out cars, working the electric shovel. But he didn't like it. It wasn't the work so much that bugged him, but Morris. Right from the start, those two couldn't see eye to eye on anything. You know Norward. He gets on good with most folks, so it was kind of an unusual situation. He sure didn't get on with Morris Randell. I'd hear them arguing, back and forth, every day:

'Jullsen. Did you sweep out those cars like I told you to?' Morris would ride him.

Norward would narrow his eyes and grip his broom tighter. 'Ya. Why?'

'Cuz there's dust and feathers all over the ones up front, that's why.'

'There's dust and feathers all over 'em cuz there's dust

and chickens everywhere, and the wind's blowin'. What did ya expect?'

This kind of argument happened every day Norward and me worked there. And every time, the tips of Morris's ears sticking out from under his cap would turn bright red. That's how you could tell he was real mad. Not a good sign.

So one day, after another fight, Morris Randell tells our brother, 'Look, you can either sweep those cars so they're clean or you can go home for the day.'

'Tough choice.' Norward thrust his broom at Morris and walked off whistling. I found him downtown later on that evening, drinking and playing cards in the back room of the livery stable. He'd won five bucks and offered to buy me dinner at the hotel.

I told Norward over dinner, 'You should've seen the look on Morris's face when you handed him that broom. He was some angry! Didn't talk the rest of the afternoon, just sat in his office scowling and drinking coffee. The rest of us kept our heads down and our noses clean.' I cut my steak. It was a little tough, but I couldn't complain. It'd been a while since I'd bit into a hotel meal, and it'd be a while till I got that chance again. I recall a fat fly circled perilously close to the fan above our heads, turning slow and casting shadows on that tin ceiling. The air barely moved.

'That guy. He thinks he can push people around.' Norward snorted and continued talking through a mouth full of mashed potatoes and gravy. 'Not me, he can't. I ain't gonna put up with that son of a bitch's shit, not no more.'

That's when I told him, 'You don't have to. He fired

all four of us: me, you and the two other fellas, that guy from Saskatchewan and that local kid.'

Our brother looked up from his half-eaten supper. 'When?' he asked me.

I said, 'Today—right at the end of the day. He gave us our pay and told us we were done.'

'Just like that?' He held his knife in one hand, his fork in the other, both in mid-air.

'Pretty much like that,' I said.

Then Norward asked me, 'He give you pay for my work?' He didn't keep eating but stared at me waiting for an answer. A bit of gravy dripped off his fork onto the tablecloth.

I shook my head and told him, 'He didn't give me any for you.'

Then, our brother wanted to know if I asked Morris Randell why there was no pay for Norward.

I explained, 'He said you walked off. He said it was your decision to leave, and he didn't have to pay you.' I finished my peas and felt a touch of relief when Norward brought his hands down on either side of his plate, still clutching his utensils, but not poised to stab anyone.

'That's bullshit. That goddamned son of a bitch!' Norward was cursing and swearing, and everyone in the café turned to look at us. He yelled again, 'That's such bullshit!' And then Norward threw his fork. It hit the wall with a clang and made a deepish nick in the flowery paper above the wood wainscoting. The gal at the cash register yelled at him to settle down, told him he'd find himself outside if he didn't. Boy, did he backtalk her. It was embarrassing.

He told her something like, 'I was goin' there anyway, little Miss Muffet. You wanna come? I got a tuffet you can sit on.' Then he turned toward the woman and grabbed his crotch. Sorry, Ellie. That's how it happened. Then our dear brother left.

I finished eating fast, and on my way out, I paid for both our suppers and gave the waitress a twenty-five-cent tip along with an apology for Norward's behaviour. She told me, 'He's an ass.'

'Can be.' I put my hat on and tipped it at her. 'Thanks. The food was real good.'

I went next door for a drink. I knew Norward was likely to show up back there soon as he'd got his money. And so I waited for him in the dim, stale-smelling room with the other tired guys who had extra money to spend on a glass of beer. Some of them slumped together at tables talking low while others, me included, sat hunched over the bar saying less and drinking more.

It wasn't too long before Norward plunked down on the stool beside me. 'You weren't at the boardin' house,' he stated.

'Naw.' I took a long draw of beer, feeling a bit sore at our brother. 'Thought you'd come here first. I was right, wasn't I? Any luck getting your money?'

'Nope. Son of a bitch wasn't home. Or maybe he wasn't answerin'. I pounded on the door a long time.' So we sat there for a bit and drank. Norward bought the beer, but he never did thank me for supper.

We had breakfast the following morning at the boarding

house, and that's when we heard what had happened to Morris Randell. Mrs. Beyer—we called her the widow Beyer when she wasn't within earshot—served the six of us poached eggs on toast sliced so thin you could've used it as a window, along with coffee so weak you could see through it to the bottom of the cup.

The widow asked those of us at the table, 'Did you all hear about poor Mr. Randell? Weren't you two working for him?' She looked at Norward and me, her chins all wobbly with concern. She knew we'd been working for him, so I don't know why she bothered asking. She went on to tell us that Mrs. Marshall from next door said that someone came to his house late the night before and whacked him with a baseball bat.'

— *Chapter 8* —

USEFUL INFORMATION

Late in September, Alan Forsbie headed to Saskatchewan hoping to land work for the winter months in the CNR's tie camp there. The train pulled into the Meadowlake station at 5:10 p.m. Alan stood up and stretched his stiff frame. He stepped off the train and onto the platform with three other men, traveling alone and Alan surmised that they were there for the same purpose as he.

Across the street, the square two-storey building that housed the local hotel looked inviting. Behind the lace curtains that hung in the windows, he could see that the restaurant was bustling with customers. Hungry and thirsty, Alan made a beeline for that establishment, looking both ways before crossing Railway Avenue, wide and dusty.

Once inside the restaurant, Alan Forsbie removed his battered hat and seated himself at a table for two near a window so he could look out onto Main Street and get accustomed to the feel of the place. This main street looked a lot like Hughenden's. Directly across the road from the hotel, on the other corner opposite the train station, was the livery barn, and next to that, a harness shop. From where Alan sat, he could see a general store and a drugstore further up the street, along with a barbershop. There were horses and wagons both moving along the street and sitting still before businesses. A shiny black Packard was angle parked in front of that barbershop, looking extravagant and out of place on that street.

It was loud in the restaurant, voices all around him, bouncing off of the walls and the high tin ceiling. Alan thought the atmosphere felt festive. The waitress had already poured him a glass of water and offered him coffee, which he gratefully accepted. He held up the one-sided paper menu and, after very little deliberation, decided on the roasted chicken dinner.

Suddenly, a towering figure approached his table, causing Alan to look up from his menu.

"I thought that was you, Alan," Stan Sinclair clapped him on the shoulder. "How've you been?"

Alan stood up and shook Stan's hand and grinned, telling him, "I've been just fine. How 'bout yourself, old man? What're you doin' here?"

Stan chuckled. "I could ask you the same thing. You eatin' alone?"

"Sure am," Alan said. "You wanna join me?"

"Yeah, that'd be good. Just came into town to get some supplies for the camp," Stan told Alan as the waitress filled Stan's water glass and coffee cup. "We're settin' up for winter work out there, gettin' everything ready for the gang. You got a job, Al?"

Alan smiled broadly, took a deep drink of coffee and admitted, "That's what I came here lookin' for."

"Then you're just the fella I wanna see."

When Alan Forsbie ordered chicken, Stan thought it sounded good and requested the same thing. The street quieted down outside the tall windows as businesses closed for the day; horse-drawn wagons headed in the direction of home, and the shiny black Packard backed up out of where it was parked and rumbled past the hotel, turning right at the end of Main Street. Gossip and coffee flowed at the table for two, and as the men tucked into their roasted chicken, conversation branched out in all directions, reaching here and there until it touched on a topic that meant something to both of them.

"You remember Cully Jullsen?" Alan asked, scraping the last of the gravy off his plate with the edge of his fork.

Stan's eyes narrowed and he set his knife down. "What about him?"

Alan didn't plan to share the fact that Cully had landed him on his ass at the Benson schoolhouse dance a month ago. Instead, Alan shrugged and casually said, "He's livin' back in Hughenden."

Stan sat rigid, stock still, listening hard to what Alan said. "How do you know?"

"I lived around there, too, this summer—over by Czar.

I ran into him at a dance in August," Alan chatted easily, but he tasted the grit of revenge in the back of his throat, felt it under his tongue. "He seems to be doin' pretty well for himself. Got a little wife and a steady job." He scoffed and emptied his water glass before saying, "Must be nice to have it so good."

"Yeah," Stan echoed. "Must be." Poison formed by his hatred dripped off Stan Sinclair's words. Alan heard that hatred, and it fuelled his own malice, searing and blinding as whiskey straight out of the bottle.

Alan felt compelled to keep the anger burning. "It was a shame—what he did to your daughter." He shook his head and refused when the waitress offered more coffee. He was ready for something stronger. "Then taking off like that. What a coward."

Stan gritted his teeth. He had ignored the waitress completely when she asked if he wanted anything else. He glared at Alan Forsbie, eyes wild with rage, fists clenched tight. "It's time for you to shut the fuck up."

Realizing, in a moment of stark clarity, that he'd crossed a line with Stan, Alan quickly backtracked, "I meant no insult to your Darlene. Sorry if it came out like that. I've got nothin' but respect for her and you, too." He considered adding something about Cully's lack of respect, but thought the better of it and stayed quiet, giving Stan space in which to calm down.

Finally, Stan's body relaxed, and he sat back in his chair. He admitted, "It's not somethin' I like to remember, that time in the camp with that bastard all over my daughter. So he's in Hughenden, eh?" Stan sat and seemed to ponder this fact for a bit before saying to Alan, "You feel like comin' next door for a drink or two? We can talk more about work this winter."

Alan grinned. "Sure thing, boss. Sure thing."

— *Chapter 9* —

THE SWING
IS NARROW

It's because of what Stella confided to her the summer before, the day they'd canned rhubarb and saskatoons, that Ellie believed the rumour. Also, it was from Cully that she had heard it, and he never passed along idle gossip. And if what Cully had heard about Stella was true, it would explain Reverend Andersen's behaviour that Sunday shortly after he'd caught Ellie's sister imitating him in the church basement.

"Hi, El." Cully stepped in the front door and set his hat on the back of the chesterfield. He sat down at the kitchen table looking dusty and tired. Ellie walked over, laid her hand on his shoulder and softly kissed his warm cheek.

"How was your visit to town?" she asked him. "Did they have what you needed?"

"Yeah," he answered. "I was able to get both the rope and the posts I'm gonna need. I picked up some more nails, too, just in case."

"Do you want water or iced tea?" she asked, setting a plate of oatmeal cookies on the table in front of him.

"The iced tea sounds great. Thanks."

Ellie brought over the jelly jars of iced tea and sat across from her husband on the freshly painted benches. She sat with her back against the wall and placed her feet in Cully's lap. He smiled and tickled her before grasping her feet so she wouldn't move them.

Cully drank half of his iced tea in one swallow. When he came up for air, he said, "That's good. Darn hot out today. Crops on the way to town look like they're withering in the fields."

"Everything's farming with you, isn't it?" She teased him and wiggled her toes.

"Yep. Everything is," he had to agree. Cully stroked the bare tabletop with his rough hand, his nails short and clean. He kept looking at his hand as he spoke, clearing his throat before he said, "El, I heard something today. Now, I'm not sure it's true but I wanted to tell you, didn't want you hearing it from someone else. And like I say, I doubt it's even true."

Ellie set her jar down and looked at him. "What did you hear? Look at me, please. Was it about me?"

He said quickly, "No. Not about you. About Stella." Cully looked at his wife quickly, and he looked away again.

"Well. Go on," Ellie pressed.

Culvar took a deep breath. "Lloyd Olson's wife saw her with Horace Williamson's wife."

"Daisie. Of course. They're friends," Ellie stated impatiently.

"That her name? Daisie? Yeah, her. Anyway," he continued. "She told Lloyd that the two of them were in Horace's backyard, sitting on that swing he hung from the willow tree for his nephews."

"So?" Ellie said irritably. "They were visiting."

Cully rubbed the back of his neck with his right hand and exhaled heavily. "They were sitting *real* close."

"I've seen that swing, Culvar. It's not big. You have to sit close on it."

"And Lloyd's wife thinks they were holding hands and that…well… that maybe they kissed." Cully said this last part fast, wanting to get it out into the air and have it float upward into the sky and out of their lives.

Ellie responded, "That is the most ridiculous thing I've ever heard, Culvar. It's just second-hand talk." She got up and took their jars to the counter for more iced tea.

"I never said I believed it, Ellie," he reminded her. "Only that I wanted you to hear it from me, instead of some busybody housewife with nothing better to do than spread talk. Can you blame me for that?"

Ellie sighed. "You know I can't. Thank you for telling me." She came back to the table and they drank a second jar of iced tea in silence.

* * *

A couple weeks later, the days remained hot with apparently no break from the heat in sight. Stella was sitting at the dressing table in her room, the room the sisters used to share before Ellie got married and moved to the house on Hughenden Lake with Cully. Stella was fussing with her hair and makeup in front of the large round mirror mounted low on the dressing table.

"For goodness sake, Stella. It's just a hayride. Your hair's going to get all mussed up anyway, and no one's going to see your pretty blouse under the coat you'll be wearing." Ellie gently smoothed the covers on the double bed they'd shared for years and then sat down on its edge.

Stella looked in the mirror and spoke to her sister's reflection. "Actually, I'm not going on the hayride, Ellie. I'm catching a ride with Mom and Dad into town."

Henry had offered to take them all on the hayride: Ellie, Stella and Cully, too. Henry's cousins from Wisconsin were visiting for a couple of weeks so he'd arranged this as entertainment for them, something to do on a long summer evening. Cully would be along shortly, and Henry would pick them up at the Pedersens'. The wagon ride would culminate at Henry's folks' house where they'd have lunch before going home. Ellie and Stella's parents had agreed to pick their daughters and Cully up from there on their way back from town. It was all planned.

"What did Henry say?" Ellie wanted to know.

"Oh, I haven't told him yet," Stella quickly admitted. "Could you mention it to him please, Ellie?"

"I suppose," Ellie said, then asked, "Where is it you're going?"

In the mirror, Stella's reflection flashed Ellie a little smile, somewhat sly, Ellie thought. "I might go see Daisie. Horace is working late at the lumberyard, and it makes for such a long evening when she's there all alone. Poor dear hardly knows a soul. You should get to know her, El. You'd really like her. She speaks English. She says there're lots of English-speaking people in Montreal."

"What do you want me to tell Henry?" Ellie asked.

If Stella heard the bitterness in her sister's question, she ignored it. She just added a little more rouge and said, "Just tell him that I decided to go into town with Mom and Dad. He'll understand." Stella turned on the stool at the dresser to look at Ellie. "Please, El. It's no big deal. I'd tell him myself but I can't. I gotta go see Daisie."

Muriel Pedersen called up the stairs, "Stella! We're going!"

"All right," Ellie gave in. "I'll tell Henry but honestly, I think you're being rude."

At this, Stella stood up, cocked her head to the side and held her hands up, palms toward the ceiling. An exaggerated dismissive gesture. "Oh, well. Mr. Henry's been rude to me more than once. What goes around…" With that, the younger sister left the room.

That Saturday night was fairly comfortable, with the evening breeze moving over the wagon and the sun slowly falling from the sky. Henry made sure that the hay was deep and clean, and he was careful to avoid the most pronounced ruts in the road so the ride was smooth. Ellie considered Henry's thoughtfulness and hoped that her little sister wasn't jeopardizing the good thing she had going with him.

When Ellie mentioned that Stella had chosen to go into town with their folks, Henry looked a bit disappointed, but her decision didn't seem to put a damper on his night. Henry joked around as he drove the horses and lead his passengers in a round of *She'll Be Comin' Round the Mountain*. His cousins were easy-going, as well. Ellie had met one of them, a girl a year younger than Stella, a couple of years earlier when she was visiting at Henry's. The other two cousins, boys, were both friendly. Ellie and Cully enjoyed listening to the jokes and stories they told about the goings-on in Wisconsin.

The following Sunday morning, a very odd thing happened. The Pedersen family was filing out of the church with everyone else, feeling relieved at leaving the close warmth of the little building. Ellie and Cully followed Ellie's family down the aisle. At the door, Reverend Andersen greeted them all and, when he got to Stella, he stopped her.

"Good morning, Miss Pedersen," he said in a way that seemed relaxed—for him.

Stella flushed. "Good morning."

"Would you be interested in reading the scripture for next Sunday?" He didn't wait for Stella's answer before telling her, "Here. I've printed it out for you. Genesis 19:3-8. It's short." He held out the paper for her. Stella didn't reach for it.

"I...I don't know. I've never done..." she stammered.

The Reverend pushed her, "I'd like to have a focus on the youth of the community. It would be very good if you could act as a representative. You're not shy, are you?" he asked.

"No, not really." It was true. Stella was not shy, but it couldn't be said that her favourite reading material was the Bible.

The preacher smiled tightly. "I didn't think so. You'll do fine." He pressed the slip of paper into her palm. "See you next week." Stella's parents looked pleased and Ellie looked worried.

Ellie and Cully said goodbye to the Pedersens out in front of the church then walked up the street. When they were a block or so away from Birdie Jullsen's house, Cully reached for Ellie's hand and asked her, "So, what do you think that's all about? Andersen getting Stella to read?" he looked at her sideways from under his hat pulled low to shade his eyes from the late morning sun.

Ellie admitted, "I don't like it. He never gets women to read. It's just not done. Culvar, you don't think he wants to get even with her, do you?"

"For her imitating him that day, you mean?" Cully paused, weighing it out, then decided, "I wouldn't put it past him."

"No. Me neither." Ellie's voice reflected the dread she felt.

Now, if it were Ellie, she would've read that passage out loud over and over again until she got it right, until she could read it through with no mistakes. But not Stella. She didn't worry about being prepared—until she realized the seriousness of being unprepared, that is. Then she panicked. Stella, the procrastinator.

That's why on the following Sunday, Stella ended up reading the passage silently in her family's pew during the

Call to Worship and the Opening Prayer. She'd made sure that she'd sat at the end of the pew, next to the centre aisle. When the time to read her assigned verses arrived, Stella stood and walked confidently up to the pulpit.

"The first reading of scripture is from Genesis 19, verses 3 through 8."

Stella's voice was strong and clear and could be heard right to the back of the church, even by its most elderly members. From where he sat in his chair behind and slightly to the right of the pulpit, Reverend Andersen smiled as Stella read.

"'And he pressed upon them greatly; and they turned in unto him, and entered into his house; and he made them a feast, and did bake unleavened bread, and they did eat. But before they lay down, the men of the city, *even* the men of Sodom, compassed the house round, both old and young, all the people from every quarter.'"

Ellie felt her mouth go dry as a jolt of recognition shot through her. She snatched up her Bible from where it lay on the polished wood pew and opened it to the first book of the Bible. As Stella continued to read, Ellie read silently along with her sister, feeling the tension build as Stella continued.

"'And they called unto Lot, and said unto him, Where *are* the men which came in to thee this night? Bring them out unto us, that we may know them.'"

At reading the word "know" Ellie's face felt hot. The word suggests intimacy, the kind shared between husband and wife. Cully, sensing her discomfort, touched Ellie's knee and gravely nodded at her as if to say, *Yes, he is getting even with Stella.* Ellie glanced up at her sister, trapped there before the congregation. If Ellie's cheeks were warm, her sister's were on fire. Ellie considered that if only they had bothered to look at the passage before today, they may've found a way to avoid reading it. Ellie also considered the rumour regarding Daisie and felt ashamed of her own gnawing suspicions.

" 'And Lot went out at the door unto them, and shut the door after him, and said, I pray you, brethren, do not act so wickedly. Behold now, I have two daughters which have not known man; let me, I pray you, bring them out unto you, and do ye to them as *is* good in your eyes: only unto these men do nothing; for therefore came they under the shadow of my roof.' "

Stella stepped down and hurried back to her family's pew, her eyes lowered. The Pedersens sat unsmiling and rigid beside Ellie and Cully. As soon as Stella was seated, Reverend Daniel Andersen launched into his sermon.

"These are hard times." He cleared his throat. "We're fortunate here, in many ways. Many of us are able to help ourselves and, at the same time, friends and neighbours in our community are not reluctant to help one another when need arises. There is an ability in our village to reach out to each other and love one another as the Son of God instructs. This, my friends, appears to be a community of love. A Christian place, a haven from the evils of the world.

"From our seat of relative safety and comfort in times of economic strain, it has become increasingly easy to believe that we are somehow immune to sin and wrongdoing.

We believe this community, *our community*, could never plummet to the depths of depravity experienced by the ancient settlements of Sodom and Gomorrah. We couldn't be more wrong. This kind of smug complacency is the type of instrument that props open the door through which sin will enter."

Stella and Ellie looked at one another. Without speaking, they shared the thought *Here it comes*. And come it did.

"You may not believe it, you may not want to accept that this community can become a Sodom, that it may, in fact, actually already be a Sodom. Don't be naïve. Don't let it fool you. Human corruption can happen at home, and it can happen in our time. Diseases of the soul are not confined to Biblical times and places—and neither is the work of evil hands. And people, evil hands are always looking for work. Beware of turning a blind eye to that which happens, that which blatantly takes place, within the perimeter of your own community, under your own noses, under your own roofs."

At this, Daniel Andersen stared hard at the Pedersens for embarrassing, uninterrupted moments, resulting in their uncomprehending looks. The Reverend went on to talk more directly about the debauchery that occurred in those places cursed and destroyed by the Old Testament God, but the sermon always circled back to Hughenden and to the threats present among them. And when the Reverend referred to those menaces at home, he'd stare again at the Pedersen family pew.

Following the service, Stella's family, along with Ellie and Cully, sneaked out of the church via the side door. In the wagon on the way home, Muriel questioned Stella.

"Any idea what the sermon was really about today? We seemed to be its topic," she asked coldly. Ellie and Cully, coming to their house for dinner, sat on the rear bench seat with Stella.

"I don't..." Stella began, but Ellie interrupted. In her view, this was not the time for the whole story.

Ellie said, "What are you talking about? How did we seem to be 'its topic'? Mom, are you referring to the way the minister kept on looking in our direction?" Ellie laughed lightly, practicing amusement the best she could. She'd been working on this story from almost the moment the good Reverend had begun his sermon. Ellie launched into it now, explaining, "Directly behind us, at the back of the sanctuary, there's that tall window with the red and blue stained glass. You know the one?"

"Yes." Muriel Pedersen turned around and gave her daughters a stern look. "What about it?"

"Well, there's a brand new crack running the length of one of the panes. A big one!" Ellie fabricated the details. "I think it drives him crazy! He can't keep his eyes off it. It makes sense, doesn't it?" Stella nodded in frantic agreement. "He was never actually looking at us, but he was looking over our heads! Dwelling constantly on that new window already broken." Ellie shook her head in mock sympathy for the preacher.

Their mother looked thoughtful, sitting there on the front bench seat next to her husband. After riding along for a while in silence, she turned on the bench, faced her daughters and Cully, and proclaimed, "That man is certainly proud of his church. 'Pride goeth before a fall.'" After quoting the book of Proverbs, Muriel Pedersen turned back around and moved in a little closer to Benson, who smiled down at his wife.

There were changes in Stella in the weeks that followed "the sermon." She was never a big girl anyway, but now she lost weight. Lots of weight. Stella's clothes hung off her decreasing frame, and her mother often inquired about her health, saying things like, "Stella, you're getting so thin! Are you dieting? You shouldn't be so vain. You were fat as a child, but you've grown out of it, dear. Here, have some more potatoes."

It was clear to Ellie that her little sister wasn't being vain. Stella obviously wasn't spending even a quarter of the time she used to in front of that round dresser mirror in her room. The girl wore no makeup around the house and no jewelry. Only if she were meeting Henry, was Stella inclined to put on a touch of rouge and lipstick. But as she wasn't seeing Henry very often anymore, her makeup stores remained amply stocked. Many times that winter, Cully and Ellie invited her along, asking her to come into town with them. Most times, she opted to stay home or chose to babysit for the neighbours.

Of course, Stella never ventured out to visit Daisie. Not anymore. One autumn afternoon, though, Ellie remembered arriving for a visit with her family and seeing a letter addressed to Stella lying face up on the table. The return address was a local one: Mrs. Horace Williamson, Hughenden, Alberta.

Later on that evening, after the letter was long gone

from the table, she asked Stella about the correspondence. "Stella, did you get a letter from your friend Daisie?" The girls were sorting old photographs into albums. Something they wanted to do together. Stella looked at Ellie blankly. "No," she said and went back to going through that hatbox full of pictures.

In February of 1935, with the weather persistently cold, and that steady wind building impassable banks of solid snow on the prairie ground, Horace Williamson found his wife Daisie in the bloody water of their tin tub. The whetting stone she'd used to work the knife blade to a sharp gleam sat there on the kitchen counter in the lantern's glow. The knife itself was found on the bottom of the tub. The water was cold when they lifted Daisie's body from it.

— *Chapter 10* —

YOU'RE NOT PREGNANT, ARE YOU?

That morning Ellie had arranged to catch a ride the short distance into town with Henry, who was going into work at the livery stable owned by his father. In the doctor's office, she let the nurse know that she had an appointment, and then sat down in one of the two stiff-backed chairs. As the nurse hurried by, she smiled warmly at Ellie, and Ellie remembered the rumour that had circulated about her. Apparently, the nurse had had an abortion when she was a young teenager—only fourteen—and was now unable to have her own children. Ellie considered the old rumour and considered the fact that the nurse did not have children. She was married, all right, and Ellie calculated that she must be in her mid-thirties. Then and there, Ellie concluded that the rumour was probably true.

Ellie felt grateful that she was alone in the waiting room. She soon gave up trying to read last week's edition of *The Hughenden Record,* the village's newspaper, and opted instead to look out the large picture window that gave her a full view of Main Street. At nearly ten o'clock in the morning, the street was quiet. Ellie noted how much it differed from the busy Saturday night shopping scene she took in almost every week.

In the café across the street, Ellie could see through dusty windows the banker—Edward Shultz—and the general store owner, whose name had slipped her mind. The man had bought the store a couple of years after she'd moved to Hughenden with her family. Ellie recalled that the former owner had moved back down to the States to look after his aging parents. She liked the old owner much better.

Ellie saw the two men lean back in their chairs. There were coffee cups on the table between them, but she didn't see either of them take a drink. They just laughed, sometimes so hard that one of them would slap the tabletop or rock back and forth in his chair.

There were a few cars angle-parked along the street in front of the shops, but in those depressed days, folks mostly walked or brought wagons to town. It wasn't unusual to see an old horse hitched to a post beside a battered truck, loaded with coveted hay upon which the happy horse would munch. That day, there were no horses on the street and only a handful of people—mostly men—hurrying in and out of stores, getting what they'd come for and going back to work. Very unlike Saturday nights, during which much time was spent browsing and visiting with the folks you met on the streets and in the crowded shops. Hughenden was a booming town, but you wouldn't know it on a Tuesday morning in mid-October. "Ellie?" Lorna smiled. She stood up and followed the nurse into the examination room and, a little later, when Ellie came out, she was the one smiling. On the spot, Ellie decided to tell her husband first, and so she headed straight for home, walking the mile or so with the sunshine warm on her face. When she arrived in their yard, Ellie walked out to the corral where Cully worked with the horse he called Maurice, guiding him round and round by a sturdy rope tied to his halter. Her husband wore his battered cowboy hat and that old coat he refused to get rid of.

When she told him the news, Cully whooped, swept her up off the dry ground, and spun Ellie around in his arms. This scared the horse, causing him to jump and snort at the end of his rope. In an empty barn stall on the property they'd rented on the edge of Hughenden Lake, Cully spread a horse blanket on the fresh hay and pulled Ellie down onto it after him.

* * *

The ride into town on Sunday morning was quiet, husband and wife treating each other with stiff courtesy and speaking only when necessary. They had argued the night before, and their shared mood was as frosty as the grass in the ditches. Cully couldn't remember what started the argument, but his wife did: it was her husband's lack of consideration. Ellie had just finished scrubbing the kitchen floor. The pail full of sudsy water sat next to the wet mop out in the porch. Cully had to have known she'd mopped. Still, he strode right by that bucket and mop and into the kitchen, boots covered in dust and who knows what else from the corrals.

As he ladled himself a jelly jar of water, Ellie stared hard at him. Then the fight began, and the couple was still feeling its effects that morning on the way to church.

The Morgan named Maurice snorted steam as he pulled their new wagon down the driveway out to the main road. Cully purchased the four-year-old gelding knowing that he could train him to pull a wagon, work to which Maurice was unaccustomed. The gelding had been a plow horse all his young life. The horse was green broke, but as Duke Reggon told Cully when he'd bought Maurice, "You can ride him, but ya gotta be really needin' to go somewheres bad. Otherwise, I'd sooner walk, just to be on the safe side." Cully knew horses, and he needed a reliable one to pull his wagon. He'd spent a little extra time with Maurice and gently brought that horse 'round to his way of thinking.

Ellie set a basket of freshly baked buns behind her on the wagon floor beneath the bench. She'd wrapped them in two threadbare towels. "Is there time to drop these off at your mom's before church?" she asked her husband. Cully stared straight ahead and answered, "Nope."

That was the extent of their conversation during the trip from their house to the Hughenden United Church where they were married not even a year ago. Now with their first baby on its way, and with that white church coming into sight, this thought crossed Ellie's mind: *Is it always going to be this hard?*

At Birdie's house following the church service on the subject of eternity (which lasted almost as long), the frost between Ellie and Cully began to melt. Ellie helped Cully's mom in the kitchen. She was mashing potatoes when Ellie noticed her mother-in-law watching her closely. The young wife tucked a wisp of stray hair behind her ear and felt the heat of the steaming potatoes on her face. After what seemed like long minutes, Birdie asked Ellie straight out, "You're not pregnant, are you?"

The masher halted in mid-mash. A glob of potatoes heavy with butter and cream splatted back into the pot. "What? Why?" Ellie asked.

Birdie smiled and touched Ellie's shoulder with her plump, work-reddened hand. "I can usually tell. Ever since I was a girl I've been able to do it. I just know—it's like a feeling." She set her paring knife down on the edge of the sink and turned to look closely at her daughter-in-law. "You are, aren't you?" The flush in Ellie's cheeks was all the answer she needed. Birdie squealed, grabbed her son's wife and pressed her into the purple bib apron she wore over her Sunday dress. Ellie still clutched the masher that had spattered the linoleum with bits of starchy white potato. Finally, Birdie released her and held the girl at arm's length. With her free hand, Ellie brushed away a tear.

Birdie marched under the archway that separated kitchen from living room. "Culvar Jullsen," she said gruffly. Cully, Franklin Simpson, his lady friend Doris

Brown and Birdie's daughter, Alice, all looked her way, silenced by Birdie's tone. Whenever she called any of her children by their full names, her progeny knew Birdie had something important to say. The visitors waited and watched as Birdie stood there poised in the archway, nearly filling it with the stance of her resolve alone. In a flash of smile that still dimpled her cheeks, her disguise of annoyance disintegrated leaving just Birdie, a not-yet-grey grandma-to-be.

Ellie stepped up behind her and grinned a little sheepishly at her husband. "She guessed."

Cully sighed and lifted his hands, letting them fall again passively into his lap. "She always does."

The mood was buoyant for the rest of the afternoon. Everyone ate too much, drank too much coffee, and stayed too late. Ellie and Cully sat close together, his hand under the table resting on her thigh. Resting inside its mother and slightly above its father's hand, the unborn baby was already exercising its power over people's emotions.

After dinner and before dessert, Birdie brought out her photo albums. The last time Ellie had seen these pictures was when she and Cully first began courting. She remembered that autumn evening he'd brought her over to his mom's house. Of course, she'd met Birdie Jullsen before—at church, at socials, on the street—but this was different. This was formal. Extra manners were taken out and dusted off. Birdie had offered the young couple lemonade in shining glasses and gingersnaps on china plates.

During that visit three years ago Norrie and Birdie Jullsen's photo sat in a silver picture frame atop the polished end table. Tough as gristle, Norrie's skinny old body was the antithesis of his wife's full figure and youthful face. An elm tree stretched out its branches behind the awkwardly posing Jullsens. Norrie Jullsen had died the same year Cully met Ellie—the winter that Cully spent working in the camp up north.

Ellie recalled seeing Norrie Jullsen in church during Christmas and Easter services when her family first moved to Hughenden during her sixteenth year. All the rest of the time, Birdie Jullsen came to church without her husband. She and her daughter, Alice, would always sit on the left side, four pews from the front. These days, Alice and Birdie usually sat directly behind the Pedersens and Ellie and Cully. Every spring and summer, Birdie donated fresh flowers from her backyard garden to place on the alter and on the steps at the front of the sanctuary. Her cookies and pies were often the first things that sold at church bake sales. Birdie taught Sunday school, also, to the older kids, the ones who didn't want to be there very much.

Birdie Jullsen loudly sang hymns of praise and thanksgiving, and meant it. And after Norrie Jullsen's passing, she sang them even louder and meant it slightly more.

Now, in this Sunday afternoon living room with a seed in her belly and with her husband sitting next to her on the chesterfield, Ellie got another look at these photo albums. Through a mother's eyes, she examined pictures of Denby, Alice, Cully and Norward, their black and white clothes worn to rags, but their hair neat and faces scrubbed clean. She saw them standing in front of scrawny Christmas trees, bathing in tin tubs before winter stoves, playing in scruffy yards, seated around the kitchen table in mismatched chairs. No bikes, no toys, no dogs. Not in these pictures or in any of the others Ellie had seen in Birdie's living room. Denby went out to work to support himself at ten, the other two boys at eleven. Alice helped her mom at home until she was fifteen. Then she got work as a domestic on Shelton's cattle ranch east of town, closer to Czar. Just recently, Alice had landed a job as a telephone operator; the position came open upon Rosie Ulstad's worsening health.

"Who's this?" Ellie pointed to the centre of the black page at a photo featuring two young boys. Her mother-in-law, sitting with her thigh pressed against Ellie's, laughed and told her the story behind the picture.

"This one's a candid shot. I'd been tending the flowers out back. It was August, and they were in full bloom. You should have seen them, Ellie. Thought I'd take a picture of the yard to send home before I cut some of those pretty flowers. I got the camera and kept working. Denby and Cully were playing out behind the house, down the alley a ways. I overheard Denby daring Cully to jump." Birdie paused in her story and gave her daughter-in-law a friendly nudge like she was letting Ellie in on a joke. "If I'd've known from *where* he was coaxing him to jump, I would've put a stop to it."

"Where was he?" Ellie asked, leaning forward slightly, attentive. Cully, sitting on the other side of his mom, answered his wife.

"I'd crawled up on top of Swenson's wood pile and got on the roof of their shed. They had a crabapple tree on the other side of that shed in their backyard, and I was going to get to it. I picked some apples—Mrs. Swenson couldn't see me there behind the leaves and branches—and threw 'em down to Denby." Cully chuckled, and his mother picked the story up right where he left off.

"Of course, he'd got up there all right, but when it came to getting down he realized he hadn't planned that part out. My son thinks ahead a lot more nowadays. Got a sprained ankle from that adventure." Birdie patted Cully on the shoulder.

Just then, Franklin Simpson started to cough, and Doris Brown went to the kitchen to get him a glass of water. Cully's mom wrapped up the story. "But Cully's brother took good care of him, picked him up off the ground, helped him down the alley. And that's when I got this shot of them both."

In shades of grey, a tall Denby stooped so that Cully could get an arm around his neck. Pain in Cully's face, concern on Denby's. Cully held his left foot off the ground, hopping on his right and leaning against his brother, the story's ending frozen in Birdie's album.

Birdie's thoughts seemed to go astray as she reached for her coffee cup and murmured to herself, "I've been meaning to get that one framed and keep it out somewhere." But she left the picture there in the album for another day. They kept turning the pages, looking through the two photo albums Birdie had put together along with another box of pictures she hadn't yet organized. At about five o'clock, the women got up to make roast beef sandwiches, cut more apple pie and brew a little more coffee.

In the kitchen, Birdie told her daughter-in-law, "You'll see what it's like now, Ellie. You'll have your own pictures, your own family's history." Right then, Ellie knew how much a baby changes everything.

— *Chapter 11* —

THE VISIT

Denby had suggested it, and Cully thought it was a good idea. They'd take the train into Edmonton and visit Norward before the snow flew. Ellie had packed them sandwiches that early morning, and Henry drove them to the train station on his way to work at the livery stable in town. The sky was a crisp, pale blue against which bare trees spread their frost-covered limbs. The wagon ride into Hughenden was a little rougher than usual on account of the hard, frozen ground. As they approached the town site, the three men watched as the grain elevators grew taller against the tree-dotted landscape.

"Whoa," Henry told his horse, and the wagon came to a stop next to the deserted platform. "You fellas greet old Norward for me, will you?" The Jullsen brothers promised they would and told Henry that they'd made arrangements with Benson Pedersen to pick them up at Birdie's house sometime the next morning.

"So we'll see you when we get back—probably Saturday?" Cully asked as he stepped down off the wagon and onto the frosty boards that surrounded the little train station at the end of Main Street.

Henry held the reins tight and smiled. "Yeah, Saturday sounds just fine." Then he reminded them about Norward, saying, "You make sure to say hello to him for me."

"Will do," Denby assured him. Henry waved, clucked to his horse and headed that wagon up Main Street to the livery barn.

Because it was cold, the brothers waited in the station on one of the three benches there—the one closest to the potbelly stove. The wood inside it crackled and hissed just for them. Only the ticket booth attendant shared the station with them, and he was quietly filling out forms behind the counter. It wasn't long before all three of them heard that old familiar whistle blast right on schedule. Tickets clutched in hand, Denby and Cully walked back out to the platform to watch the train arrive, their footsteps echoing in the quiet air.

"Here she comes," Denby commented as the engine appeared from the east, a solid black shape looking smaller than the volume of its horn suggested. As the locomotive neared the Hughenden station, the brothers heard the train slow, and the wheels began to screech on the rails. Finally, and with a sharp release of steam, the engine pulled to a stop and the engineer waved to the two men standing on the lonely platform.

Denby and Cully stood near the station building waiting to be called aboard after any passengers arriving had disembarked. In the passenger car almost directly in front of them, Cully noticed someone stand up—someone familiar but out of context in this setting, his hometown. She adjusted her hat self-consciously and clutched a small suitcase close to her body. Suddenly, in one lightning-quick motion, Cully pulled his hat down low, snatched Denby's sleeve, and dragged him along the platform and around the corner to the west side of the station—out of sight of Darlene Sinclair.

"What the...?" Denby muttered as he was nearly pulled off his feet by Cully's forcefulness.

"Shhh," Cully hissed at his older brother as he pressed his back against the station's cold exterior wall. From there, Cully peeked around the corner of the building to where the train sat and to where Darlene took the conductor's hand as she stepped down from the dark green passenger car. On the platform, she glanced quickly left and right, and then headed into the station.

Denby was irritated by his brother's behaviour. "What're you doing? We're gonna miss our train. Let's go," he urged and grabbed Cully's sleeve, asking, "What's going on with you?"

Cully shook his arm free from Denby's grasp and told him, "Let's just get on the damn train."

In the passenger car, Cully kept his hat pulled down low and was careful to sit on the left hand side of the car, the side farthest from the platform. Denby sat in the seat right behind him. He didn't know who they were avoiding, but Denby followed his brother's lead and sat where he couldn't easily be spotted from the platform. He barely looked up when the conductor asked for his ticket. Only when the car began its slow forward roll and the whistle ceased to blow, did Cully sit up straight and watch the land begin glide past the window.

When the train was a little ways down the track, Denby leaned forward over the back of Cully's seat. "Now tell me what the hell's going on here," he whispered harshly.

At this, Cully sighed heavily, stood up and slid into the seat behind him next to Denby, feeling the cold of the wicker weave. He shot his older brother a sideways glance, grimaced and asked, "Did I ever tell you about Darlene Sinclair?"

"Nope," Denby answered, "But I have a feeling you're gonna now."

Cully made a long story short and left out quite a few details, but by the time he was finished, Denby had the gist of what went on between his brother and Darlene Sinclair.

"So that's why you slugged ole Alan Forsbie at the Benson schoolhouse the night of our fishin' trip," Denby said and nodded, adding, "Makes sense now that I know the story." Then, dropping his tone, Denby asked, "Do you think you *are* the father?"

Cully shrugged and looked pained. "I suppose I could be. Me or Stan. It'd be better if it was me. For Darlene and the kid, I mean."

"Not better for you, brother," Denby reminded him.

"No, not better for me."

Although the sky had been clear when they left that morning, as the train neared the city, making stops at every station along the way, the sky had clouded over. Now, later in the day, it was a solid grey, high above the earth and non-threatening. Occasionally, a small, dry snowflake would float down past the train's windows foreshadowing the white winter to come. For now, though, the land was encased in shades of brown and grey, nature's green a long-forgotten colour.

In downtown Edmonton, Denby and Cully walked the many blocks from the station to the prison where they would see their little brother. As the two strode along, more flakes fell, melting on the sidewalks as soon as they hit, making the walkways slippery and the roadways muddy.

"I hate the city," Denby muttered under his breath.

Cully turned up his collar against the sharpening wind and agreed, "Me too."

When the Jullsens entered the low concrete building, they were greeted stiffly by a large man seated behind a long counter. Denby told him they were here to see Norward Jullsen.

The large man eyed them suspiciously before asking, "Who're you?"

Cully answered, "His brothers."

After considering this information for a moment, the large man behind the counter said, "Take a seat, gentlemen," and stood up slowly as he spoke. "Wait right here. I'll see what I can do."

To Denby and Cully, sitting there in that stark, silent room, it seemed that the uniformed man was gone for a very long time. Neither of them said it, but both understood that Norward may be denied a visit today. Finally, though, the man returned and told them in that same cold tone, "He's in there waiting for you." With a baseball glove-sized hand, the man indicated the grey double doors at the end of a short cinderblock hallway. "Just go through there."

Seated at one of the metal tables with matching metal chairs, was their brother. Two guards stood unsmiling in the room, one on either side, neither one acknowledged the Jullsens nor each other. Near the ceiling, there were two small windows through which the grey sky could be seen.

"Hey, brother!" Denby called out and walked quickly towards Norward.

"Hey yerself!" he answered. It was when Norward rose awkwardly to greet them that his brothers realized his right leg was manacled to a table leg. His hands were free, though, and with them Norward grasped both Denby's and then Cully's hands, a tear appearing in the corner of his eye.

"Sit down, sit down," he invited, as if they were guests at his own kitchen table. Denby and Cully pulled the metal chairs out and sat down, the legs scraping hollowly against the painted but deeply scarred cement floor.

Norward leaned forward with his elbows on the table, his prison uniform as drab as the rest of his surroundings. Always the best conversationalist of the three brothers,

Norward launched right in with, "Now that you're here, tell me somethin' I don't already know."

And so Denby and Cully told him all about Darlene Sinclair to which Norward softly responded, "Oh, son of a bitch." He uttered each word in its own space, speaking deliberately. Neither of them, Denby nor Cully, could have put it better.

Norward went on to tell his own stories. Standing there unmoving and unsmiling, the two guards let him talk, allowed him this rare visit from his brothers. "You hear if Gunnar and his missus still havin' trouble with ghosts over there at their place?" he asked Cully.

Cully smiled. "Yep, now and again," he answered.

Norward had his own ghost story from the Olmstead place to tell. Cully had already heard it—right after the incident had happened—but this particular ghost story was new to Denby, who told Norward, "Let's hear it, brother."

And Norward was more than happy to oblige him.

"That was a crazy night and I felt like hell the next day." You had to hand it to Norward. He knew how to start a story, knew how to get his listeners hooked. "I was lookin' after the place for Olmstead and his wife a coupla months after they'd tied the knot. Ole Gunnar was gonna take her fishin'" Then to Cully, "Can you imagine your missus on a fishin' trip with you?"

For one guarded moment, Cully looked only slightly offended and then the three of them chuckled at the idea of Ellie going fishing. It seemed as likely as any of the three of them doing petit point.

Norward continued with his story. "Anyway, I'd slept at the house that night when I'd finally made it home. I slept it off most the day on their chesterfield in the livin' room. When I woke up, I realized I was missin' a boot. So I headed back into town wearin' a pair of Gunnar's old gumboots and carryin' my one leather boot, hopin' to find the other along the way somewheres. I thought I'd head over to Mom's and see what she'd made for supper.

Makin' my way up the main street, I located my boot, but I could see right then I'd be wearin' Gunnar's for a while, at least till Bryton's Ladies Wear opened up on Monday mornin'."

Denby laughed and asked, "Why's that, brother?"

"Because there in that big glass window stood a girl mannequin, decked-out in a loose-fittin' dress, came down just below her knees. Round her neck was a long stringa pink pearls and in place of her delicate little head was my left boot." Norward paused while his brothers laughed, then he delivered the punch line. "On the heel was the model's blonde wig. I couldn't remember anythin' from the Saturday night before. Nothin' to help me fill in the blanks. So upon examinin' the situation closer, I decided not to claim the boot on Monday after all—or ever. I decided it all looked too incriminatin'."

At this, Denby hooted and slapped the tabletop. A guard spoke up, sternly warning, "Keep it down."

Norward picked the story back up where he left off. "I ate supper at Mom's then headed back over to Gunnar's place. It was those same old gumboots," he said, looking at Cully, "That I wore out to the barn to do chores that evenin'. Didn't take me long to milk the cow, fork her some hay, feed the chickens.

"Anyway, when I got back in from milkin', I didn't notice anything diff'rent at first." He looked directly at Denby and described the sequence of events, "I took off Gunnar's chore boots in the porch and hung up my coat, as usual. Went to the icebox, put the milk and a couple eggs in there and got a glass of milk for myself. I got a bit of a start when I turned to sit down at the table. On it was Missus Olmstead's biggest bowl with a wooden spoon stickin' out of it. There was two bakin' pans just sittin' there like someone was thinkin' of makin' up a batcha cookies."

"Where'd they come from?" Denby asked.

"Hell if I know," Norward answered and continued, "So I yell out, thinkin' maybe they're home. 'Hello! Anybody here?' And I hear nothin' 'cept dead, dark silence.

"I drank my milk in the livin' room, listenin' so hard for noises that I could hear my own heart beatin', but that's all I heard. Thought maybe I'd just not seen the stuff there earlier—the pans and the bowl. I was kinda hung over when ole Gunnar and me was visitin' before he left. I wasn't really payin' attention.

"Anyway, I drunk down the rest of my milk, and went back toward the kitchen, aimin' to rinse out my cup and put the bowl and the pans back in a cupboard somewheres. My feet felt nailed to the floor when I hit the archway joinin' the two rooms. That yellow table top was bare as a baby's arse."

Denby and Cully shook their heads in disbelief.

Speaking again to Denby, Norward explained, "They'd joked about their ghost before, but I knew they liked to tell stories, Gunnar and the missus, make 'em bigger than they are. Stories are fun. I obviously like tellin' 'em, too. But sometimes ghosts are real. Then it's nothin' to laugh about." Clamping his hand on Denby's shoulder, Norward added, "And believe you me, brothers, I wasn't laughin'."

"So what did you do?" Denby pressed.

Cully laughed softly and said, "Don't worry. He'll get to it."

And he did. "Not wantin' to cross through that dark kitchen to get to their room upstairs, I set my milk glass down on the coffee table, put my boots back on and went out the front door 'round to the back. It leads on into the kitchen, too. This was the way to get to the staircase and upstairs without havin' to walk past that kitchen table in the dark. Outside, I kicked off Gunnar's chore boots on the stoop, tore open that screen door and bolted up the stairs. Leavin' the door at the top of the stairs open, I slammed their bedroom door shut, and hopped outta my pants and into bed."

"Hey," Cully joked. "Did the Olmsteads give you permission to sleep in their bed?"

Norward responded with mock irritation, "Shut up, would ya? I'm tryin' to tell a story here."

"All right, all right," Cully teased, "Keep goin' with your longwinded story. I see Denby's still awake. That makes one of us."

Norward grinned and kept going, "Hadn't laid there

long, still listenin' hard and feelin' my heart finally slow down when, all of a sudden, I heard somethin' loud enough to stop it all together. Crack!" For emphasis, Norward smacked the tabletop with both hands. This garnered him a glare from both the guards, but neither of them said anything. Norward elaborated, "Sharp enough to be a gunshot, but you know what it was?" Norward asked Cully and Denby.

"What?" they both asked.

"It was the door at the top of the stairs bangin' closed. Then I heard the hinges creak slow, and in my mind, I could see that door openin' again. Then—crack! This time I shot outta bed, grabbed my pants off the floor and pretty near leapt down the staircase, my feet touchin' wood maybe twice on the way down."

"He's the dramatic one in the family, isn't he?" Cully grinned and commented as Denby hung on every word Norward said.

"Out the back door I went, not botherin' with the boots I'd left out on the step not even half an hour ago but runnin' in my sock feet out to the middle of the front yard, grass soft and wet on my soles. Blood pounded in my ears and I was gaspin' for breath, strainin' to hear more slammin'. Nothin'.

"I waited there, safe outside, for quite a while. When I still didn't hear nothin' more, I went back into the house and got that patchwork quilt that was settin' on the rockin' chair. I made my way back out to the barn, forked some clean hay into a pile and laid a coupla old horse blankets down. Spread that quilt over myself and slept that night in the hay. Slept there for the next coupla nights. Me, the cow and them chickens, cozy like that." Norward paused here for effect before finishing, "And durin' that time, ev'ry night, 'round eleven, I heard that door slam twice, real loud, over in the house. After that first night, it barely woke me up."

As if they, too, had wanted to hear the end of Norward's ghost story, the guards now spoke up. "Time to say your goodbyes, fellas," the one nearest the double doors told them.

Then, the one standing by the single metal door which lead back into the prison said, "Make it quick."

— Chapter 12 —

DAMSEL IN DISTRESS

Early that same morning, the morning that Denby and Cully boarded the train for Edmonton, Birdie heard a knock on her front door. She opened it up to the early light and a beautiful dark haired woman in her early twenties. The young woman looked exhausted and nervous and, Birdie thought, perhaps a little rough around the edges.

Birdie smiled and greeted the stranger, "Good morning." Cully's mom had been mixing bread dough and wore her favourite apron, the one with the purple flowers on it. "What can I do for you?"

"Morning, ma'am. The folks at the hotel café told me to come here." She studied Birdie's face, searching it for someone she recognized. Then she asked, "Are you Mrs. Jullsen?"

Birdie stood a little straighter in the doorway and held a little tighter to the screen door handle. "I am. And who are you, miss?"

At Birdie's question, the young woman's face crumpled. She dropped her suitcase onto the frosty grass beside the front step as her hands flew up to hide her tears.

"Now, come," Birdie told the girl. "It can't be so bad that a good strong cup of coffee won't put it in perspective." Taking her gently by the arm, Cully's mother guided the young woman into her kitchen, telling her, "Here, sit down right here, dear. I'll get your suitcase."

Birdie Jullsen set the little blue suitcase down in her tiny entryway and walked to her stove to put on a fresh pot of coffee. She glanced at the distraught woman seated at her kitchen table, eyes red, her hands lying despondently in her slightly plump lap. While the coffee brewed, Birdie pulled out a chair across from her new acquaintance and warmly invited her, "You're here now, so you might as well tell me all about it."

In a voice blurred by tears, Darlene Sinclair relayed to Birdie Jullsen some of the details—but not all the details—regarding her relationship with Cully. Darlene explained how they had met while both she and Cully were working in that CNR railroad tie camp in northern Alberta, located somewhere between here and nowhere. She told about the cold, the snow and about cooking for that many men.

As Birdie poured coffee and set out yesterday's cinnamon buns, Darlene poured out her story, telling Cully's mother, "Your son was really kind to me, treated me like a lady even when I sometimes didn't act like one." Darlene hadn't yet gotten to the part about her child, but she was getting there, building up to it. By this point in the conversation, and without Darlene telling her so, Birdie knew there had been a baby, her first grandchild. Call it intuition. Birdie always knew about such things. Darlene sipped the creamy coffee, and over her cup she complimented Birdie, "It was always easy to tell that Cully had a good mother."

At this, Birdie gave Darlene's forearm an affectionate squeeze, saying, "I did my best. That's all any of us can be expected to do—including you."

Darlene Sinclair began to sob again. Cully's mother waited patiently, and when Darlene was able to speak again, she told Birdie about the recent death of her own father, Stan Sinclair.

"A couple of months ago, there was a heavy rain in the woods," Darlene recounted. "It rained so hard that everything just got slick. The logs and the ground were both really slippery." She inhaled raggedly and kept going, saying, "I guess the men were cold—it was hard to work with the weather like that. They don't know exactly how the load became loose, but it did. All those logs rolled off the back of the wagon and crushed my dad. They tried to help him, all the guys, tried to pull the logs off him, tried to get him out. He was yelling, and then all of a sudden he was quiet." Darlene took another sharp breath and exhaled the truth, "I knew then he was dead."

"Oh, honey," Birdie tried to console her. "That's a terrible thing that happened. I'm sorry." She asked the young woman, "Where have you been for the last little while?

Do you have family? Is there anyone?"

Darlene nodded. "Back in Saskatchewan. Stan's... Dad's parents. My grandparents. They own a hotel there, and I've been cooking in the restaurant. They hate me being there!" This last bit came out in a gush, gilded with sorrow. Birdie didn't say anything to contradict what Darlene told her. The younger woman wouldn't have said it if it wasn't true. It was too painful to be an embellishment.

For a bit, the two women sat in silence, Birdie taking in the new information and Darlene gathering the strength she'd need to tell her next piece of news.

* * *

After Darlene finished her coffee and two cinnamon buns, and after telling her story of the child that she said was Cully's, Birdie suggested the young woman stretch out on Alice's bed and have a sleep. Birdie's guest was very pale, her skin looking almost translucent, with dark shadows beneath her tired eyes. Alice was at work that morning at the telephone exchange, and she wouldn't be home until late that afternoon.

Darlene was grateful for the invitation to rest, saying, "Thanks, I think I will. It was impossible to sleep on the train last night." And then, less certainly, "Are you sure you don't mind?"

Birdie smiled warmly. "Of course I don't mind. I wouldn't have offered if I minded." She paused, weighing her words carefully, before adding, "After all, you're family now."

Darlene was settled into Alice's little bedroom off the living room with the door closed. Her host judged that the young woman would be asleep as soon as her head hit Alice's pillow. Birdie punched down the bread dough that had risen on the countertop over near the stove and looked out the window past the trees in her yard to the bare hills beyond. Although the sky was pale blue, Birdie thought the air felt like it held snow. There was that crisp, new quality to it that made her brace herself for change. It would come without concern for whether any of them were ready.

Darlene stayed overnight in Hughenden, sleeping on the chesterfield in Birdie's living room. "I brought money for a hotel room," she told Cully's mom, "That's where I planned to stay."

"Save your money, dear. We've got room for you here. There's no point in you sitting all alone in some hotel room and eating your supper by yourself in an unfamiliar restaurant." And so it was settled. Darlene spent the night. In the morning, long after Alice had left for her very early shift, Birdie and Darlene sat down to breakfast. Darlene had just tasted the fried egg on her fork when Cully called out from Birdie's front entry.

"Hello! Mom? We're back!"

Denby's voice added, "Smells great in here. What's for breakfast?"

Birdie wished there was some way she could have warned Cully, prepared him somehow, but perhaps that's always how a mother feels. Right now, in that moment, there was nothing she could do to cushion the blow.

Cully froze at the threshold into his mother's warm

kitchen. It had snowed during the night while the brothers rode the train back from Edmonton. Now, bits of snow fell from the cuffs of Cully's pants and slowly melted on the linoleum, leaving little clear splotches of water.

Denby, stuck behind his brother and wanting the bacon and eggs he smelled, gave Cully a push from behind and said, "Get movin'. I'm starving—aren't you?" Upon seeing Darlene, Denby was stopped in his tracks, too, right beside his brother. "Hello," he greeted her, and then to Birdie, "Mom, I didn't know you had company." Denby didn't ask who the attractive brunette was. He knew. Judging by Cully's reaction, she had to be the girl they'd hidden from at the train station yesterday morning. Darlene Sinclair was still in Hughenden. Here she was at Birdie's kitchen table.

Without speaking, Cully turned abruptly and walked out of the Jullsen house, a burst of winter cold coming in as he went out, filling the empty spot where he'd stood.

"Denby," Birdie commanded her eldest son. "You go after him." When he didn't move, she specified, "Now!"

Denby ran out of his mother's house and looked up and down the street. He spotted Cully headed south and turning left towards Main Street.

"Hey! Hold up!" he called out to his brother. Cully didn't stop, but he slowed his pace allowing Denby to catch up. Denby fell in beside Cully, his own long stride matching his brother's. Theirs were the first footprints in the new fallen snow at the side of the road. They walked along like this for a block or so before either of them spoke.

"What are you gonna do, little brother?" Denby finally

asked Cully as they walked down Main Street.

Cully sighed a hard sigh and said, "Damn it all! Stupid. I've been so stupid!" He spat out the words, coated thick with self-loathing.

Denby patted him on the back. "You're not alone in that club, brother. There's a mighty big membership. You just got caught being stupid, is all," he told Cully in an effort to console him before suggesting, "Shall we go back and face the music, as they say?"

"Who says that?" Cully responded, shooting his brother a sardonic look.

Denby laughed and shrugged, admitting, "Who fuckin' knows." With that, the brothers turned around and walked back up Hughenden's main street in the direction of Birdie Jullsen's house and back to Darlene Sinclair.

The atmosphere in the kitchen was tense while Denby and Cully ate breakfast with Darlene and Birdie, but the brothers' mother tried to relax it the best she could. Birdie tried to ease the young people into conversation hoping that would help break the ice.

"Darlene," At the sound of her name Darlene looked up. She'd been staring at her eggy plate and wishing she were somewhere else, anywhere else at all. "Why don't you tell Cully here what you were telling me about your son," Birdie encouraged her softly.

Darlene looked directly at Cully. His hair was slightly longer than she remembered, a dark shock of it falling into his eyes. Her voice trembled as she told him, "His name is Thomas. He'll be two on December third." Darlene took a deep breath and added, "He has your eyes."

Cully set his fork down on his plate, his breakfast half-eaten and cold.

Without emotion he said, "I'm sorry for your troubles, Darlene, and sorry I couldn't have been there for you. I didn't know." In a way, it felt like absolution, saying these words in the presence of both his mother and brother. Cully picked up his fork again and cut a rubbery fried egg with the edge of it before saying, "I thought the boy might have your dad's eyes."

* * *

While Denby helped his mom wash up the breakfast dishes, Cully and Darlene sat a good distance apart on Birdie's chesterfield.

Cully asked her, "How've you been? Where's Stan?"

At his question, Darlene's shoulders slumped and Cully saw a tear drop into her lap to form a wet dark spot there on her skirt. Without looking up, she replied, "He's dead, Cully."

And before he could stop himself, Cully responded, "Good."

Darlene's head shot up, and she glared at him. There was that spark, the same spark Cully remembered, the fire he'd been missing. "Is it really?" The words had a jagged edge, ready to cut. "Is it really good? How can you say that? Where were *you*? What did *you* do to help?" she spat. "You *knew* what he was doing—saw him do it—and you let him do it. Let him do that to me. So you don't tell me what's good. Who else did I have? And who do I have now? Certainly not you, Cully Jullsen."

Resolutely, Darlene stood up from the chesterfield, and Cully grabbed her wrist and pulled her back down closer to him, saying, "Stop, Darlene. Just stop. I'm sorry."

She turned her head away from him, refusing to look at him. Still, Cully held tightly onto her wrist. When she tried to pull away from his grip, he pulled her closer and whispered near her ear, repeating, "I'm sorry. I should've…" Her hair smelled clean and her perfume like flowers. Cully didn't know what he should have done. Taken Darlene away from the camp? Confronted Stan? Kidnapped his daughter? Married her instead of Ellie? He'd asked himself a million times, and a million times, he came up without an answer.

Without turning her head or looking at him, Darlene asked Cully, "Are you going to tell your wife about me?"

Cully shook his head and said, "I don't see how that would help anything. If you believe Thomas is mine—and there's no way of knowing -" he said, "Then I'm willing to help you out. But Ellie doesn't need to pay the price for my actions." Cully almost said "mistakes" but was able to catch the harmful word before it escaped. He squeezed Darlene's wrist gently and asked for her acquiescence. "Agreed?"

Darlene said softly, shame replacing the fiery pride, stooping her shoulders, and weighing down her response. "Agreed."

Each month, Cully would pay Darlene as much as he could to help she and Thomas to live. He'd mail the money to Saskatchewan, and Darlene promised not to contact him directly. If there was ever an emergency, a need to get in touch, Darlene could do so through Birdie Jullsen.

When Benson Pedersen arrived at Birdie's house to pick up Cully after the breakfast dishes were done, Darlene stayed out of sight, sitting with Denby in the living room. She left for Saskatchewan that afternoon, boarding the train alone in the softly falling snow.

— Chapter 13 —

JUST LIKE US

For December, the day was fairly mild. Upstairs, all the windows were open for ventilation. The afternoon breeze blew fresh air in, and the paint fumes found their way out. Ellie hoped she had enough of the yellow paint left to cover the walls in that little room tucked there above the living room. Usually, they'd left its door shut after they'd moved in, having nothing with which to furnish it and enough other work to do in making the house on Hughenden Lake livable. Last Friday morning, Ellie had opened that room up and struggled with that stiff window until she was able to prop it open with a brick. She had swept and mopped the floor, and washed the walls. It took Ellie an entire day to prepare that room for painting, but she'd done a thorough job.

Ellie had tied her hair up with an old scarf. There was a yellow streak across her bare forehead, and her fingers were sticky with paint. It was noon, and she'd finished three of the four walls. She'd made sure to complete the largest surfaces first, hoping to stretch the paint far enough to finish the job. All that was left to paint was that short wall beneath the ceiling's sharp southern slope and the cupboard doors. If worse came to worse and she ran out of paint, the doors could wait. Standing up, she stretched her back and felt it crack. Her knees ached from kneeling on the floor, the floor she would paint when more paint came her way—hopefully before the baby was born. She heard a knock on the back door. The sound echoed right up the stairs.

Ellie raised a hand to touch her hair and instead, felt the scarf. She set her brush crossways over the opening of the Roger's syrup can that held what was left of her paint. On the other side of the screen door stood two men Ellie had never seen. Her heartbeat quickened, and her palms became instantly moist. The strangers wore dungarees and shabby coats, their hats held in hand. Because they were bearded, their hair longer and unkempt, Ellie couldn't tell if they were in their twenties or thirties. One of them, the man with the black hair, had several threads of grey in his beard. Ellie didn't open the door. Instead, she spoke to them through the screen.

"Yes?" she asked them coldly, trying to sound busy, not scared.

"Afternoon, ma'am. My companion and I are wondering if there's any work you and your husband need done?

We'd be happy to work for food and perhaps the opportunity to sleep in your barn for the night." The one nodded seriously as his taller friend did the talking.

"Sorry. No work for you here" Ellie told them.

The men thanked her and immediately turned away as if that's the answer they were expecting. They stepped off the stoop into the snow. They put their hats back on, and Ellie watched them head off.

They'd made it as far as the driveway, and she pictured them walking slow in heavy boots, the cold at bay but the wind confrontational. Ellie had risen earlier than Cully that morning to peel potatoes and boil eggs. On top the woodstove, while the potatoes boiled hard, she whisked eggs, sugar, vinegar and dried mustard together to make a thick sweet-sour dressing for the potato salad. Now, as she stood still in the porch, imagining the slow retreat of the jobless men, that salad waited cold and fresh in the icebox. Ellie's heart pounded and her brain began to tingle.

Ellie flung the screen door open, bounded off that makeshift step and hurried around the porch, the bare lilac branches brushing her shoulder. The snow came in through the tops of her shoes. "Hey!" she called. The stooped figures halted and looked back over their shoulders, their shadows ink black on the white ground. "Are you hungry?"

They came back, and Ellie gave them that salad, fetched them the wool blanket that she used to keep warm in the wagon and sent the two men out to the barn. She instructed them, "You can clean the horse's stall and milk the cow for me. When you're finished, there are nails and a hammer just inside the door. Nail up those loose planks on the corral fence. My husband will be glad not to have to do it. Then you can fetch some water and fill up the horse's and the cow's trough." She paused, and they continued to listen. "Make sure you fork some fresh hay for yourselves. You can sleep in the empty stall."

With the mild weather, Cully had decided to ride Maurice over to the Whitlock's that morning. As the horse trotted down their driveway, Cully thought about how well Maurice had done that day, no bucking or shying. He leaned forward and stroked the gelding's neck. Just then, he noticed the two men working on the corral fence to the north of the barn. Cully also noticed how much they reminded him of his own brothers.

Cully stamped the snow off his feet in the porch, and Ellie appeared in the doorway. "Hi," she greeted him.

Cully kissed her forehead. "Hi. I was just out to the barn. See we've got visitors. Friends of yours?" He smiled crookedly, warm and relaxed, and Ellie felt quiet relief spread through her.

"They came to the door while I was painting." When her voice began to falter, she was surprised. "I...I told them to go." Ellie took a sharp breath, "But then I couldn't let them." She began to sob full out. Slumping forward, her head hit her husband's chest, and his fingers stroked the scarf that covered her hair. Ellie looked up at him and cried, "Oh, Culvar! I don't want our baby to be a hobo!"

Cully laughed and held his wife at arm's length. He studied her tear-stained face and told her, "Ellie, our baby won't be a hobo. I promise."

She sniffed. "How can we know? What if he ends up like them?"

"I guess we can't know. He'll be what he'll be. Or she. It may be a she. That's the thing about having a baby. It's a leap of faith, my wife. But I think it'll turn out all right." He put his arms around her, brought her in close, and gave her a gentle squeeze. "One thing's for sure. That baby'll have one terrific mother." He released her and began taking off his boots while Ellie wiped her red eyes with the hem of her apron.

"We don't have another old blanket around we could give those guys, do we?" Cully asked as she followed him into the kitchen. He ladled himself a jar of water and downed it standing by the basin at the counter.

"I don't think so." Then she remembered the cupboard in the nursery, the old bits of bedding and scraps of forgotten clothing. "On second thought, there may be something upstairs. Let me go look." It was Ellie's turn to kiss his salty forehead smelling like horse and December. "There's still some of those cookies left and some coffee on the stove," she told him, then headed back upstairs.

Sure enough, behind those unpainted doors on the east wall Ellie discovered two more tattered blankets and a thin, musty patchwork quilt, along with a buttonless shirt, three mismatched socks, and a shredded pair of overalls. She brought them downstairs and set them on the floor in the porch by the wringer washing machine.

"I'm gonna bring these blankets out to those guys and see how they're making out with the chores." Cully paused, putting on his work coat. "How'd you feel about me asking them in for a visit?—if they seem all right, that is. It's warm for this time of year but still pretty cold. And who knows how long it's been since they ate anything besides your famous potato salad. Maybe they'd like to try some of your famous baking powder biscuits."

"I don't know." Ellie bit her lip, her back against the counter, hands braced along its edge on either side of her.

"Well, you asked them to do some work. They're probably happy with that, so it's up to you."

"See how they seem to you. They seemed nice enough when they came to the door. Polite." Ellie was silent for a few moments, and Cully could tell that his wife was weighing it out. When she spoke again, Ellie said, "You're a good judge of character. And besides, there are lots of my famous baking powder biscuits to go around."

Those very biscuits were just coming out of the oven when Cully came back into the house, the two ragged men behind him. A pot of water sat on the stove. Ellie had been saving it for dishes but thought to offer a wash to the men instead. She'd set a bar of soap and one of her older towels on the counter, rinsed out the enamel basin and filled it with warm water. Cully fetched two more coffee cups and invited one of the men to wash up and the other to sit down at the table.

The shorter man, the one to wash up first, after graduating from the University of Alberta in 1925, worked as a banker in Edmonton. There he married Betty Doyle, and they bought a little house overlooking the North Saskatchewan River. Their son was born when they lived in that house. David Campbell lost his job at the bank in 1931, despite taking cuts in hours and wages for two years, and he finally sold his house and moved his young family into a rented room. When he got the news in November, Betty took their son and went to live with her parents in Leduc. Their son died at four-years-old of pneumonia in February of 1932, and Betty became dead-eyed and speechless. David said he visits her in the extended care ward whenever he's passing through.

Maynard Milne had had a simpler life, and had, one might say, less to lose than David Campbell. At thirty-seven-years-old, he remained a bachelor, contented in his work as a construction foreman, overseeing projects in and around the growing city of Edmonton since 1925. As construction slowed and dried up, so did Maynard's livelihood. He got work when he could now, helping to build and repair barns, fences, livery stables and general stores in towns along the railway line. At first, he'd enjoyed the opportunity to travel and to see the country.

"But now it's tough to ride. Not safe anymore. Those cops, they're getting rough. They want to get us off the line when before it didn't seem to matter." Maynard Milne had wolfed down three biscuits with molasses and coffee, thanking his hosts between bites and praising the food.

"Yeah, I got a couple brothers who ride. They say the same thing about the railway police. Riding's not as easy as it used to be," Cully acknowledged.

David Campbell spoke up over his coffee cup. "Say, you're not related to Norward, are you?"

Cully's eyebrows raised and he responded, "Yeah, actually. He's my little brother."

Monday, December 13, 1934

Dear Norward,

I'm sending this letter with fellows who know you. They came and did some work here for us. I hope you get this. I sure enjoyed our visit with you in November. Things here are good. Ellie's got the house nice and I'm training that horse we bought this fall. I ended up naming him Maurice. I thought you would think that was a good name for a horse. Mom is good but I have not seen much of Denby since we visited you together. I hope he is doing good. Maybe we will see him soon. He might show up for Christmas. You know how he is.

— *Chapter 14* —

SWEET CHILDHOOD MEMORIES

David Campbell and Maynard Milne had gone out to the barn to sleep on old blankets laid over a heap of deep hay. It was to be the best sleep either of them had had in weeks, soft and warm with their bellies full of biscuits and potato salad. The next day, they'd continue in the direction of Edmonton. They would work and ride and spend Christmas time with the family and friends still living there in the city.

Cully sat alone at the table staring at the incomplete letter in the lantern light. His pencil rested beside the paper, and his head rested in his hands. Ellie had gone up to bed more than two hours ago, and he'd told her that he'd join her soon, but the words were slow in coming and, as a result, he was slow in getting to bed. He sat in the circle of light that enveloped the table, waiting for the words' arrival and remembering his childhood. The unfamiliar chair feeling hard beneath him (Birdie had found five of them—all matching—at an auction sale and presented them as an early Christmas gift) and with the fire burning low in the stove.

It seemed that this same memory would always haunt Cully every time he thought too much about Norward. His drunken father bursting into their room, screaming at them all, and Alice hiding under her cot in terror. Alone in the kitchen in the house on Hughenden Lake, Norrie Jullsen's words echoed again, as fresh as if they'd been spoken yesterday: "Y'know, you wouldn't have any place to live if it wasn't for me. You wouldn't have this bed or food on the table. You'd have nothin'. You'd be nothin'." Again, Norrie shoved that same tobacco-yellowed finger into Cully's face. "You *are* nothin'."

And Norward defending his big brother: "That ain't true. Cully *is* something." That smack, the dots of blood across pajama tops and blankets, the broken nose, the white lies told in the doctor's office.

Only when a fat tear splashed onto the tabletop, just missing the letter, did Cully realize he was crying. He swiped at his eyes with his sleeve and wondered how life would've been different for the two brothers had their father cracked Cully's nose instead of Norward's.

Weather has been pretty mild. We are going to go out tomorrow and find a tree. We asked Mom if she would like us to have Christmas Eve dinner here, but she said no of course. It will always be Mom's job to have everyone over at Christmas.
Did you kill Morris Randell?

The question stared up at him, bold and embarrassing. Cully erased it, leaving a grey smear. His brother was in jail because he was a rough-living guy with no steady job and no constant home. He wasn't the only one that had found himself in prison because he had trouble fitting in elsewhere. Who knows? Maybe he'd always be in and out of prison. Maybe it wasn't so bad.

By the time this letter gets to you and I hope it does, Christmas might already be over. I hope you had a good one and that you are not in there for long.
Merry Christmas.
Your brother,
Cully Jullsen

Norward's older brother folded the letter and tucked it into the old Christmas card envelope Ellie'd found for him. The envelope had never been sealed. Cully stuck out his tongue and tasted glue, his taste buds shivering their disgust. He stood up stiffly, turned down the lantern's wick and made his way up those stairs in the dark, leaving the letter lying there on the bare tabletop.

— *Chapter 15* —

SIMPLE ELEGANCE

"This is what I would suggest. It's perfect! Simple elegance."

Cully reached out and touched the edge of the linen tablecloth Florence Adamson held out for him to inspect. It looked like most other tablecloths he'd ever seen or that he'd noticed, which weren't many.

She mistook his blank look for disinterest and set the linen cloth behind her on the counter by the register.

"Or how about this?" The store clerk walked across the floor to the back of the shop toward a glass fronted cabinet that held several pieces of flowery china. "You could choose a pattern and buy a different piece for each occasion: a cup and saucer for this Christmas, a serving dish for your anniversary, that kind of thing. But you'd need to let us know a few weeks ahead of time so we could place the order for you. It's too late now to get this in for Christmas but maybe for Ellie's birthday?" Mrs. Adamson paused for Cully's response, got none and so prompted him. "What do you think?"

Cully blinked. "Mrs. Adamson, I think you've got really good taste, and whatever you wrap up for Ellie's gonna be fine."

The store-owner's wife smiled her relief. "So shall we go with the tablecloth?" She lead him back up to the long counter, her perfume leaving a thin trail of scent behind her, not unpleasant.

"Sounds good. And maybe order something china for me, too, and just keep it here till her birthday," Cully instructed her.

"Sure," Florence Adamson looked pleased with the additional sale. "Which day in January is it?"

"The nineteenth."

* * *

Ellie's mom, Muriel Pedersen, and Florence Adamson both belonged to the Woman's Association of Hughenden United Church, and Mrs. Adamson sold California Perfume Company products that she'd bring out to the farm for Muriel to sample. Over talcum powder, tiny bottles of *Daphne* and rose oil fragrance, cups of coffee and oatmeal cookies, the women grew into confidantes. Family histories were shared and troubles discussed. What worked best in removing saskatoon or cranberry stains from clothing? What about grass stains? How do you encourage men not to drink? How do you get your daughters to choose good husbands? Is it wrong to be angry with your husband for forcing your "marital obligations" upon you if you've made it clear that you're not feeling well?

"Well, Florence, I think it's like the Bible says, that woman wouldn't exist if it weren't for Adam's rib so I just try to remember that, in a way, I owe my life to my husband. That and the commandment, 'Be fruitful and multiply.'"

Ken Adamson's wife looked skeptical. "You and I are both far past being fruitful and multiplying. I've produced my fruit, thank you very much." She took another cookie from the yellow plate in the centre of the table. "These are good. I'm not so sure about owing my being to Kenneth, either. Between you and me, there're days I'm not sure that man could get dressed without my help."

Ellie's mother frowned. "I don't like to question the Word." She shifted uneasily in her chair.

Florence chuckled, reached out and laid a hand on Muriel's wrist diplomatically. "Honey, I'm not suggesting we question the Lord. All I'm saying is that we question the way the world works. Don't you ever do that, Muriel, not against the Lord or even with the Father in mind? Just wondering why?"

"I try to always keep the Father in mind, no matter what else I may be engaged in." This reply was stiff, unyielding. "Would you like more coffee?"

Florence Adamson accepted half a cup more and opened the cosmetics company's slim catalogue, moving the conversation from God to the less emotional subject of what smells good this season. After her friend left, Muriel cried into her folded arms alone at her kitchen table until her head throbbed. When she was finished crying, Muriel Pedersen resolved not to buy any more of what Florence Adamson had to sell.

* * *

Cully had Mrs. Adamson wrap that tablecloth in paper and leave it behind the counter. He was meeting Ellie at Bryton's Ladies Wear after he was done at Adamson's Dry Goods store. He planned to pick the Christmas gift up on Saturday of next week. The bell above the dress shop door tinkled when Cully pushed his way in from the cold. Ellie was browsing near the door, apparently waiting for him.

"Hi." Her fingers trailed down the sleeve of a burgundy cardigan and she gave him a little smile. "Ready to go?"

"You bet." Cully scanned the store. "Where's Stella?"

"She went along with Henry to the drugstore. Want to meet them?"

Cully shrugged. "Sure."

They got home late from their evening of visiting and shopping, and headed straight to bed where Whitlock's old lantern cast its soft yellow glow on the walls. As Cully turned back the covers and crawled into the bed, he breathed in deeply the fresh scent of the bedding.

"Mmm. Clean sheets."

Ellie laughed softly, got in beside him and snuggled in close, leaving the lantern lit. Beneath the blankets Cully ran his hand up and over Ellie's thighs until he found the slight swell of her belly, growing a little every day. He laid his hand there and kept it still while he talked to his wife.

"Guess who's got a cradle we can have?"

Ellie sighed in mock exasperation. "Mrs. Whitlock."

He laughed, moving his fingers in a gentle tickling motion over her midsection, and Ellie wriggled with pleasure. "Nope. My mom. It's my old cradle. Guess it goes to the first of her kids to have a baby. That's us."

"That we know of." She regretted the words as soon as they were out. Where had they come from? From the depths of quiet suspicion, that's where. "Oh, Culvar. I didn't mean…" But it was too late. How she wished the words were still there, suspended somewhere in the darkness just before her eyes, so that she could snatch them back before they entered her husband's ears. Except he'd already heard them, been cut by the accusation. Cully reached over his wife without touching her and turned down the lantern's wick.

He turned his back to his wife. "Good night, Ellie."

She didn't answer him. The lump in her throat wouldn't let her. In the summer, they'd argued in the kitchen, and the wounds from that dispute were deep and still tender. What started that argument—the seed of this one— was Ellie commenting on the seemingly carefree lifestyles of Cully's brothers. There in the desolate dark Ellie remembered that original conversation.

"Do you ever think that you may already be an uncle?" They had been drying dishes together after supper earlier that evening, a chore with which Cully often helped. Ellie held her largest pot in the warm water of the basin nestled into the countertop, its red rim flush with the scratched Formica surface. Two weeks before, Cully had cut this neat hole into which the basin fit perfectly.

"What do you mean by that?" Cully's voice grew cold. He'd stopped drying the tin mug he held and was looking at her.

"I don't know." Ellie gave a little lift of her shoulders and turned to move the butter from the counter to the icebox. "You know the way they live, Culvar. Don't you think there's a chance they've fathered children they don't even know about?" It was a rhetorical question.

"Why do you always have to criticize them, Ellie?" He set both the mug and his tea towel down on the worn counter. "They've had a hard life, harder than yours. The only reason you can pretend you're better than they are is because of your raising. Your mom and dad made you work, taught you to take care of yourself, all the time making sure you'd always have somewhere to go when you needed it. My brothers and me, we never had your opportunities. And through all this, neither of them's been on the dole—just like I haven't."

"Culvar, that's not true and you know it." Ellie wiped her hands on her apron. "I'd consider lining up at the soup kitchen in Edmonton the same as being a charity case, wouldn't you?"

"No. I don't suppose I would. They were hungry. You ever been hungry, Ellie? I mean, really hungry so that your bones and your teeth ached? And I'm not talking about diets and such. Your mom's always taken real good care of her kids. Your dad, too. You never found yourself having to swallow your dignity so that you could force down free food." He leaned one arm on the counter and left the other hanging by his side, twitching imperceptibly.

Now Ellie's hands were on her hips, and an ice wall, almost visible, was forming between she and Cully. "That's exactly what I'm talking about, Culvar. Dignity. I agree they've set theirs aside a time or two. That's what I'm saying. I bet they've forgot their dignity with a different girl in every town along the line. I'm telling you, you could easily have nieces and nephews. More than you know and more than they'd ever take responsibility for."

"This is stupid," he told her. "I'm going outside."

She stewed around the house that evening, dusting and organizing drawers and shelves while Cully worked out in the barn, coming inside later on to read sullenly in the living room. That night in bed they made up and whispered sorrys as Ellie's tears streamed in the dark. Cully kissed her neck and rubbed her back until she fell asleep, murmuring, "I do like your brothers, but I'm so glad you're not like them."

And now, tonight in the bedroom, the ice from that fight had returned to cover over everything. Ellie saw now that it would take a long time for it to melt.

Cully had always been blessed with easy sleep, and although hot anger thundered out of his heart on into his veins, the night, insulated and deep with soft snow, wrapped itself around him and pulled him under. The thunder was stilled, and within fifteen minutes Cully's breathing was steady. His body relaxed into his wife's, but his back remained toward her. Ellie stared up into the shadows forming before her eyes as they adjusted to the dark. For her, sleep would never come as willingly.

— *Chapter 16* —

A LITTLE TIRED TODAY

The weather was warmer that night than it had been for months. The snow was sticky when Ellie walked over to Birdie's, and it clung to her boots. Above her, the coal-black sky was full of stars that seemed much closer to earth now as spring inched its way toward a winter-weary people. Cully would meet her at his mom's after he and Henry had dropped a load of lumber off as a favour to Horace Williamson. There was a new construction site on the east edge of the village. A service station would be built and running by the time the grass was green again. Cully warned Ellie that Horace might want to repay Henry and Cully's kindness at the hotel tavern. Ellie didn't like the idea, but Birdie had told her to come to the house when she was done her Saturday night shopping.

Tonight of all nights, Ellie missed her sister. Stella had come around before Ellie's birthday, an unusual burst of energy and enthusiasm, but besides that, she had refused every invitation that involved any fun whatsoever. That evening, Ellie browsed the shops alone, visiting with neighbours and friends as she wandered from building to building, and made her way toward Birdie's.

She walked up the snowy boardwalk and rapped on the front door of the little white house west of the main street in Hughenden. Ellie opened the door, stuck her head inside the porch and called, "Hello! Birdie? Are you home?" Still no answer. Ellie was certain that her mother-in-law would be home any minute and so she stepped into the cramped entry and pulled off her wet boots in the darkness. She felt around on the kitchen wall until she found the switch. The room filled with a cozy, amber light. At Birdie's table, Ellie shrugged off her coat and left it hanging from the back of a chair along with her hat before she put the coffee on.

While the coffeepot simmered on the stovetop, Ellie relaxed at the table, her stocking feet up on the chair across from her. Idly, she browsed through the mail on the round wooden table. From beneath the latest edition of *The Hughenden Record*, a white envelope peeked out. The return address in blue ballpoint pen and elegant script prodded Ellie's curiosity, waking it rudely. Saskatchewan. She slid the envelope from under the weekly newspaper and removed the letter. Ellie read:

March 15, 1935

Dear Birdie,

How are you? Thomas and I are well and I hope you are too. I'm writing to you because the money Cully sent last month won't be enough. I wouldn't write and bother either of you with this if it wasn't an emergency.

Stan's parents kicked us out and we will need some help getting settled elsewhere. They said I could keep working in the restaurant but that they do not want me under their roof. I will try to find another job as I do not want to be beholden to them any longer.

When the front door opened, Ellie blinked hard and folded the letter, tucking it back into its envelope. She replaced it under the newspaper just as Birdie called out, "Ellie? Is that you, dear?"

Ellie swallowed hard and blinked again. She tried her voice. "Hi, Birdie." It worked. Birdie stamped the snow from her boots and greeted Ellie as she stepped into the kitchen.

"Hello, Ellie. I'm glad you made yourself at home." Birdie tossed a light parcel wrapped in brown paper and tied with string, onto the kitchen table. "I thought I'd be home sooner, but I got to visiting down at Bryton's." She raised an eyebrow and said to Ellie, "You know how that goes."

Ellie smiled weakly in response, and with her voice

weighted with concern, Birdie asked, "What's the matter? Are you feeling all right? You're awfully pale." Birdie took off her coat and hung it from a hook in the tiny entryway before coming to sit by Ellie at the table.

"I'm feeling well enough," Ellie lied, then edited. "I'm a little tired and nauseated today, though." Birdie nodded her understanding. It was convenient for Ellie to have this pregnancy to blame for her suddenly ill appearance. Ellie didn't want to talk to Culvar's mother about what she'd just read sitting there at Birdie's kitchen table. How could she even bring it up? Ellie would have to admit snooping through Birdie's mail first, and then she'd need to swallow the lump of hot shame she already felt burning in her throat. Ellie wouldn't do either. She couldn't.

"Can I pour you some coffee?" Birdie asked her, standing up to get the pot from the stove and cups from the cupboard.

"Sure," Ellie said. "I'll have half a cup while I'm waiting. Culvar should be along right away." She didn't say so but at that moment, Ellie didn't care if she ever saw Birdie's middle son again.

* * *

"How could you have lied to me about this?" Ellie didn't yell. Instead, her voice was tight like barbed wire being pulled taut around an old post. The kitchen was dark except for the lantern that glowed in the centre of the table. It was cold, too, as neither of them had yet started a fire in the stove for the night. Ellie had silently kept her thoughts to herself on the long ride home to Hughenden Lake, pleading exhaustion when Cully asked her why she was so quiet. Inside her body and mind, Ellie was boiling, and almost as soon as they'd entered the house, the roiling heat of her anger made its way out.

Cully exhaled audibly and told her, "I didn't lie, El. I didn't know. It was…"

She cut him off, choking out the words, "Don't tell me you didn't know. You've obviously known for a while. And Birdie too. She was in on it." Ellie's rage poured out in hot tears, the poison of liquid betrayal wetting her face.

At her weeping, Ellie's husband touched her shoulder and said, "El, I'm so sorry." Without warning, she whirled around and slapped him hard, the sharp sound echoing in the stark dimness of the room. Cully stood there for a moment, unable to move, a rush of fury flooding him. He raised his hand to strike his wife in retaliation. At his reaction, Ellie stood straighter and turned her cheek to him. She closed her eyes and waited for the sting, the hurt that would confirm that she was right to hate him this much, this deeply. Instead, she heard Cully's footsteps retreat across the floor, and Ellie flinched at the hollow slam of the back door.

There, alone in their kitchen, her hands and feet numb from the cold inside the house, Ellie collapsed onto a kitchen chair. She cradled her head in her hands and cried. Her shoulders heaved, and the sobs tore out of her like she was vomiting each one up and out. Finally, after forever, she stood up weakly and took that lighted kerosene lamp up the staircase to her bedroom.

Ellie was awakened the next morning by the smell of coffee and the crackle of a newly laid fire. She heard the quiet movement of pots and pans as they were shifted from kitchen shelves and onto the stovetop. Quickly, Ellie swung her legs off the bed and into the crocheted slippers there on the rag mat. From the chair against the bedroom wall, she snatched up her pink robe and headed downstairs, calling, "Culvar?"

But upon rounding the corner at the foot of the stairs and into the kitchen, it was Birdie that Ellie saw working at the stove. "Ellie," was all she said, Cully's mother's voice heavy with remorse. Ellie paused there, deciding whether to go back upstairs or enter the kitchen. Birdie didn't coax her either way. She just put the ham onto fry and waited.

Without speaking, Ellie walked over to the rough table adorned with a fresh tablecloth boasting a million tiny green checks. She pulled out a chair and sat down. Birdie set a steaming cup of coffee down before Ellie, brought her own coffee to the table and joined her daughter-in-law. Birdie waited for Ellie to speak, and after a while, she did.

"Why didn't you tell me?" Ellie asked, not looking at Birdie, but instead focusing on the careful cross stitches on the tablecloth. To Birdie, the young mother-to-be sounded drained.

"I'm sorry, Ellie," Birdie admitted, "It was poor judgment on my part. I wanted to protect you. Now I understand that I only hurt you more. Can you ever forgive this foolish old woman?"

Ellie looked up to see tears shining in her mother-in-law's eyes. This made Ellie cry again, too, her shoulders slumped, and through her tear-blurred vision she saw the pink fabric that covered her lap. Birdie grasped Ellie's wrist where it lay limp on the tabletop. At this gesture, Ellie looked up, eyes red and swollen, tears staining her face.

"I wish you would have told me," Ellie said. "I had a right to know."

Still gently holding Ellie's wrist, Birdie agreed quickly, "Of course you did, Ellie. I'm sorry," she repeated.

The back door opened, and Cully came in from the barn where he'd forked Maurice a little hay and milked Bossie. In the porch, he stomped off his boots before pulling them off. He took his time, not wanting to walk into that kitchen, not wanting to see his wife. Cully had taken the wagon back into town following his argument with Ellie the night before and had slept on Birdie's couch. Before he went to bed, though, Cully and his mother decided that she would come to the house on Hughenden Lake with him this morning. Birdie told him, "I helped you make this mess. I'll help you clean it up."

Alice, who was home from shopping by this time, as well, asked, "What mess?" and stormed into her room when neither of them answered her.

"Morning," Cully greeted Ellie and sat down beside her after pouring himself a cup of coffee at the stove. Ellie looked at him then looked away, not answering. The tension was making her heart pound and her head throb. She took her first sip of strong coffee and hoped that it would straighten her tangled thinking.

Birdie got up and flipped the ham in the frying pan. When she sat back down, Birdie asked them, "How are we going to solve this?" Both sat staring at their coffee cups and not answering her, and so Birdie pressed, "We need to discuss this, to air it out and decide how to handle the situation," then she added, "Together."

It was Ellie who spoke first. "If it's your child, Culvar," she said his name like it tasted bad, "then you have a responsibility for it."

"There's a chance Thomas is not mine at all," Cully stated this fact, and Birdie looked surprised.

"What do you mean?" she asked. "Do you know this for certain?"

Cully took a deep breath and prepared to tell the unsavoury truth he'd told Denby on their train trip, but that he hadn't shared with his wife or mother. It was hard enough to tell your own brother about witnessed incest, but it was a hundred times more difficult to broach the subject with your mother and your wife—at once. The words came out on a rush of air. "Stan Sinclair could be the father, too." There. It was out.

Ellie asked, disgusted, unbelieving, "Darlene's *father* could be the father?"

Birdie demanded, "How do you know this?"

"I caught them together. In the cook shack." Cully said it simply, praying to himself that the women wouldn't want more details than that.

The ham's sizzle seemed louder now, filling all corners of the kitchen, as the three of them sat silent. Birdie pushed out her chair and brought the eggs from the icebox. She moved the ham to one side of the frying pan, stacking it up, and cracked eggs one by one into the dark salty pan.

Ellie looked Cully in the eyes and asked, "Did she want...?"

Cully shook his head and answered, "She thought it was her duty. She thought she owed him."

"Oh," was all Ellie could say.

— *Chapter 17* —

TEMPTATION

Now, on this day near the end of May, Ellie sat outside in the shade cast by the porch. She realized that it'd been six weeks since she and her husband last had relations, but that was to be expected when she was this far along. Sitting there on one of their old kitchen benches, her back against the whitewashed porch wall, her feet in a tin basin of cool well water, Ellie was too uncomfortable to miss him. Lately, she'd been spending her days talking to her baby, coaxing its arrival, begging it not to kick, and to please ease up on her spine. "Listen, baby, if you'd shift to the right then maybe…ahhh, that's it. Thank you sweetie pie. Mommy loves you."

Besides talking to her unborn child, Ellie engaged God

in several conversations during that hot, parched spring when loneliness clung to her skin like sweat. She went back inside, her feet leaving little wet tracks up the stairs and knelt on the floor in the nursery she'd painted that winter. Cully's cradle sat in the corner, the lone object. This room would have to develop into itself as the baby grew and developed into who it would be.

"Will it be a boy or girl, Lord?" Ellie prayed out loud, her words bouncing off the walls in the mostly empty room.

Then the answer came, a voice in Ellie's head but not sprung from her imagination. "It's a boy, daughter. A blessed baby boy."

The floorboards hurt her knees. A fly landed on the back of her neck, slightly below her hairline and stuck there until Ellie swatted it away. While she had God's attention, Ellie had to ask, "When will he be born, Father God?"

"Soon, child. Soon. June twentieth. Pack your things the day before. Always be prepared and you'll be all right." God paused before adding, "You've got to get organized, Ellie, or you're not going to be much of a mother."

Ellie knew this was true.

As the mother-to-be stood up, her spine cracked loudly. She placed her hands on her lower back, braced it and groaned softly. On hips that felt divorced from their sockets, she wobbled downstairs to see if her bread dough had risen high enough to punch down. Beneath its damp tea towel covering, she could see the yeasty swell. Ellie washed her hands at the basin and smeared them with butter before slamming her fist into the glass bowl that sat on the table. There was a knock on the door. "Hello? Anybody home?" Denby Jullsen called through the screen door.

At the familiar sound of his voice, Ellie's loneliness lifted. She called out to him, "In here!" and began to scrape the bits of dough and greasy butter from her hands at the basin. By the time her brother-in-law had pulled his boots off and entered the kitchen, Ellie was wiping her hands on a tea towel.

Denby smiled broadly and made the astute observation, "Wow. You *are* pregnant."

She smiled back and offered her brother-in-law some iced tea. He accepted and started to pull out a chair at the table before she stopped him. "No. Let's sit outside," explaining, "I can't stand it in here today."

At the counter, Ellie poured iced tea into two jelly jars from the glass pitcher. Drops of condensed water dotted the clear glass and splotched onto the countertop as she poured. Those jars and the unbearable heat together pushed the words out of Ellie's mouth, "I hate drinking out of jars. I can't wait till we finally get some decent glasses. Here you go." She handed Denby his iced tea and told him, "Come on out." Denby followed her to the bench she'd set in the shade.

As Ellie eased down onto the bench, the jar in her lap, Denby noticed the tin basin, half full of warming water, drowned bugs and bits of dry grass floating on its surface. Denby set his own jar on the bench beside Ellie, picked up the basin, walked over to the garden and poured the water gently over a row of young pea plants before returning to the well for cooler, fresh water. He set the basin on the ground in front of her puffy feet. "Thanks." Again, Ellie smiled, sighing as she dipped her feet in the water.

Denby sat down beside her and took a long drink before commenting, "Your knees are red. You been washing floors? Kinda far along for that kinda work, aren't you?" Concern edged his voice.

"No. I've been down on my knees talking with the Lord." She rested her head against the exterior porch wall then turned her head to look at him. "Do you ever do that, Denby? Talk with God?" she asked, her tone serious.

"There's been times." Memories of cruel women and mean men flashed through his mind, quick and sharp like pain. "Life does that sometimes. Forces you to your knees and I figure, once you're down there, you might as well pray."

"Amen. I'm glad you're here." Then she asked, "Where've you been, brother-in-law? We missed you at Christmas." Ellie stared out over the hills that lay to the west of the house, brown and drying already, young leaves stunted, some shriveling.

Denby shrugged and finished his iced tea before saying, "I been around."

"Met anyone?" Ellie meant women. Had he met a woman.

He grinned and shook his head. "You always could read me like a book, Ellie. Yeah, I met someone." He brought a closed fist up and over the left side of his chest dramatically. "But she broke my heart—so I guess I came back here to lick my wounds, like I always do."

"When're you going to find someone nice, a good girl, and settle down, Denby?" She sincerely wanted to know.

He looked at her. "When I meet someone like you. That's when I'll settle down." His grin was gone. The two of them sat there in silence, both thinking about what Denby had admitted, both holding their empty jars, both wondering how much he meant it. A huge bumblebee hovered nearby, finally landing on the bench between them for an instant before continuing his work.

Denby lifted his empty jar. "Want some more?" he asked Ellie. "Sure. Thanks." He took the empty jars and disappeared inside. While her brother-in-law was gone, Ellie's baby, resting atop her bladder, convinced her to waddle across the grass over to the privy. When she came out, that door creaking shut behind her, Denby was at the well filling her kitchen pail. He wasn't wearing his boots or his hat, and he'd rolled up his sleeves. The sun caused strands of his sandy blonde hair to shimmer and, as he pulled that bucket up out of the well, the muscles of his forearms were sharply defined in the afternoon light. In that moment, Ellie noticed that he was perfect.

Walking with difficulty, Ellie breathed out long and deep, but her breath didn't release any of her sudden acute longing for Denby. The exiting air merely gave desire more room inside her to expand, and it filled her chest cavity, causing her heart to panic and her blood to rush. Shame coursed through her veins, also, following right behind her lust.

"Your tea's on the bench." He called to her, watching her make her ungainly way back toward the porch. "I'm just gonna set this inside," indicating the pail. "Need anything from in here?"

Ellie paused in her slow journey toward the shady bench and thought for a moment, tilting her head to one side. "Could you bring that old bowl on the shelf to the right of the window? And the knife? The big one with the wooden handle. We might as well cut some rhubarb while we visit, if you don't mind."

"I don't mind," Denby said and disappeared into the house.

Ellie's feet were once again soothed by cool water and her body by the shade. Unfortunately, the shadow cast by the porch was retreating as the sun moved nearer the western horizon. Soon she'd need to move the bench round to the other side of the house, nearer the garden. Ellie wasn't going to go back into the house—the heat in there would be unbearable.

When Denby came back out carrying the bowl, the knife resting in it, she asked him, "Should we move this bench? Before we lose our shade completely?"

Denby looked at the sky. "Not a bad idea."

So Ellie carried the bowl while Denby picked up the bench, walked around to the garden-side of the house and set the bench there beneath the branches of the willow tree. Ellie pointed out the rhubarb patch to him, sitting where it did on the edge of the garden.

Denby said, "It's big already."

She laughed. "It was here when we moved in. That

rhubarb's probably been here for years. It'll likely live here long after we're gone, too." Ellie began walking toward the garden, bowl and knife still in hand. Denby intercepted her.

"Why don't you let me cut it, and you can sit in the shade and slice it up?" He took the knife from her, and together they walked to the garden, Denby slowing his pace to match Ellie's. Denby cut several stalks, handed them to Ellie and she brought them into the shadow beneath the spreading willow boughs, laying them on the grass near the bench. Then she settled herself beneath the thickest branch of the tree. There, close to the trunk and protected from the wind, sat the red birdhouse Cully had made for her. She couldn't help but think of her birthday already four months past.

* * *

It's true that Ellie had had high expectations for her first birthday as a married woman—especially after the beautiful linen tablecloth Cully had given her at Christmas. After that refined, thoughtful gift, Ellie wondered what her husband had bought for her birthday.

Ellie awoke that morning in January with more energy than she'd had all month. Cully had turned to her as soon as she stirred, kissed her cheek and murmured into her hair, "Happy birthday, El." She'd got up then, dressed quickly and headed downstairs, leaving her husband to sleep until breakfast was ready. All that bright blue morning, she floated around the house, cleaning, baking cookies, and even working on the baby quilt she'd started. Just before lunchtime, Stella arrived at her door having ridden over on horseback. The sisters sat at the kitchen table eating those freshly baked cookies and speculating on what Cully's plan for Ellie's birthday might be.

"I wonder if he's in town today picking up your gift." Stella dipped an oatmeal cookie into her coffee. It dripped onto the tabletop and then onto her blouse on its way to her mouth. "Or maybe he's hid it here in the house somewhere? Have you looked?" She raised her eyebrows.

Ellie replied shortly, "No, of course I haven't looked, Stella. I don't want to find anything. I want to be surprised."

"Oh, come on," Stella coaxed honesty from her sister. "You can't tell me that you haven't even *thought* about taking a peek around? You didn't check under the bed or in those cupboards in the baby's room? Maybe he put it in the barn somewhere. In that empty stall, under some hay?"

Ellie seemed to be considering this possibility. "Well, maybe…" Suddenly, Ellie leapt from her chair with Stella close behind as she dashed up the narrow staircase. The two women reached the bed at the same time, fell down on their knees on either side and peered into the darkness beneath it. All they saw were each other's wide eyes. Ellie got up and threw back the curtain that served as the door over their bedroom closet, and Stella craned her neck to see if anything sat on that high shelf, perhaps near the back while Ellie searched the floor behind her three-paneled dressing screen. Nothing. Next, they moved across the hall into the nursery to check the cupboards, their doors still bare of paint. Empty. The shelves were as bare as they'd been when Ellie had passed on those remnants of clothing and scraps of blankets to the homeless banker and foreman who had eaten her biscuits and potato salad, and then slept in the barn.

Next, the sisters dashed downstairs. Stella searched beneath the rickety chesterfield while Ellie looked between the pages of the western novel Cully was presently reading. Neither of them bothered to look in the kitchen. Hiding a gift there would be akin to hiding a hen's eggs in her nest.

"Let's go look in the barn!" Stella fairly squealed her enthusiasm, and Ellie got caught up in it. Stella, who had been gloomy for months now, was fairly beaming, and Ellie let herself soak in her sister's levity. They bundled up in the porch, Ellie pulling on her boots and chore coat, both of them wrapping thick scarves around their necks.

Single file with Stella in the lead, they walked along the deep, narrow path leading to the little barn. They'd both already forgotten that in the autumn with just a dry skiff on the ground, it seemed the snowfall that year would be minimal. How things had changed in the months in between. Now, the banks on either side of the path were at least a couple feet deep. Without warning, Ellie's little sister flung herself off the trail and into an expanse of pristine snow, spreading her arms and legs energetically, repeatedly.

"C'mon, Ellie! We know you can make a baby, but can you make an angel?" she challenged.

"Just watch me." Ellie shielded her eyes from the sun's glare on the snow, found an unmarred spot and flopped down. Beneath its hard, sparkling crust, the snow was light and moved easily above and under her limbs. Stella stood up first, extending a mittened hand to her sister and together they stood on the path, assessing their artwork.

Ellie laughed lightly. "I haven't done that since we were kids."

Stella giggled and gave her shoulder a muffled pat. "Honey, we *are* kids." Then, playfully she kissed the end of her sister's nose. "Let's go check that barn—see if Horsie's discovered anything." After the glinting white that shut their pupils to pinholes, the women needed to wait just inside the barn door for their eyes to adjust. After a moment or two, they were able to see into the dark interior of the barn. Horsie snorted and softly stamped at the hay there on the floor of her stall giving the impression she was happy to see Ellie and Stella. That evening, Horsie would follow Cully's wagon back home to the Pedersen place, Stella riding in the box instead of on the young mare's back. It was to be an anomaly, this burst of energy from Stella. She wouldn't ride bareback again until the summer.

Inside the stall, Ellie forked a little more hay to the Pedersen's horse while Stella rummaged through the clean hay in the unoccupied stall, feeling around through the wool of her orange mittens for anything resembling a birthday gift. Still nothing. They felt along the tops of beams, braces and planks, finally giving up and returning to the house for more coffee. There, they'd wait for Cully's arrival so that they could all head on over to their mom's for Ellie's birthday dinner.

Ellie understood her husband, and because of this understanding did not expect that he'd give her a birthday present while anyone else was around, not even Stella. "It's silly," Ellie confided to her little sister, "But it seems to make him embarrassed or something."

This surprised Stella. "Hmm. That's funny. He's such a confident guy."

"I know, I know. Culvar's just shy about some things." Ellie shook her head. "I can't understand it either so I guess I'll have to accept it."

Stella reflected, "That's what marriage is, isn't it? A whole lotta accepting minus understanding why." Then she lifted her tin mug in a toast,

"To marriage!" and she and Ellie clunked their mugs together.

Ellie was right. Cully didn't bring out his gift for her until that evening, after they'd arrived home from the Pedersen's farm. He hadn't picked it up in town that day nor had he paid too much for it. He'd made it in Whitlock's shop from scrap lumber, finishing it with the red barn paint leftover in an old gallon can from beneath Edward's workbench. When he'd finished it the day before yesterday, he'd left it there at Whitlock's, waiting to bring it home the day of Ellie's birthday and hiding it in the barn just before hitching Maurice up to the wagon. He'd talked to Mrs. Adamson at the beginning of the week. That flowery china he'd ordered before Christmas wouldn't be in now until February.

"Oh. A birdhouse."

Cully's jaw clenched at his wife's reaction. "You don't like it."

"No, Culvar. No. I do." Ellie faltered. "I was expecting something different. That's all. Something like you got me at Christmas. Something nice."

Her husband didn't tell her that he had ordered "something nice," but it hadn't yet arrived at Adamson's store. He didn't tell her that he'd noticed how much she enjoyed the birds or how he loved working with wood, creating something just for her. Instead he told her, "I did my best to make you happy. Sorry I didn't. Maybe nobody can." And with that, he disappeared upstairs leaving his piece of birthday cake they'd brought home from the Pedersen's half-eaten on the kitchen table.

Ellie set the birdhouse by the back door and then sat back down at the table and cried.

* * *

That crack in their marriage formed by Darlene Sinclair hadn't ever repaired itself—not like the other fissures that seemed to mend with time or a smile. Ellie felt it now, knew that it was this wound that Denby was coming through, the force of his entrance making it bigger, harder to heal.

Denby strode up with an armload of rhubarb, interrupting her memories. Ellie hadn't been paying attention, or she would've stopped him at about half of what he'd cut. Too late, and so she thanked him and said, "I'm going to get a smaller knife and a little water." She began to stand, but he laid a heavy hand on her shoulder.

"You stay put, little lady. You can start cutting the tops

off these with the big knife." The wind tossed his hair, and for the first time, Ellie noticed those few large freckles across the bridge of his nose. She thought about kissing those freckles as she lopped the broad green leaves from their thick stalks. Tomorrow, they would have rhubarb pie, and perhaps they'd take one into Birdie, as well.

"Here." Denby handed her the paring knife and sat down in the shady grass, placing the topped stalks into the basin of water he'd brought. With his fingertips, Ellie's brother-in-law gently scrubbed the traces of soil from near rhubarb's bases. He set each clean one up on the bench beside Ellie. She sliced the stalks quickly into the bowl, grateful for the shade and for her bare feet in the dry grass. For a while, neither of them spoke, just worked in the easy afternoon, the quietness between them soft and warm as the air after a good rain.

When Denby had finished cleaning all the rhubarb, he moved that basin with its silty bottom closer to Ellie. Then he picked her feet up out of the grass by raising her ankles and lowered her feet into the water. Ellie sighed before she could stop herself, and Denby chuckled. He sat on the bench next to Ellie, rested his hand on her thigh, leaned in and kissed her on the mouth.

"Hey! How are you, brother?" Cully lead Maurice into the yard just as the kiss ended.

Startled, Denby quickly moved his hand from his brother's wife's leg and over to the stack of rhubarb leaves and began shuffling them into a neater pile. Ellie, her own cheeks flushed, heart racing, marveled at his outward calm—not a calm she shared.

"Hey," he grinned. "I'm good." Denby Jullsen stood up from the bench with a bunch of rhubarb leaves in one hand and clapped Cully on the back with his other. "I was just helpin' your wife with the rhubarb, makin' myself useful." Denby flashed a smile at Ellie.

"For a change," Cully teased him. "And how're you, my wife? Hot?" Cully bent and kissed Ellie lightly on the top of her head.

"Oh, so hot. Hey!" she called out as Maurice stepped quickly forward upon spotting the basin of water and thrust his long nose between Ellie's feet, snorting hard. With a surprised yelp, Ellie pulled her feet from the basin. She would've toppled over backwards off the bench if Denby hadn't caught her by the upper arm.

Cully laughed hard, pulling back on Maurice's halter shank. "C'mon fella. Let's go find you your own water." And then over his shoulder, to Denby, "Are you staying for supper? If you do, you might as well stay the night."

"Thanks. I'd like that," Denby told his brother. There, alone again in the shade of the willow tree outside the kitchen window, Denby looked at Ellie. She concentrated hard on smoothing her faded house dress over her knees.

He said, "Sorry about that…earlier."

"I'm not," she responded, looking out over her garden, not at Denby.

He wasn't sorry, either. Not really.

— *Chapter 18* —

SHADOWS

"You been to see Norward in your travels?" Cully meant had Denby been to the prison in Edmonton to see their brother. Cully relaxed back into the shady grass. The three of them had eaten supper beneath the willow tree out by the garden. Roast beef sandwiches (the roast beef leftover and brought home by Ellie and Cully from Birdie Jullsen's last Sunday), a green salad from the garden complete with chives and radishes, and a jar of iced tea each. The men had offered to make the salad, picking the lettuce and the other vegetables, washing them at the well and placing the whole works in a smaller glass bowl. Now there was Johnny cake with Roger's syrup and coffee for dessert. And, sweeter than all that put together, was the evening coolness.

"I did see our brother." Denby was carefully pulling up strands of grass and chewing their light green stems, sweet and untouched by the sun. "Stopped in at the jail a few weeks ago."

"How is he?" Cully sat up, and his brother shrugged.

"You know Norward. He does all right wherever he lands. Don't know how. He just does." Denby shared, "Norward was telling me that there's some new evidence against that guy from Estevan. The police are looking to pick him up and question him again. But for now, our brother's still stuck in the clink."

Cully grinned. "That's better news than I thought you'd have for me."

Again, Denby shrugged. "I don't know. Until Norward's out of there, I wouldn't get my hopes up too high."

Ellie came across the lawn carrying the coffeepot. "I was just tellin' your husband about Norward."

"You saw him? In prison? How is he?" she wanted to know.

"I was gettin' to that." Denby continued his story as Ellie poured coffee and then sat back down on the bench to listen. "He makes friends everywhere that guy. Makes himself enemies, too, don't get me wrong. But he sure gets to know people. When I was visitin' him up in Edmonton, he had a million stories to tell about the guys he'd met in there. Hardly told me anything about himself, only that he hadn't been into court for a while. Said that things were up in the air, that they suspected that guy from Estevan, too now, after talkin' to some other folks around Wetaskiwin."

"Well, that could be good news, couldn't it?" Ellie asked.

Denby said, "Maybe. Maybe not. It all depends. I don't even know if they've talked to that guy from Saskatchewan. I don't figure things are gonna move too fast. They'll just let him sit in there till they decide. Not much anybody can do."

Cully held a plate of cake in his lap. "Did he get my letter?"

Denby's face brightened. "Yeah. He did. He said to tell you thanks, and then we talked about Christmas. This was back in February when it was so bloody cold. We'd both missed being here for it. Maybe next year."

"Yeah. Maybe next year." Cully sounded unconvinced.

"It would be so good to have everybody together again." Ellie broke in. "It's not Christmas without family."

That night, Denby slept stretched out on that old chesterfield in the living room, the wool blanket rolled up under his head. Upstairs, husband and wife shared the uncomfortable space their bedroom had become since Ellie found out that Cully may already be a father. In that time between then and now, Cully had developed phantom backaches that seemed to ease if he slept downstairs, where Denby was now. Their breathing was the only sound in the room. Outside, Maurice whinnied.

Cully stabbed at the silence with a question: "You like how my brother looks at you?"

This came out of nowhere from her husband lying there close but far away, stiff and covered by cotton pajamas even in the sweltering heat. Sparked by anxiety, Ellie wondered if Cully had seen them kiss. "Pardon me?" Her offended response hung motionless in the air above the bed.

"Don't be too flattered," he pressed on, adding, "He looks at pretty much every woman that way. That's just how he is."

"I don't know what you're talking about, Culvar. Your brother doesn't look at me any way in particular and if he did, I certainly would not be flattered." Cully didn't answer, but Ellie felt him stiffen and move a little farther away. With his suspicion aired, Cully's breath soon became deep and even, and the rigidity left his limbs.

Ellie couldn't relax. Instead, she lay awake remembering the rough warmth of Denby's hand on her thigh, the sweet surprise of his kiss. It had comforted her, that intimacy. Excited her, too, woke her up to the blue of the sky and the singing of the birds. She missed that kind of emotion, the kind she'd sometimes felt with Cully in those days before and after their wedding. After Cully's indiscretion with Darlene Sinclair but long before Ellie knew about it.

Ellie thought about her husband's bitter words: "That's just how he is." She knew it was true. Ellie understood Denby's charms and was aware that he'd known many women, but she wouldn't guess exactly how many. She judged that the number was much larger than she'd like to know tonight. Denby had seemed so real, so present to her, that she didn't want to think about all the others that he'd appeared to in that same way. When she talked, she loved the way he listened. She ate it up. Denby listened intently, focusing on nothing in deft concentration, sometimes leaning slightly toward her and watching her face. He'd offered to do for her those little things that never seemed to cross her husband's mind; Denby had helped her in the garden, fetched well water for her swollen feet, sliced bread for the sandwiches.

Cully helped with the dishes, but that was it.

Ellie lay in the darkness for what must have been more than an hour. Her tired eyes traced the crack that ran wildly across the ceiling, spidering out in the corner by the door as if from that spot it aspired to gradually take down the entire room. Beyond the open window, its sheer curtains hanging listlessly, the coyotes begun their ceaseless yipping, echoing and imitating one another. And again, the baby sat directly upon Ellie's tight bladder making it impossible for her to ignore the uncomfortable sensation for a moment longer. The chamber pot was under the bed on her side, but mostly she used it with reluctance, worried that Cully would wake up and see or hear her. Sometimes, especially when the weather was bitterly cold, Ellie would carry that chipped porcelain vessel into the empty room across hall, reserved now for newborn children. Tonight though, sleeplessness and the heat together prompted Ellie to ease her big body from the bed and into her slippers. Cully's breathing continued on, deep and steady.

She tiptoed down the stairs and into the porch. Ellie took off her slippers and considered putting on her gumboots for a moment before her swollen feet begged her to go barefoot. Outside, the grass brushed the soles of Ellie's feet with dewy kisses. She wondered how such dry air was able to produce enough moisture for even the lightest film of wet to cling to those stubborn blades of grass. And yet, there it was. Another miracle sent down from heaven.

Ellie raised her eyes and above her saw the endless blackness that was generously peppered with dots of bright. Souls and angels, or perhaps street lamps reflecting off the golden and pearly surfaces of the kingdom she imagined. She touched her belly and wondered if the heavens missed her baby now that he had chosen her. Fear sparked through her. She couldn't bear to think of her baby's return to heaven. At the passing shadow of that saddest of thoughts, the coyotes howled Ellie's heart's mourning.

She made her way to the privy, and the feeling of dread passed. When she was out, Ellie took a tour of her moonlit garden and tugged a few weeds from its perimeter. From there, she walked back around the house under the willow tree, past the front door, along the west side of the house and back into the porch. She knew she should, but Ellie didn't head up those stairs leading back to bed. Instead, Cully's wife moved softly on bare feet into the kitchen and ladled herself a jelly jar of water from the pail Denby had refilled after supper. She sipped it slowly, staring out the window above the counter. Without admitting it to herself, Ellie hoped that Denby would wake and come join her in the kitchen. He didn't, but she could hear his steady breathing in the living room.

Ellie set her jelly jar on the counter, and at the doorway to the living room, she stared through the gloom until she could just make out the man lying long on her chesterfield.

The same moon that had inspired the coyotes to sing now shone its fullness through the lace curtains to land softly across Denby's body, caressing his features. He wore both his underwear and his undershirt, his head twisted at a sharp angle against the blanket balled up between the top of his skull and the couch's arm. Because of the heat or a dream, Denby had kicked his clothes from the arm of the chesterfield onto the floor. He had flung one arm over his head. Ellie noticed the dark thatch of hair there under his arm, where it poked out from beneath his bunched-up sleeve. She noticed, too, the finer, lighter hairs on his legs, how there was less on the thighs and slightly more below his knees.

When she shopped with her sister on Saturday nights, Stella would often reprimand Ellie for longingly fingering the bolts of fabric, for running her hand along the smooth of slips and the satin of full skirts. In fact, Ellie often thought of what it would be like to plunge her hands deep into a barrel of hard, white beans as far as they'd go, or to slap her palm with a black licorice rope. The yearning to feel was always there, persisting, but someone was always watching. "Ellie, do you have to touch everything?"

Ellie thought that maybe it pleased her little sister to find something for which to scold her, as it was generally Ellie's job to do the scolding. "Yes, I do have to," she'd answer. "And I'd touch more if you weren't here spying on me."

Stella placed her hands on her hips. "Spying on you? *Spying?*" Ellie laughed. It was the reaction she'd wanted, and to get it was gratifying. Stella recognized this and laughed, too, imitating and exaggerating from then on Ellie's tactile habits, wrapping herself around bolts of fabric, sighing, "Oh, isn't this the most extraordinarily soft cotton!"

As Ellie watched Denby sleep, that urge to touch him all over grew stronger than it'd ever been. She craved running her hands lightly, so lightly over his ribcage and feeling the curve of the bones giving shape to his silk skin. Ellie wondered if the bottoms of his feet were smooth or more calloused, like her own, and considered what the area on the inside of his thighs, just below that dark and intimate place, would feel like. Under her tongue, would he taste salty after their afternoon together in the sun? Was his hair soft, ruffled by the breeze and bleached by the sun, or would it feel dry and coarse as autumn's grass? Would she taste the bitter of coffee and the sweetness of syrup in his mouth?

Denby shifted slightly in his sleep, and Ellie froze where she stood, balanced on the balls of her feet next to the wood box, praying that he'd keep sleeping and hoping with a deeper part of herself that he'd wake and bring her to him. He splayed his toes, bent his right knee and remained asleep.

Carefully, quietly, as if in a dream, Ellie walked across the living room floor. She paused when her toes felt the worn braided rug, but then she kept going. In the darkness, wrapped softly in the shadows drawn by the moon, Ellie bent and kissed Denby on his forehead and then lightly on his cheekbones. As he shifted and woke, she placed her hands on either side of his face and kissed him deeply on the mouth. Reaching out, he guided his brother's wife gently down onto the cushions beside him. Denby and Ellie kissed deep and slow until her aching body wouldn't let her lie in that position any longer. Without speaking, she brought herself out from under Denby's hand on her hip. All Denby said was her name: "Ellie."

She turned away and found the path across the kitchen. Numbly, she tiptoed up the stairs and eased her round body into bed. Cully hadn't moved in the time she was gone, but as she settled in, he sighed heavily and murmured through his dreams, "I love you, Ellie" and she let her tears soak into the pillowcase.

Denby hung around Hughenden for a couple of months, stacking wood in the lumberyard and helping with painting the buildings downtown: the bank, Adamson's, Bryton's, the livery stable, the drugstore, the new filling station. It was a big job that provided a few lucky men with some steady summer work. During those months while Cully spent long days away tending cattle and mowing hay at the Whitlock's, Denby clipped the dying grass around the Hughenden Lake house with a mower borrowed from Birdie's neighbour in town. He brought water into the kitchen, cleaned Maurice's and Bossie's stalls and forked clean hay.

All this time and when Cully wasn't around, Denby treated Ellie affectionately. She didn't stop him, either. When he'd kiss the top of her head or touch the back of her hand, Ellie would smile and accept what Denby gave her. Of course, these gestures dried up as soon as Cully came home at night. But the moment he was out the door in the morning, the tenderness flourished again.

While they had never made love, several times they'd slept together on the old chesterfield covered by the wool blanket, arms around each other. The sun would make its way through the curtains in the living room and throw lacey patterns across their bodies, intertwined and unmoving. At the peak of her pregnancy during the long cool spring afternoons, Denby and his brother's wife, rested like this, sheltered from the world and its realities.

It was a Tuesday afternoon in mid-June when Ellie's brother-in-law nailed down the loose shingles up on the roof while she prepared dinner to the rhythm of his heavy footfall and steady hammering. Her hand stopped kneading the biscuit dough when a sudden gush of fluid coursed down the insides of her thighs and onto the floor she'd scrubbed clean the day before.

"Denby! Help me!" Her answer wasn't Denby's voice but the sound of his boots scrabbling on the rooftop above her. Just before he crashed through the back door and into her kitchen without removing his boots, a jolt shook her, contracting her abdomen and burning up her spine so that she was forced down into a chair. He fell to his knees beside her.

"Ellie?" Denby stared into her face, trying to read her pain.

"It's time." She couldn't help it. She began to cry. "What are we going to do?"

He thought fast. "Well, we got the wagon here. I'm gonna go quick and see if I can borrow us a horse." He kissed her forehead. "Hang in there. I'll be right back."

As God had instructed her, Ellie had packed a suitcase the night before and set it by the back door. Cully had gently teased her about it. "Always so organized, my wife. You can try, but you can't control everything." She knew. Her feelings for Denby had taught her that. She hadn't told him about her message from God. Her husband was a believer, but he was also very practical. Cully wouldn't believe that God would view her disorganization as sinful, that He Himself had some doubts about her ability as a mother. And so she followed the Lord's directions but chose not to tell Cully about it. Now it was June twentieth and labour pains engulfed her, moving in thick as purple clouds heralding a sudden summer storm.

With Denby gone, having disappeared down the driveway at an easy jog, Ellie talked again with God. "Father God, please let Denby get back here with a horse before this baby comes. Please let me live. Give me strength. Oh Lord, I'm so scared," Ellie pleaded from where she sat perspiring at the kitchen table.

In less than an half an hour, Denby returned riding a livery stable palomino with just a blanket thrown over her back. He tethered the horse to the poplar tree by the well and ran in to check on Ellie. She was at the stove bringing from it a pan of biscuits, hot and golden brown.

"What are you doing?" Denby stopped and stood stock-still there in the middle of the kitchen floor, his eyes fixed in disbelief, his heart still thudding following the race for the horse.

"I wanted to get these done." Ellie smiled. "I didn't think you'd find a horse so quickly that I wouldn't have time to finish this baking. Now Culvar can have these for breakfast. You haven't got the wagon ready yet, have you?"

"No. I wanted check on you first." For a moment, Denby was irritated by Ellie's calmness and what he perceived to be her demands, but just as quickly, the irritation evaporated and gave way to a laugh. "Why don't you get those put away, and I'll get the wagon ready. I'll only be a couple minutes," he warned. "Don't start baking bread as soon as I step out of the house."

Ellie just smiled and laid her hand on his arm. "I'll be ready when you are."

When Denby pulled the wagon up to the house, Ellie was sitting on the boards that formed the makeshift stoop, clutching her tiny suitcase, weathered green. Denby hopped down from the wagon, took Ellie's suitcase and tucked it under the bench. Then, he helped his sister-in-law into the wagon. Running back inside, he brought out the wool blanket from the porch and as Ellie stood up, Denby tucked it under her. "There. Now you'll be comfy." He grinned up at her and naturally, easily, like a husband, kissed her forehead. Denby sprinted around to his side, jumped up onto the bench seat, and the two of them rumbled off in the glare of the afternoon sun, as bright and piercing as the pain that had torn through Ellie and would again and again.

As he clutched the reins, Denby told Ellie, "Henry was working at the livery stable. He's gonna get Alice to call over to the Whitlock's to let Cully know that the baby's on its way." He glanced over at her. "How're you feeling? You look like you're hurting." Denby touched her shoulder.

"I'm all right. I've had one more bad pain since the first one in the kitchen. It happened right when you took off to get Goldie here. Thank goodness the biscuits were already in the oven." Ellie was mostly joking about the biscuits. She told him, "And by the way, thank you." She smiled at her brother-in-law from under her hat brim.

"Hey, anything for you." Denby laid his hand for a long moment on her thigh and added seriously. "I mean that, Ellie. Anything. Ever." Then his tone lightened, and he took his hand from her leg. "Besides, what was I gonna do? Let you have that baby right there on the kitchen floor? What kind of family would I be then?" Denby snapped the reins and the palomino doubled her gait.

And Ellie doubled over in pain. In his peripheral vision, Denby saw her straining, saw the red in her face beneath her hat, heard her teeth grinding.

Alternately, Denby watched the road and watched his sister-in-law, the woman he loved. "Ellie! Ellie! How are you doing?" She didn't look up at him, just shook her bowed head, not allowing a groan to escape her lips. Not yet. It would get worse before it got better.

She had broken out into a heavy sweat and could feel it streaming down her back and out from under her arms. The salty excess ran into Ellie's eyes, stinging her while pain wracked the rest of her body. Her skeleton seemed made of glass, and she could picture it on the verge of shattering each time a wheel struck and bounced out of a concrete-hard rut. Ellie couldn't know how fast Denby was driving, lashing at the palomino's soaking wet back, yelling his rough encouragement. "C'mon! C'mon! Go goddamnit! Go!"

Ellie wasn't aware of anything beyond the pain of her labour. She couldn't be. She didn't even hear Denby taking the name of her Lord in vain. The rushing hurt seemed to fill her ears, like her head was being held beneath the surface of a springtime river. Ellie gasped for breath but couldn't get enough air. Denby couldn't tell if the drops on her face were sweat or tears or a mingling of both. "Hang on, darlin'! Hang on! We'll get you there!" He was trying desperately to reassure the both of them, horse and passenger, that they would all make it to town, to Dr. Stromquist's office. Denby was failing to reassure anyone—especially himself.

"Denby. Stop. Please stop." And when he didn't, Ellie yelled, "Now! Stop it! Stop this damn wagon! Now!" She'd felt a resistance, an unyielding pressure begin between her legs. "Ohhh...I don't think we can make it, brother-in-law. Pray that I'm wrong! Pray, Denby! Pray!" she screamed at him.

Denby didn't pray. Instead, he tied the horse's reins to the leg of the bench seat and asked Ellie, "Do you need to lie down? I can put you in the back? On the blanket? Would that help?" He responded to her rapid nodding by helping her to stand and by tearing that blanket out from beneath her, in one swift motion. With one hand, he spread that blanket out over the rough planks of the wagon box's floor. Denby scooped her up almost gracefully, lifted Ellie over that bench and set her almost gently onto that blanket. Upon standing up straight, Denby scanned the sun-drenched road for any traffic, any sign of help. No one. "Shit!" This time she'd heard.

Through clenched teeth, she inquired, "Do you have to?"

"Sorry. It's just I...I don't know..."

She cut him off. "I know. I know. Me neither, but how many calves have we, between the two of us, brought into this world?" Ellie yelled at him. "I've helped bring three! Three baby cows!" Now she screamed, a strangled sound, as she attempted to stifle it.

It was Denby's turn to count the calves he'd delivered. His lips worked silently, franticly, until he came up with the number as close as he could remember. "Forty-two!" he bellowed triumphantly. "Forty-two calves!"

"Then how hard can this be?" Ellie forgot her need for modesty and removed her freshly donned panties—her best ones—and stuffed them in a corner beneath the wagon bench in front. Ellie didn't have to think about spreading her legs. They opened up widely, automatically as her muscles worked and clenched, contracting with a might she'd never imagined was possible. Denby's vision strained. How many times had he walked or ridden this damned road and met one or two, sometimes three neighbours on their way to or from town? Still, the road remained deserted, and the palomino patient.

"What can I do, Ellie? Tell me. Tell me anything. Tell me," he urged through clenched teeth. He tried to sound calm.

"Reach into my suitcase and get out my nightgown.

We'll need something to wrap the baby in and something to clean me —" With a hiss, she inhaled sharp and short. Denby retrieved the long cotton gown and made it back around to sit between Ellie's knees just in time to guide that round, red head out followed by the tiny, wrinkly body. Ellie wept now, and so did Denby. He gently covered the baby where it lay on Ellie's stomach with her long flannelette nightgown.

Just then, near the wagon, someone called out, "Hey!" It was Cully. He rode up to them and pulled back hard on Maurice's reins. In one motion, Ellie's husband halted the horse alongside the wagon, leapt out of the saddle and into the wagon box. "Didn't make it to the doctor's?" They hadn't heard him coming, and Denby was amazed that he hadn't seen his brother on the road. Later on, Denby would wonder if he hadn't seen his brother because Denby didn't want to be rescued. Denby would wonder if he had wanted to be the hero for Ellie.

"Nope. He came quick." Denby smiled broadly, like a proud father.

"And two weeks early. He all right?" Cully asked.

Denby shrugged amiably. "He looks fine to me, but what do I know about babies?"

Cully laughed. "Probably not enough to be delivering them in the middle of the road."

Ellie didn't speak. She just smiled and held her baby close to her belly, and the two, mother and son, stayed joined as no one in the wagon had the nerve to cut the shiny umbilical cord. Denby indicated the red string of flesh that kept the baby attached to Ellie. "Thought maybe we should leave that to the doc. Whaddaya think, Daddy?"

Cully agreed. "Yeah, that's a good idea. Let's wait. You check his nose for mucus and stuff?"

"Yeah, he's good. He's breathing fine." Denby chuckled. "You know, once you get over being scared to death, it's not so different from calving."

Now Ellie spoke. "Oh, really. I must say, brother-in-law, I disagree with you entirely." With her tired eyes, she smiled at him.

Cully had tied Maurice to the back of the wagon, and now the black gelding followed with a light gait, seeming happy to have lost his frantic passenger. "How're you, my wife? You got your baby." Cully took her hand, stroking the back of it. "I should've been there, but I thought the baby knew his due date." Her husband stroked Ellie's hair and told her, "Sorry, honey."

"I told you that he'd be arriving any time, husband…" Ellie scolded Cully gently and even laughed lightly, happy to be rid of the fire that ripped her open. She gripped Cully's hand, holding her baby with the other. The fire was replaced by a dull, throbbing pain and Ellie was relieved to see the tops of Hughenden's grain elevators appearing in her line of sight just above the wagon box's edge.

Denby kept his eyes fixed on the road, staring straight ahead and holding the reins hard. He was suddenly alone, and he understood it like never before. From behind him in the wagon, Denby couldn't help but overhear their soft conversation.

He heard his brother, the brand new father, laugh and agree with Ellie, "You did tell me. You sure did. I love you."

"I love you, too, Culvar." Then and there, Ellie meant it. And both Cully and Denby knew she did.

Cully squeezed her hand and asked, "Are you hurt?" The wagon bounced as the wheels turned across the railroad tracks.

"I think so." She winced. "Are we almost there? I want the doctor."

"Nearly. Just hang on a couple more minutes." Cully watched as a shadow of fear moved across his wife's face. Denby slowed the wagon to pull up beside the doctor's office, still open for the day if near closing. If the office had been closed, they would've done what everybody did: they would have dashed up to the Stromquist residence, banged on the door and cried, "Help!" It was something the doctor was used to. Having a baby born roadside half a mile from town arrive at his office, all shriveled and sticky with blood drying on his skin, was not.

The bell above the door tinkled when Denby opened it. Doctor Harold Stromquist looked up from the file he'd been perusing. "Yes?" he asked, looking at the two men who had just come into his office. The doctor stood behind the tall counter looking at the brothers over his thick, wire-framed glasses that rested part way down his nose.

Cully whacked Denby on the back and told the doctor, "Ellie's out in the wagon with our baby boy. My brother here brought him into the world just up the road. Guess that baby couldn't wait. What do you think of that?"

"They're both in the wagon?" The doctor sounded alarmed. He set the file folder down and stepped out from behind the counter. Dr. Stromquist pushed up his glasses.

"Yup," was Cully's answer.

"Well, we'd better bring them in here."

The three men hurried out into the late afternoon and stepped across the boardwalk to the wagon. Dr. Stromquist stood on tiptoes and leaned over the edge of the wagon box, his veiny hands resting on the weathered wood. "Hello, Ellie. How are you doing?" She was lying there on the rough floor, the grey wool blanket spread beneath her.

She smiled up at him weakly, clutching her baby close and not daring to move. "We're fine, doctor. I think we'll be just fine."

"Of course you will." Cully had leapt into the wagon box and was leaning over his wife. He kissed her forehead and told Denby and Dr. Stromquist, "Here. I'll help her up and out, and then you two can let them down to the ground." Cully handled Ellie as if she were breakable. He hooked his hands beneath her arms from behind and slowly, ever so slowly, stood her up. He guided his wife and newborn son to the side of the wooden box that was closest to the doctor's office door. From there, over the wooden box side, cracked and greyed by years of sun, cold, and precipitation, Denby and Dr. Stromquist caught Ellie and the baby, and brought them safely to the ground. Ellie balanced between the doctor and her brother-in-law as they walked her into the office, with Cully following closely behind. "Don't let her walk too fast," he instructed, and when they got to the wooden step, he told them, "Careful! Careful!"

At the sound of his brother's voice, Denby felt a heat

in his stomach and a tightening in his belly. He recognized this feeling as something akin to jealousy, but stronger and much deeper. Denby concentrated on Ellie, on getting her into the examination room at the rear of the building.

Seemingly unaware of Denby, Ellie managed a laugh and turned her head to look at her husband. "Culvar! I'm all right."

"But you're sore?" he asked.

Her voice still sounded happy, but now her words were lightly ringed with impatience. "Yes, yes. I'm sore. I just gave birth, Culvar. But I'm not going to die. Not today."

Once inside Harold Stromquist's office, Cully stepped in front of his brother and said, "Thanks, brother. I'll take over from here." Denby stood there alone for a moment staring at the closed door of the examination room, his hands hanging uselessly by his sides and beads of sweat gathering on his palms and on his brow. His heart beat hard and, for the first time in his life, he wished Cully were dead. Denby didn't let them know he was leaving. They wouldn't care. Not now. So he turned and walked out of the office, following the sandy road up Main Street and over to Birdie Jullsen's and a place at her supper table.

— *Chapter 19* —

THE REVIVAL

"A lot more people here than last year," Cully commented and slowed Maurice, pulling back on the reins. Together, he and Ellie scanned the wagons and cars for Stella and Henry or anyone else they knew. The weather had been hot and dry for so many months now that people seldom ever mentioned it anymore. It's news that gives rise to conversation, and there was nothing new about this weather. Pretty much everyone had stopped waiting for it to change, deciding instead to get on with life.

The huge tent was set up on the picnic grounds not far from the lakeshore, its broad green and white canvas stripes shaking and snapping while the tight lines and deeply driven stakes kept the canvas structure anchored against assailing winds. The late afternoon sun glinted on the lake's surface bestowing a golden tip upon each tiny wave and stretching the shadows of the thirsty poplar and aspen trees across the lifeless grass. People from communities up to fifty miles away milled about the lawn area outside the tent, gathering in laughing, chattering clusters. Anticipation hovered low, touching everyone, making them weigh less and smile more.

"There's Stella!" Cully had steered their wagon into some of the rare shade left when Ellie spotted the bright yellow sleeve waving frantically in their direction above the crowd. At the sound of Ellie's voice, Kristoffer squinted up at his mother from beneath the brim of the white bonnet tied snugly beneath his chin.

"Hello, baby boy. You're awake." Ellie brushed his cheek with the back of her index finger. "Are you hungry? Mommy's brought a bottle. Would you like it? Hmm? Would you?"

Cully had jumped down from the wagon and unhitched Maurice.

He smiled up at the two of them. "If you're waiting for him to answer, you're gonna be waiting awhile."

"Culvar, you're supposed to talk to your babies. Just because you don't, doesn't mean I shouldn't." Already, she was on the defensive.

Ellie's husband stood up from where he'd stopped to tie the end of Maurice's rope to a grey poplar trunk. His jaw worked, and his smile was gone. "It was a joke, Ellie. Calm down." Cully walked away into the swarm of believers just as Stella reached the wagon.

"Hi, Cully!" Stella called and in reply, he touched the brim of his hat and kept on going. She turned to Ellie and asked, "What's up with him? I thought he'd have more to say than nothing. I haven't seen him for a week."

Ellie had seen Stella's disposition improve as spring moved on into summer. She had gained back the weight she'd lost, her cheeks were healthy pink and she was spending more and more of her time in Henry's company.

Stella held her arms out, and Ellie handed Kristoffer to her sister. "Come say hi to Auntie Stella, little man. That's right. You have more manners than your daddy, don't you?"

Ellie lowered herself from the wagon as Stella gingerly held the baby. Once on the ground, Cully's wife commented on his behaviour. "I don't know what's with him. I think we're both tired. He doesn't get up with Kristoffer in the night but, careful as I am, I know I wake him. He gets so cranky."

"Kristoffer?"

"Culvar."

"Oh." Stella handed the infant back. "Did you explain that babies are a lot of work? That at first they're going to cry at nights? It's what babies do?"

"It's like he doesn't hear me, you know? I'm tired, too. And I'm the one who gets up all the time. I got three hours of sleep last night, Stella." Ellie inhaled sharply and breathed out the admission, "I'm beat." The young mother felt angry with the tear that, without permission, slipped down her cheek.

"Aw, sis." Stella reached out and wiped the dissident

drop away with her fingertip. "Come on. You know it'll turn out all right. Cully loves you, and Baby will be sleeping through the night soon enough. Why don't you let Mom come stay for a few days. She still wants to, El. It'd be good for you. Give you a chance to rest." She ran her hand reassuringly down the length of her sister's arm and felt some of the tension leave Ellie's body. Stella tilted her head toward the groups of folks starting to slowly enter the tent. "Let's go join them, shall we?"

Ellie swallowed her emotions and nodded, looping her free arm through the crooked arm her little sister offered. Ellie cradled two-month-old Kristoffer in her other arm. It wouldn't be long until she would need both arms to hold him—he was growing so quickly. At the thought, Ellie felt a jab of sadness at the centre of her heart.

"Henry!" Stella had spotted her boyfriend just ahead. "Wait up!" She waved and then spun around to tell Ellie, "Oh, this is so exciting! Rachel said that this year at Camrose people were healed and some saw visions. For sure we'll hear some speaking in tongues. That always happens. Really, it's better than the fair!"

"Stella! It's the power of the Lord!—it's nothing like the fair," Ellie corrected her sternly.

Her sister backtracked. "I meant it's better than the fair because it's holier than the fair." She rolled her eyes quickly, less exaggerated than when truly annoyed. "Sheesh. You take everything way too seriously."

"Afternoon, Ellie. So this is the little guy?" Henry had stood by the tent entrance, pausing in the jostle until they'd caught up. Now he bent to look at Kristoffer, lifting a massive hand to touch the end of the infant's upturned nose. "Hello, little fella. How are you? You sure are cute, aren't you? Aren't you? Yes you are!"

"You've got to speak with my husband about babies," Ellie told him, marveling at how high and small the big man had made his voice when talking to her baby. How silly and sweet!

Stella let loose Ellie's arm, grabbed Henry's hand instead and tugged. "Come on, you two! Let's get a good seat." Henry just chuckled, squeezed her hand and trailed along behind. Ellie followed them, her eyes darting about the dark interior of the tent looking for her husband.

"Henry?" Stella's tall boyfriend looked over his shoulder at Ellie, and she asked him, "Can you see Culvar anywhere?" She stood up on her tiptoes and craned her neck in an effort to spot Cully in the crowd.

"I thought I saw him come in here with the Whitlocks... Oh, yeah, there they are." Henry waved from his superior height over the crowd.

"Now they've seen us. Stella. Slow down. Go that way. Cully's sitting over there." Stella veered off in the direction Henry suggested, and she pushed through the people. There was room on the hard seat beside Cully and the Whitlocks for Ellie and baby Kristoffer, but Henry and Stella had to sit on the benches directly behind them. Within minutes, Muriel and Benson Pedersen slid in close beside Henry and Stella, peeking over to catch glimpses of little Kristoffer. Ellie located Birdie Jullsen and Alice fanning themselves to the right of where she and Cully sat and a little farther back. Soon everyone was settled in, the enclosed space already sweltering hot, dust drifting out of the air onto the hopeful folks. Every inch of bench was occupied, sweaty limbs pressed together in rows, knees touching the benches in front. Several people stood at the rear of the tent. The canvas flaps were tied wide open, enabling those folks left outside to see straight up the narrow aisle, carpeted with defenseless grass, newly trampled. Others lined the walls of the tent forming a tight, single line on either side right from the back and on up to the platform at the front.

Through a smaller canvas flap to the rear of the wooden stage, a well-dressed man and woman stepped up onto the rough boards to face the crowd, both smiling broadly. A respectful silence fell. The man, called Pastor Andy, spoke first.

"Good afternoon, brothers and sisters! God be with you! The Lord is in this place. Do you feel His presence? Hallelujah if you do!" He raised his hands to encourage the congregation.

"Hallelujah!" The response reverberated through the tent. It wouldn't be necessary to warm up this crowd. They were ready to worship, aching to believe and to give voice to their faith in that revival tent surrounded by those low hills, browned to done by the sun.

"Amen!" Sister Patricia echoed. In her right hand, she held a tambourine which she immediately began to shake. As if bidden by the rhythmic jangling, a voice sweeter than a honey-dunked harp came from her, not from her vocal chords and not from her diaphragm, either. This song sprung from her soul. "Do Lord, do Lord, do you remember me? Do Lord, oh do Lord, do you remember me? Do Lord, oh do Lord, do you remember me? Way beyond the blue...Join in, if you know the words," she called out through painted red lips, inviting everyone to sing. Next, Sister Patricia turned to the man beside her, "That means you, too, Pastor Andy. Grab your guitar and show the Lord Jesus you love him and remember the sacrifice he made for you! Hallelujah!" She said all this, each word, to the beat she kept with her tambourine, striking it on the heel of her left hand, the hem of her dress flouncing up and down to match the cadence of her song. The familiar hymn began again, this time with accompaniment from Pastor Andy and two hundred and fifty voices.

I got a home in glory land, outshines the sun.
I got a home in glory land, outshines the sun.
I got a home in glory land, outshines the sun.
Way beyond the blue!
I took Jesus as my Saviour! You take Him, too!
I took Jesus as my Saviour! You take Him, too!
I took Jesus as my Saviour! You take Him, too!
Way beyond the blue!

Sister Patricia led them all in song for over half an hour, the temperature in the tent rising with the heat of the hymns. Fortunately, as the evening dissolved, cooler air began to seep through the wide opening in the back. About fifteen minutes into the lively song service, ninety-four-year-old Mrs. Morrison from Amisk toppled over. Her grandson Troy, six foot three, two hundred and thirty pounds, and handsome as a thousand dollars, scooped her up deftly and carried her limp body down the aisle never breaking from the tune he sang, his baritone voice almost perfect, "Shall we gather by the river..." Even as he laid her gently in the shade of the closest tree and patted her hands until she came to, he continued to hum.

Her eyes opened and the first words out of Mrs. Morrison's mouth were, "Troy. I saw Jesus and a host of angels. Jesus was coming for me! Praise God! Praise Him!" It wasn't a statement- it was an order. A scant two weeks following the tent revival, Jesus came again for Mrs. Morrison, but this time the old woman's eyes remained closed after Troy carried her down that one last aisle.

But at the outdoor service, she was still alive and well. Mrs. Morrison commanded her grandson to help her up and to take her to the front of the tent. The singers and dancers cleared the narrow walkway as they passed, that tiny, shrunken woman leaning determinedly on the elbow of that gorgeous, towering man. When she reached the edge of the stage, Troy encircled his grandmother's waist and hoisted her up. Above the music, she trumpeted, "Jesus is alive!" Sister Patricia ceased banging her tambourine, and Pastor Andy stepped to the side of the stage playing softly now, providing a lilting auditory backdrop for the first testimonial of the evening.

"Tell us, sister!" Patricia encouraged, smiling invitingly at Troy who smiled back and then lowered his eyes to look at her legs, slim and strong, visible beneath the hemline of her dress.

"I was singing and praying, my hands uplifted to the

Lord!" She demonstrated this shaky pose, "When He came to me! Jesus flooded my brain and filled me! I don't remember falling because I was looking at his face! Upon my Saviour's countenance I gazed! Praise Jesus! He is alive!"

Sister Patricia threw an arm around Mrs. Morrison, squeezing her until she felt something shift and crack. The song leader released her grip. Pastor Andy had set his guitar back in its stand and was now poised next to Sister Patricia, her cue that the time had arrived to give the stage over to him. He leaned in and asked loud enough for the audience to hear, "What's your name, sister?"

"My name's Mable Morrison and I saw Jesus!"

"Hallelujah, you did! And what did our sweet Lord and Saviour say to you, sister?" Pastor Andy asked.

"He didn't say anything. He just beckoned to me." The elderly woman answered him firmly, holding up her right arm, imitating Christ's beckoning motion.

"He told you to enter His kingdom! To come into His everlasting arms! To live with Him in heaven! Amen?"

"Amen!" Almost everyone in the tent added their voices to Mrs. Morrison's crackly one, fading now in the blinding light of Pastor Andy's dead certainty.

Pastor Andy gave Mable Morrison's shoulder a soft nudge and a look that told Troy to get his grandma off the platform. "Is there anyone else here today who has felt the presence of Jesus here in this place or anywhere in your lives? Come forward now and share with us how the Lord has touched you! We want to hear of the glory of God almighty! The miracles, the lives altered, the souls redeemed! Jesus moves within us! Praise Jesus! God moves within us! Praise God!"

And as Pastor Andy spoke, and others echoed his praises, a familiar figure loped to the front. It was Wilma Bryton, co-owner of Bryton's Ladies Wear in Hughenden. Although she was in her mid-fifties, she bounded onto the stage like a teenager, speaking to the crowd, and for the moment, ignoring Pastor Andy's presence. "Jesus is at work in my life this very day. For a long time now, my heart's been suffering from a broken friendship. And then, just last week, my friend and I patched things up. She came to me and said straight out that she missed me and was sorry we weren't friends anymore. She didn't say it was Jesus that moved her to apologize to me, but I know it was because I had prayed to the Lord, saying, 'Lord, I miss Louise so much. Just please bring me an apology from her so that I can forgive...'"

A shrill voice from within the congregation cut Mrs. Bryton off before Pastor Andy could. "Wilma Bryton! I did *not* apologize to you! I said I was sorry that we're not friends, but I am *not* sorry for anything I said or done. If anything, *you* should apologize to *me*. I told you that before, you...ignorant woman! And if you think things are still all right between us, you'd better think again!"

Without bidding, Sister Patricia knew to step forward and place a gentle arm around Mrs. Bryton's shoulder, guiding the crying woman through that flap behind the platform leaving Pastor Andy to put out the fire.

He raised his arms high above his head and looking at the tent's ceiling, cried out, "Almighty God, Heavenly

Father, hear our prayers tonight. Help to heal this friendship between these two, your daughters. Remind all present here that forgiveness is your will and your gift. Mend our hearts, Saviour God, so that we can love each other. Amen!

"Now, my brethren, let's turn to one another and greet each other with a blessing and a kind word. Let's share God's love here on the shores of Czar Lake as Christ did on the shores of Galilee. Brothers and sisters in Christ, friends, family, neighbours…" Folks were already shaking hands far around as they could reach and embracing those close to them. Backs were slapped heartily and shoulders touched reassuringly. As he made his way through the crowd toward the woman who had spoken up against Wilma Bryton, Andy shook hands rapidly and beamed until his cheeks hurt, never giving up his directed stride. It took him less than two minutes to reach her.

Pastor Andy grasped her hand and didn't let go. "What's your name, sister?"

"Louise." The woman stopped pumping his moist hand.

"Louise, today the Lord is calling to you. Will you choose to answer Him or will you let Him down this day?" Pastor Andy pressed her.

"Oh, my. Of course I'll answer. Praise God, I'll answer!" The conviction in her words built as she spoke. While she replied to Pastor Andy, he'd begun steering the hefty grey-haired woman up to the platform. The people around them continued their chatter, cheeks flushed from joy and the heat, and from the connection they'd made with each other.

When they'd made it to the front of the tent, Andy told her, "Sister Louise, our Father God has instructed us as His children to forgive one another." Behind the tent, in the cooling air of evening's onset, Sister Patricia had calmed Wilma Bryton down. At that very moment, she reminded the store owner from Hughenden of forgiveness. Not four minutes later, the women embraced and wept in one another's arms atop that platform, and all present witnessed firsthand the power of God manifest in forgiveness. To a soft chorus of "amens" and "praise the Lords" the women returned to the benches occupied by their families.

The reconciliation between the two friends seemed to fuel the group's desire to publicly proclaim Jesus Christ as their Lord and saviour. Several people testified at the front with stories of abstinence from alcohol and abstinence from women, with stories of easing arthritis and of healed gout, of strong marriages and deep wells, of faith and strength granted by God in times of adversity. People brought their prayers forward, too, as evidence of their faith and in the hope that all the others there at Czar Lake would share in their prayers.

Cully waited until the time felt right, until he was sure that the Lord had called him forward. Then he moved to the front and stepped up onto the stage. Cully Jullsen prayed loudly and clearly, his hands at his sides and eyes tightly shut. "Heavenly Father, hear my prayer for my brother Norward in prison in Edmonton. Dear God, please forgive any sins he's committed, and wash his soul clean. Bring him home, Lord. Just bring him home. Amen." Several people added their amens, and Cully went back to his seat feeling that now he'd done all he could do for his brother. He'd set this decision in the Lord's hands, and His will would be done.

Near the end of the worship service, a middle-aged man recognized by Ellie and Cully, worked his way slowly to the platform from the very back of the tent. When the man arrived at the edge of the stage, Pastor Andy extended his hand, pulling him up and asking, "What's ailing you, brother?"

The man spoke softly so that only those nearest the front were able to hear. "I got a bum leg. Always been that way, ever since I was a kid." Cully faintly remembered seeing the man at the general store, remembered his pronounced limp and then remembered his name: Rufus Kent.

Pastor Andy looked sympathetic. He asked, "Have you accepted Jesus into your life, my friend?"

The man swallowed hard so that the crowd could see his Adam's apple rise and then fall. "I did today. Yes sir. I did today." The corners of Sister Patricia's mouth lifted softly as the man scraped away a tear with his claw of a hand.

Pastor Andy wanted to know, "Do you believe the Lord can heal you? Do you have faith?"

Rufus Kent nodded. "I got faith." Then he shrugged. "Guess if it's His will, it'll happen. If not…"

"But you must believe! Believe without a doubt that the Lord can cure the weakness in your leg. Can you believe, brother? Can you?" the preacher urged.

Rufus Kent paused and then made up his mind, confirming, "Yes sir. I can."

With that, Sister Patricia moved in behind the crippled man as Pastor Andy instructed him, saying, "Now just relax. I'm gonna put my hands on you, lay my hands on you, and pray that the love of Jesus Christ flows through me and out my fingertips into your leg. I believe that love can heal you, but you've got to believe it, too." The pastor held his arms out in front of him and looked at them as if they were shockingly unfamiliar. His eyes were wide, and the rest of his body looked somehow removed from and yet attached to his upper limbs. "Oh, I feel the faith warm like the streets of Jerusalem. Here comes the faith, flowing wide and deep like the river Jordan. Hold on, brother. You ready for the power of the Lord?"

"Yes sir," Mr. Kent answered.

"I said, are you ready for the power of love, the power of the Holy Spirit?" Pastor Andy coaxed the man farther.

"Yes sir! I am ready!" The crippled man shut his eyes so tightly that his nose crinkled and rivulets of lines spread out from the far edges of his eyes, spilling onto his face and creasing it more. The man looked like a wrinkled child concentrating hard on making a wish. Beads of sweat grew on his brow. Pastor Andy's hand hovered slightly above the man's thigh for moments, and then, without warning, the preacher grabbed the leg with both hands and squeezed. The lame man's eyes flew open as Sister Patricia braced herself behind him.

Pastor Andy screamed toward the sky, with his mouth wide open and his throat bare and exposed. "Jesus! Saviour of us all! In the name of the Lord God almighty, heal this man!" The preacher reeled backwards as if he'd been kicked in the stomach and, at the same the time, Rufus Kent staggered backward into Patricia's arms. He stood there stunned for a few seconds while she stoically held him up.

On the other side of the stage, Pastor Andy shook his head like a determined but losing boxer who'd just taken a solid hit. Finally, he stood up straight and asked, "Did the Spirit move in your body, brother? Are you healed?" As Pastor Andy spoke, he moved toward the man still leaning a little on Patricia. The woman took her hands from beneath Rufus Kent's bent elbows and took another step back. The lame man stared at Pastor Andy and then down at his own worn boots, their soles free of their usual manure and prairie dust.

Tentatively, Rufus Kent moved his leg. Still looking down, he took one step, then another. He brought his gnarled hands to the tops of his thighs and rubbed up and down before turning to face the preacher. Everyone held their breath, their thoughts suspended, their prayers circling around and around inside the tent, like birds looking for escape.

"My leg," said Rufus Kent.

"What, brother? What is it?" Pastor Andy was kneeling before him, pleading.

"It feels same as the other one." He grabbed the preacher's shoulder and took a few quick steps in succession. Then, in one simultaneous rush of carbon dioxide, the crowd breathed out their awe. The lame man let go of Pastor Andy and leapt from the stage. He cried, "I can walk! Praise the Lord! Oh, praise Him!" Tears streamed down Rufus Kent's weathered cheeks as he rushed down the aisle and out the tent door. Onlookers, those gathered outside around the tent's opening, watched stunned as the formerly crippled man ran past them and down the dry dirt road toward the main highway.

Following Rufus Kent's retreat down the grassy aisle, a flood of folks approached the stage with every ailment from hiccups and nasal congestion to broken bones and alcoholism. From within their cramped seats, people praised God, burst into song and spoke in tongues. As Pastor Andy healed the sick and hurt in spirit, Sister Patricia passed around four tin pie plates. The congregants gave what little they could from each pocket. The coins and bills heaped altogether in those baking tins spoke to the glory of God.

The sun was low in the sky by the time they all headed down to the lakeshore. A few people had left at this point, having previous obligations to fulfill, but anyone with a choice stayed and joined the horde that followed Sister Patricia with her tambourine and Pastor Andy in his white gown, the one he'd pulled over his Sunday shirt before he left the tent. The crowd gathered on the shore as the preacher strode out into that muddy, shallow lake inhabited by enough leeches to suck him dry within twenty-four hours, if he'd just stay put.

About ten or so feet out, the pastor turned to face the crowd and opened his arms wide in invitation. "Anyone here tonight who desires new life through Christ is welcome to come into this water. Right now, folks, this water is just water. But together, you and I will ask our heavenly

Father's blessing upon your lovely lake. Then, through God's power, this water will become holy, and in it, brothers and sisters, you shall be born again." He finished this last sentence to a hearty chorus of amens, and Pastor Andy began to pray.

Ellie and Cully along with baby Kristoffer and Birdie, stood near the back of the crowd. Cully watched the people around him watch the preacher man in knee-deep water. Pastor Andy's white gown billowed up and floated all around him. Cully saw hope frozen on their faces, sensed it on his own and thought about how good it felt. Beside Cully, Ellie had her eyes shut, her head tilted back and her arms reaching toward heaven. She mumbled and then sighed. The words were nothing her husband could understand. Beside Ellie, Birdie Jullsen held tightly to little Kristoffer, speaking to him softly, cooing, also in gibberish. Baby talk. Although Cully couldn't recognize Birdie's words as anything intelligible, he recognized their intent as she soothed her grandson. Cully for sure didn't understand the point of Ellie's strange speech.

Stella and Henry had a spot a little closer to the lake and were signaling Cully and his mother to come stand with them.

"Ellie?" Cully touched his wife's sleeve. No response. "Ellie? We're going to move over there by Stella. Over towards the dock." His wife didn't stop her swaying and humming, and she didn't answer him. Cully released his grip on her cotton blouse, letting his hand fall heavily to his side. "All right, then. You come see us when you're ready, all right?" At this, Ellie backed away from him without opening her eyes, moving farther onto the open lawn away from the lake. Bringing her arms down and spreading them wide, Ellie started to slowly turn circles and to hum her mantra more loudly. Reluctantly, Birdie and Cully moved to where they could better witness the baptisms, leaving Ellie isolated with her prayers.

"Does she want Kristoffer here baptized?" Birdie asked Cully, without taking her eyes off the infant's face.

"I'd think so," Cully said.

Birdie Jullsen narrowed her eyes. "I'm not sure about that water. It's pretty dirty." She paused, weighing her words and her feelings carefully. "I'm not sure about that preacher, either. He might have the same problem the water's got."

Cully examined her face. "What's that?"

"Impure and with the potential for bloodsucking." Birdie lifted her head quickly as she caught a glimpse of someone familiar out in the lake with Pastor Andy. "Muriel's going in. Would you look at that." And Cully did, straining forward and looking for Ellie's mom in the water. Then he glanced over his shoulder to see that Ellie had stopped spinning. Cully felt a little relief at this. Ellie was now just holding her palms pressed flat together and vertically, fingertips at her chin, her eyes still closed.

"Hang on a minute, Mom," Cully said. "I'm gonna go ask Ellie if she still wants to take Kristoffer in."

"Very well," Birdie replied. "We'll be right here." And then to Kristoffer, "Yes we will, won't we?" The baby smiled and gurgled at his grandmother.

Cully dodged people on his way to Ellie, doing his best

not to obscure anyone's view of the lake as he moved through the spectators. The moment Cully reached her, Ellie's eyes flew open, and she stared at him as if she didn't recognize her own husband. Soon, though, light filled her eyes, and she came back to him. "Hi," she said.

"Hi." Cully laid his hand on her arm, and this time Ellie returned his touch. "Do you wanna baptize Kristoffer today? The preacher's doing it now." Cully nodded past the gathered crowd to the lake where Pastor Andy stood in the water.

"Yes," Ellie told him eagerly and looked around, concern shadowing her face. "Where is Kristoffer?"

"The baby's with Mom—over there. C'mon." Cully took her hand and lead his wife over to Birdie Jullsen.

When she saw the young couple, Birdie smiled and held the baby out to his mother, stating, "He's hungry."

"I'll feed him while we wait our turn. Who's been baptized so far?" Ellie asked. "Anyone we know?"

Birdie told her, "Just Mrs. Bryton but she goes in every year. Oh, and your mom. She's out now. He's slow at it, this one. Not that many have gone in yet." Birdie shaded her eyes with her right hand and pointed with her left to the grassy lakeshore. "It looks like you go stand over there if you want to be washed."

"You coming, my husband?" Ellie squinted at him against the sun slanting its way sharply across the lake, the land, the crowd, and Cully put his arm around her shoulder.

"Let's go," he said.

Birdie was right. Pastor Andy took his time with each

immersion, saying a lengthy prayer over each of the drenched faithful with their Sunday clothes plastered to their skin and their shoes sitting on the shore. While the couple waited behind the twenty or so people ahead of them, Ellie rummaged in the bag she'd retrieved from Stella so she could feed baby Kristoffer his suppertime bottle. When he was done, there were less than ten people waiting to be baptized. Ellie held the infant over her shoulder, and as she gently rubbed and patted his back, Kristoffer and his daddy watched one another closely. Cully was the first to smile.

"Can I hold him a bit?" He asked his wife. She looked both surprised and pleased, and laid the infant in Cully's stiff arms.

Ellie laughed. "Relax, Culvar. He won't break."

Cully looked unconvinced. "You sure?"

"I'm pretty sure," Ellie assured him.

He'd held Kristoffer before, shortly after he was born and other times when Ellie needed him to for a minute or two, but this time felt different. This was his son. His son was looking at him and everything else vanished: the wet believers, the preacher and his attractive assistant, those observing and those feeling the Lord's presence or wanting to, oh so badly. Kristoffer noticed Cully anew, as well, looked into his eyes, studied his face.

"Hello. I'm your daddy," Cully whispered close to his son's face. "I love you, baby boy," he told him, employing the same title for the child he'd heard Ellie use often. Ellie herself wasn't listening. Her attention was focused on Pastor Andy and a very tall woman from Wainwright being dunked, with the help of Sister Patricia, into the murky depths of Czar Lake.

"Sister, I baptize you before all these witnesses in the name of the Father and of the Son and of the Holy Spirit. Whoever believes in Him shall never die but have eternal life," proclaimed Pastor Andy. As each member of the Holy Trinity was listed, the tall woman heard only the dull blur of water filling her ears, the pressure against their taut drums causing muffled noise, the noisy sound of nothing. Three times the preacher man and Sister Patricia lifted her out and submerged her again. When it was over, Ellie watched the woman drip, and acknowledged the peace in her drawn face. "Heavenly Father, see your daughter Delores and bless her and keep her, let your face shine upon her and be gracious unto her. Grant that she may work toward your Kingdom and that one day she may join You there and gaze upon your blessed countenance. Take her and keep her, grant her love and wisdom and knowledge of what is right and good and true. Oh, Lord God, bring Delores out of the darkness she has dwelt in too long. Bring her to the light, the light and glory of your love. Change her life, we pray, Father God, with the power of your spirit and your grace. In Jesus Christ's name, all present pray. Amen."

Ellie murmured her "amen" and stepped forward as Delores exited the water. Ellie gave thanks that as the line of those seeking baptism moved along, the pastor's prayers had become shorter. At the edge of the lake, on the narrow seam of sand between grass and water, Ellie handed her baby to Sister Patricia, who exclaimed, "Oh!

What a darling boy! What's his name?"

"Kristoffer Denby Jullsen."

Sister Patricia, wearing a gown matching Pastor Andy's, waded the short distance out to him and set baby Kristoffer resolutely in his arms. Ellie didn't move from the water's edge. Instead, she stood perfectly still and intently watched the scene before her. It was then that a high pitched buzzing sound started small at the front of her skull and grew steadily, blocking out Pastor Andy's voice, the gentle splash of the water, the "amens," the "praise the Lords," the "hallelujahs." Everything. Gone. Ellie's palms were damp with sweat; her head swam and her heart thudded. Upon the third splash of water from the preacher man's cupped hand followed by his blessing, Ellie saw through eyes wide with wonder, a dove ascend from the waters to pause over Kristoffer's head before returning to heaven.

— *Chapter 20* —

EVERYBODY ACTS IRRATIONALLY NOW AND THEN

"Cully?" Stella sat on the edge of her kitchen chair. There were circles under her eyes, and Henry held her hand on the table's top. "Is Ellie all right?"

Cully had just come down the narrow staircase and entered the kitchen. To Stella, he suddenly looked ten years older. Before answering, Cully moved across the kitchen floor, patting Birdie on the shoulder when he passed her chair. He took the one remaining mug down from the shelf, organized and covered in paper by his wife, *his* wife who now lay upstairs senseless and tranquilized by Dr. Stromquist over an hour ago. At the stove, Cully filled his mug with the coffee Birdie had brewed for them all. Then he sat down with a sigh in the chair nearest him, the only empty one at the table.

Cully answered Stella, "I dunno. It's hard to tell how she's doing." He swallowed hard, forcing that lump down and down into his stomach where it grew. Cully shook his head and sipped his coffee. It burned his tongue like acid.

It took Stella to say what they were all thinking. "I didn't understand what was going on when Ellie grabbed little Kristoffer out of that woman's hands and ran. I thought maybe she was getting sick or something."

"Looks like you were partly right." This was Birdie speaking. She didn't look at anyone, instead Birdie's eyes settled on the darkness in the living room beyond. She was remembering that blind, panicked look in her daughter-in-law's eyes, the way Ellie had clutched her child and then hid Kristoffer under that blanket in the wagon.

Later, when they asked her why, Ellie's voice shook as hard as the rest of her. She told them, "I don't want God to find him."

As if picking up on Birdie's thoughts, Stella continued them out loud, saying, "And what did she mean when she said she didn't want God to find Kristoffer? Lord of mercy, I thought Ellie was going to smother him with that blanket, the way it was so close over him. And laying him on the wagon box floor like that…"

"Under the bench," Henry added. He, too, shook his head at Ellie's actions, both condemning them and bewildered by them, stating, "Hard and cold for a baby on that floor."

Birdie heard and understood Henry's tone. Coming to Ellie's defense, she reminded each of them, "Everybody acts irrationally now and then. It's just how people are sometimes. That young woman's been under a lot of duress lately, and I think what she needs now is not for us to figure out her mind, why she's behaving the way she is, but to help her through it."

Birdie turned to her son. Cully hadn't attempted to drink anymore of his coffee, and the mug sat mostly full in front of him. Birdie told him, "I think it'd be best if we could take turns being here for you and Ellie, if it's all right with you. You know, to help you out. Do the laundry, make some meals, make sure the garden gets took in—if she's..." Cully's mother paused, searching for the right word, "...unwell for that long. Stella, I can stay tonight and for the day tomorrow. Can you do the next day and ask your mom if she can come on Wednesday?"

Cully interrupted his mother's planning. "Look. I don't know if all this is necessary. Ellie probably just needs a good night's sleep, and then everything will get back to normal." He looked and sounded exhausted.

"Culvar." She said her son's name, and Birdie's voice was unmoving as she refreshed his memories of the evening's events, emphasizing their seriousness. "Ellie hid her infant son from God. She somehow thought she needed to run away from the Lord, that He was a threat to her baby. Your wife was terrified, and she needed medicine to calm her down. Trust me, son," Birdie spoke firmly, certainly, "This isn't something that a good night's sleep alone is going to cure."

Stella reached over and gave Cully's forearm a squeeze. "I agree with your mom, Cull. I don't think Ellie's that bad. She'll be fine, but not in the morning. Chances are, she'll be like herself in a couple of days, but I'd like to help. Please. Let me help."

"That goes for me, too," Henry offered. "If there's anything I can do, let me know."

Cully's face felt hot, and he squirmed a little in his seat. "I…"

Birdie stood up and pushed in her chair. "It's what families do." The matter was settled. Birdie looked at Stella and Henry who immediately caught her meaning and stood up, as well.

Henry told Cully, "Yup. We'd better get going. I'll stop by on Tuesday, if Stella's gonna be here. Maybe have supper." The big man donned his hat in the porch, saying, "Night, Cully."

Cully said, "Night, Henry, Stella." Then he stood there and watched their shadows through the screen door as they got into the wagon and headed down that bumpy drive out to the main road.

Back in the kitchen, Birdie had already started washing up the coffee mugs and was obviously prepared to settle in. She glanced over her shoulder at Cully when he came in from the porch and asked, "Where do you keep your extra bedding? Is there a pillow I can use? If I need to stay over later on in the week, I'll remember to bring my own. Maybe a blanket or two…"

Cully started to argue. "Mom, you don't need to stay. Not tonight. Not later on. Not ever. I can handle it." His face was stone, both hands gripping the back of a chair.

Birdie looked at him, a dripping fork in her hand, and

spoke resolutely. "I love you and Ellie, and I refuse to leave either of you when you're in trouble."

Cully's stone exterior crumbled. His shoulders slumped, and he pulled out the chair he'd clung to, sitting down heavily in it. A fat tear twinkled beneath his eye. Cully took in a sudden, sharp breath. "What's wrong with her, Mom? What's going on?" Another inward breath, then, "She was fine. She was, and now she seems...crazy." There it was. That word. The one that best described Ellie's condition and the word nobody wanted to say. As he felt the weight of the word "crazy" lift from his mind, Cully hated himself for uttering it.

Birdie Jullsen set her dishtowel down and took a seat along with her son at the table. She didn't touch him. She left her hands folded before her on the tabletop and waited a few moments, giving Cully a chance to regain control.

When it seemed he had, Birdie told him, "These things happen, Culvar. More than you think. People just don't talk about it, that's all. Think about it, honey. When it's done, and Ellie's used to being a mom and gets things settled up with the Lord, will you share this memory with other folks? Do you think Henry and Stella will talk about her breakdown to the people they know? Of course not! Nobody says a word, but women go—they get sick all the time. It's too much for us sometimes. Work, families, marriages. There's no room to breathe, and after a while, it's easy to lose your mind from lack of peace."

Culvar looked at his mother's face in the lantern light. "You talk like you know about it. This happen to you?"

Birdie shook her head, looking haggard in the light

cast by the low-burning flame. She confided, "To my mother, back in the States when they'd first moved us out to the homestead from town. I remember coming in one day from playing out in the yard with your Aunt Violet and finding her curled up like a baby on our dirt floor that she'd been trying to sweep clean. I was ten, your aunt was eight and the twins were three. She must've been pregnant at the time because three or four weeks after I'd found her there curled up like that, she was in a lot of pain one night.

Mother was howling, almost, and Dad was pacing up and down. We kept quiet, your aunt and I, and finally things quieted down. Mom spent the next two days in bed. It was hard on us kids because she'd just started recovering, you know, getting up in the morning, helping with breakfast, feeding the chickens, hanging out clothes." Birdie Jullsen lifted her shoulders in a sad "what-can-you-do?" kind of shrug. "Anyway, the next morning Violet and I walked down to the river to look for gooseberries. On the way, your aunt spotted some fabric stuck under a clump of wolf willow bushes. I wish now that we would've left well enough alone, but we were curious kids."

"Why? What was it?" Cully leaned attentively toward her, his elbows on the table propping him up.

"It turned out to be our mother's nightgown all bloody and drawing flies. I tugged at the edge of it and felt a weight wrapped in its centre." Birdie looked at him hard, an explanation of lunacy clear in her eyes. "Oh, Culvar, it was a tiny perfect dead baby."

"What did you do?" Cully asked his mother.

"Nothing. We did nothing, and we certainly didn't say anything. The next day we went back to check, and it was gone. Dad or someone must've come and gotten rid of it. Or maybe a coyote dragged it off, but I don't like to think of that." Birdie shuddered.

Cully asked, "What happened to Grandma?"

"It took her until the fall, but then she went on like nothing happened. We all did. Your Uncle Leonard was born big and healthy the following spring."

Mother and son sat for a while without speaking, Birdie remembering, Cully taking in the new information. Finally, Birdie stretched her arms over her head and asked, "How's that old chesterfield of yours for sleeping?"

Cully managed a crooked smile. "It's not so bad. Let's go round up a blanket for you."

After Birdie had made up her bed on the chesterfield downstairs, Cully headed up to his own bed. He undressed in the dark and slowly crawled in between the sheets. Ellie didn't move, her breath coming steady and deep. Cully thought he could've picked the bed up and flipped it over without waking his wife. Before very long, he, too, was sleeping as though drugged, the day having depleted his energy. Cully slept without changing positions until Ellie's screaming woke him.

"You're not going to take my baby, you son of a bitch!"

Ellie was on her feet with Kristoffer in her arms before Cully, heart pounding, was able to sit up.

Startled out of sleep, he yelled, "Ellie? Ellie! What're you doing? Put him down. Ellie? Where are you going with him?"

She ignored her husband. It seemed like she didn't even hear him. Ellie had snatched little Kristoffer out of his cradle by the bed, scaring him and causing him to cry out, and was now crushing him against her body as she fled from their room. Because Ellie didn't respond to his voice and just kept muttering half-formed curses at God under her breath, Cully wondered if she was sleepwalking.

Cully swung his legs out of bed and followed his wife, hesitant to touch her because he recalled what someone had told him one time about the dangers inherent in waking a sleepwalker. Instead of trying to halt her movement, he leapt in front of Ellie and grabbed their infant son. And as he did, Ellie's eyes, flaming with rage, met his and locked them solidly to hers.

"You're on His side," Ellie accused him in a normal tone of voice, even and trimmed with disbelief. The words not shouted nor spat out.

"On whose…" With speed and accuracy Cully never knew she possessed, Ellie moved suddenly forward, sinking her teeth into the left side of her husband's face. It worked. Cully released his grip on Kristoffer, and Ellie dashed into the nursery with her baby. Her intention was to hide him in those cupboards, the ones with the unpainted doors.

"Oh, my…What on earth is going on up here?" Birdie had finally made it up the steep stairs, puffing at the top just as Ellie broke Cully's grip on the baby. Birdie saw Cully standing in the rectangle of moonlight shining through their bedroom window. He was bent at the knees and waist, clutching the left side of his face. By the light of the moon, Birdie saw the shining dark patch on the hand held to his face and understood instinctively that it was blood. "Where is she?" Birdie asked.

"In the nursery," Cully answered, his words strained by pain and panic. Birdie walked past her son and into the little room Ellie had been painting fresh yellow that winter day the hobos came to the back door. Cully followed his mother, his face tingling then going numb.

Ellie stood at the nursery's tiny window and stared up at the full moon, hugging herself tightly with both arms. She did nothing to acknowledge the presence of either her mother-in-law or her husband. She just stared up at the stars outside that window and softly cursed her Lord. From behind the unpainted cupboard doors, Kristoffer howled his fear.

Birdie walked up and set a tender hand on Ellie's elbow. "You talking to God, honey?"

Ellie nodded solemnly, informing Birdie, "He wants to take Kristoffer. He wants him to save the world." Then Ellie turned toward Cully's mom, her eyes becoming clear and then focused. "Birdie, I don't want my son to be a saviour. I just want him to be a sinner, safe and alive."

"Oh, Ellie." With Cully looking on, Birdie stroked Ellie's upper arm in a motherly way and told her, "I've been talking to the Lord, too."

"Really? Did he tell you that my baby's going to save the world?" Ellie asked.

"Mmm-mm." Birdie slowly shook her head, looking doubtful, saying, "He said Kristoffer was going to save some of the people in his own world, in his family, in his circle of friends. This baby will bring them joy. They won't be able to imagine life without him. Sometimes, he'll even bring them peace." Birdie glanced at the cupboard doors that began where the sloping ceiling ended and the short wall began. "No one here's going to be sacrificed—not in a big way, anyway."

"He lied to you," Ellie told Birdie flatly. "He lied to you to get to my baby."

Again, Birdie shook her head patiently and asked Ellie to consider, "What's our Lord going to do with a baby boy? Oh honey, Jesus himself wasn't any use to God till he was thirty or so. It's true. I can't guarantee you that nothing will ever happen to that sweet helpless child, but I'm pretty sure the only scary thing happening to him tonight is his mommy's panic."

"I just love him so much." Ellie's voice was dead.

"I know you do, Ellie. We love him, too." Birdie motioned to Cully to bring the baby from the cupboard. "Should we take Kristoffer out of there, put him back to bed?" As Birdie asked Ellie's permission, Cully was already opening the doors and lifting his screaming son from the cupboard's dusty lower shelf.

Birdie reached up and put her arm around Ellie's shoulder, giving her a snug hug. "Let's all go get some sleep."

The next day, Ellie remained asleep until nearly noon. Birdie draped the old wool blanket over the curtain rod in their bedroom to block out the day's sun. She brought baby Kristoffer downstairs for his morning bottle and a diaper change. While the baby slept on his quilt on the braided rug in the centre of the living room floor, Birdie made up a batch of bread dough and set it to rise before lifting Kristoffer up and heading outside to give the garden a little water. A few teasing clouds lay on the northern horizon above Hughenden Lake, seeming to grow and then shrink back until they decreased into shapes no larger than cotton balls. Birdie left the baby lying in the shade of the willow tree on his blanket, sucking on his pacifier (a gift from her) and practising forming his tiny hands into fists. She brought two buckets, three-quarters full, up from the lake and watered first the beets and peas, thinking they looked driest. Next, Birdie sparingly watered the two rows of carrots and thought about the damage Ellie had inflicted on Cully's face. Birdie had washed the wound with soap and water last night, bandaging it the best she could with rags. She'd instructed her son to stop in town before heading to the Whitlock place to let Dr. Stromquist take a look at it. As she emptied the second bucket, Birdie hoped he would.

While Kristoffer napped in a corner of the long rickety chesterfield following another half bottle, Birdie punched down the bread dough, did up the dishes and washed the kitchen floor. She was shaping the dough into loaves when Ellie appeared at the foot of the stairs. Birdie's hands never lost their momentum but kept on working the dough as she greeted her daughter-in-law and asked her, "How're you feeling, dear?"

Ellie sat down at the table. "Tired." Her voice remained as flat as it had sounded the night before.

"That's one doozy of a flu that's been going around. I wouldn't be surprised if you'll need to lie low for a few days at least. A couple of people I know in town caught this or something like it and ended up in bed for a week!" At Birdie's fiction, Ellie face showed neither relief nor disbelief, but remained expressionless. At the basin, Birdie washed the butter from her hands and set a fresh cup of coffee in front of Ellie. "You feel like eating anything?"

Ellie didn't answer, and she didn't touch her coffee, just stared at the tabletop, her head bowed. Still, Birdie chatted easily, checking the woodstove's temperature and sliding Ellie's bread pans into its warm insides. "We'll have some bread to go with our soup at supper. Hope you're hungry by then. I have to say, Ellie, you sure keep your little kitchen here tidy and organized. My son's lucky to have a woman with such homemaking skills."

She ran a dishcloth over the discoloured countertop and put the butter back in the icebox. She didn't mention the bite Ellie'd taken out of Cully's cheek, talking instead of routine things, the life of the house and the community of Hughenden. Her talk didn't illicit any response from Ellie. She didn't expect it to. Birdie wanted to make her feel comfortable, to keep her calm. And so she talked on and peeled vegetables for the soup, listening all the while for any sounds Kristoffer might make.

In the middle of a story about the canning Birdie planned to do tomorrow, Ellie interrupted her in a loud, lifeless tone, asking, "He's gone, isn't he?"

Birdie set her knife down and turned to look at her daughter-in-law. "Who?"

Ellie clarified. "Kristoffer. God's taken him." Although her face was calm, Birdie could see Ellie's hands working in her lap, wringing and scraping one another. The young woman's building agitation was beginning to frighten her, and so when there was a solid knock on the front door, Birdie jumped and baby Kristoffer whimpered through his dreams. Ellie seemed not to hear it. She continued working her hands, red and rough, against her nightgown, her body's salt having made the flannelette nearly as stiff as laundry starch would. Birdie strode across the living room and opened the front door to Harold Stromquist.

"Good morning, Doctor," Birdie greeted him.

"Morning, Birdie. Culvar came to see…" The woman he'd been acquainted with for years pressed an index finger to her lips and stepped out onto the makeshift stoop, closing the front door quietly behind her.

"Is she awake?" the doctor asked in a lowered voice. Birdie nodded and Harold Stromquist watched her face. "Not doing too well?"

"No. Not well at all." She was wiping her hands on Ellie's oldest apron. "Did Culvar come to see you this morning?"

"Sure did. That's quite a bite she gave him. I gave him some ointment to put on it, but it'll take time to heal. Shouldn't scar, not too badly anyway. What's Ellie like today?" he asked.

"She just got up. She didn't say much till right before you came along. Then she asked if God had taken Kristoffer away," Birdie said.

"Still on that from last night? Hmm." In his right hand the physician clutched his medical bag. Birdie noticed for the first time his Model T in the driveway and wondered how on earth she'd missed hearing the doctor drive in. It was then Birdie that realized just how involved she'd been in trying to make the situation seem normal to Ellie. She'd been concentrating so hard on her light tone, on providing evidence of the mythological flu, on keeping the house and garden in shape, and keeping Kristoffer content that she hadn't heard the grinding of the automobile's engine and the bumping of its tires along the rutted drive. Something always has to give.

Birdie opened the front door and gestured for Harold Stromquist to go in ahead. Baby Kristoffer was awake now, eyes wide open and looking at his fists. "Hello." With one of those fists, the infant grabbed the finger the doctor extended. The elderly man chuckled, set down his bag and removed his hat, commenting, "Strong. That's good." Kristoffer released his grip, and Birdie lead the way into the kitchen.

Birdie said, "Ellie. Look who's stopped by for a visit. Doctor Stromquist heard about your flu bug and wanted to check in on you. Wasn't that thoughtful?"

Ellie hadn't moved from the table and didn't look up when the other two entered. Immediately her fidgeting caught the doctor's attention as did her tangled hair and bare feet. Concern creased his forehead below his hairline, white and continuously thinning.

"Hello, Ellie. How are you feeling today?" No answer, no eye contact. Harold Stromquist thought it best to go along with Birdie Jullsen's flu story. She was a wise woman and knew how to communicate well with anyone. Not a talent he himself always displayed.

The doctor smiled at Ellie and told her, "Birdie here's

mentioned that you've got some symptoms of influenza. May I take your temperature?" Birdie handed the doctor his bag which she'd fetched along with Kristoffer, who now rested comfortably on her hip. It was then Birdie realized that Ellie wasn't acknowledging her baby. As Dr. Stromquist opened his black bag, Birdie got the remaining half bottle of formula from the icebox and set it gently in the saucepan of lukewarm water she'd left in the stove's warming compartment up top.

When the doctor brought out his thermometer, Ellie looked dully at it and then back at him. She opened her mouth and held the instrument obediently under her tongue until the physician removed it. In the light from the window, he interpreted the results.

"Well?" Birdie asked Dr. Stromquist from where she stood by the stove holding the door slightly open and peeking in at the baking bread.

"She's a little above average, all right." Then to Ellie, "You have a fever, Ellie. That's a sure sign of the flu. I've got some medicine here that will help you sleep. That's how we'll get your temperature down." He turned to ask Birdie for a glass of water, but seeing both her hands full, asked instead, "Where does Ellie keep her glasses?"

Birdie gestured with her chin. "There on the shelf. Those little jars. And the water bucket's on the floor."

"Thanks." He pulled the tea towel from over the pail and ladled a jar of water for Ellie. The doctor set the water and a tablet on the tabletop in front of his patient. Now Ellie looked hard at him.

"God's taken my baby," she informed him.

Harold Stromquist, not knowing how to respond said, "Uhhh…"

Birdie came to his rescue. "Ellie, your boy's right here. I'm just getting this bit of formula warmed up for him. Would you like to hold Kristoffer for a bit? Maybe feed him?" The sick woman's mother-in-law approached her but stopped short when Ellie told Birdie, "That's not my baby."

"Ellie!" Harold Stromquist and Birdie Jullsen chorused, and Birdie continued. "This *is* your baby! This is Kristoffer." Then she tried another tact. "Remember, Ellie? I talked to the Lord. He told me He wouldn't take Kristoffer. I promise that's the truth, honey. Really. Would you like to hold him? Then you'll know for certain he's yours." But Ellie turned away and surprisingly swallowed the tablet along with a deep drink of the water Dr. Stromquist had poured for her. Then, without speaking, she slowly got up from her chair and made her way back up the stairs.

After Kristoffer had finished his bottle and Harold Stromquist's car had rumbled down the rough drive, Birdie tip-toed up the stairs to look in on Ellie. She was sound asleep in the stuffy room with her mouth open, a little moisture at its corner. Birdie carefully moved across the bedroom floor, picked up Kristoffer's cradle and returned downstairs with it under her arm.

That evening, Henry and Stella pulled into the yard, sitting close in his wagon. She had one hand resting on his thigh and the other held her large suitcase by its handle. The couple stayed and shared the supper prepared by Birdie, vegetable soup and fresh bread, and after the dishes were done and things squared away, Henry drove Birdie back into town. Stella brought a clean sheet and two extra quilts out of her suitcase along with the gift she'd brought for her sister.

"I'm not so sure we should be waking her up," Cully cautioned, the ointment Dr. Stromquist had given him to help heal his wound reflecting the lantern light, making his cheek shine.

"I just know this'll make her feel better. Please, Cully. Let's try, and if it seems to bother her too much, then I'll let it go," Stella promised her brother-in-law. At this, Cully gave in, and together they ascended the stairway with him carrying the lamp and Stella in the lead. In the bedroom, Stella took the woolen blanket down from over the window and opened the window wider to let in the evening air.

Stella leaned over her sister and said softly, "Ellie, honey? Can you wake up a minute? It's me. I brought you something nice that might make you feel better. C'mon. Wake up and I'll show you."

At Stella's prompting, Ellie opened her eyes and half sat up, staring groggily for a moment before collapsing back down onto her pillow. Cully set the lamp on the floor by the bed, telling Stella, "I'll go get your bed ready." He left then, moving too quickly down that dimly lit flight of stairs.

A moment later, the screen door creaked open and flapped shut. From behind her back, Stella brought out a nightgown, white and floor length, with eyelet lace trim on the cuffs, neckline and hem.

"Do you like it? Found it at a thrift sale in Czar. I thought it was so cute I just had to pick it up, but the whole time I was thinking to myself, 'Stella, do you really need another nightdress? Really, you've got so many already.' And it's true! I do! So I decided to give this one to you. You being the married one, you have to look good in bed. For now, I can wear just any old thing. C'mon. Try to sit up for me, will you?" Stella pushed the covers off her sister and was greeted with the faint scent of body odor, a smell she'd never in a million years would have associated with Ellie. Then Stella said, "Hang on a second, sweetie. I just gotta go ask your husband about something. I'll be right back." Ellie didn't answer, and it was unclear whether she had heard.

Stella found Cully sitting on the back step. "Hey, brother-in-law." She sat down beside him. "I gotta bath her, Cull. She'd been sweating and, well, you know. Could you help me get her tub ready? And we might need to bring her downstairs—I mean, carry her." Stella paused and looked at Cully, saw his arms dropped down despondently between his knees, his head hanging low. "Oh, Cully! I'm sorry." She put her arm around his shoulder, and he kind of slumped against her, leaning there until he'd regained his strength. Finally, Cully stood up tall and stretched, and told Ellie, "Well, you'd better bring me that pail from the kitchen so we can get a bath going. I think it's a good idea."

Stella handed him the pail and asked, "Will we use the laundry tub?"

"It's all we got," he confirmed.

She told him, "Then that's what we'll use. I'll put the water on and haul that tub out into the kitchen."

"Sounds fine."

It took them forty-five minutes or so to prepare Ellie's bath. While doing this, Stella popped her head into Cully and Ellie's room a couple times and each time, her sister was in a different position, twisted and looking uncomfortable. Stella brought a cloth she'd wet and wrung out, folded it and laid it across Ellie's forehead. Next, she headed back downstairs and into the living room to check on little Kristoffer. Birdie had fed him just before she and Henry left, and now he was sound asleep in his cradle.

After several heated buckets of water, the old laundry tub was finally nearly half full. Stella had shampoo, soap, a towel, a washcloth and Ellie's hairbrush all lined up on the kitchen counter when Cully brought his wife downstairs, not carrying Ellie but steadying her. He brought her to stand by the tub set up by the stove. As Stella began to lift off Ellie's salty nightgown, Cully shuffled his feet uncomfortably and ran his fingers through his hair.

He told Stella, "Uhh...I think I'll let you two be. I was thinking I'd sleep out in the barn tonight."

Stella looked a little alarmed. "Why?" And then, after having considered his reasons, the most obvious one being the big bite Ellie had taken out of his cheek, Stella asked, "Are you sure, Cully?"

"Yeah, I'm sure. Think I'll be more comfortable out there. I'll just grab that blanket and my pillow from upstairs. Call if you need me, all right?" He ducked into the dark living room and bent down to kiss Kristoffer on his warm forehead before heading to the barn.

As it turned out, Stella didn't call. Cully came in at about ten o'clock for a glass of water and to ask how the bath went. Ellie was upstairs sleeping and Stella was cleaning up. "Hey, you're just in time," she greeted him. "I thought we could lug this thing outside and use the water on the garden. What do you think?"

Cully looked doubtful. "I think it's too heavy that full of water. Let's scoop a couple of buckets out and pack them to the garden. Then we should be able to drag it out the door. Ellie and me always…" He stopped himself, remembering how just last week he and his wife had struggled with that half-full tub, emptying it pail by pail onto the garden until it was light enough to carry outside.

Stella, leaving him with his thoughts, dipped the kitchen pail into the soap-cloudy water, its surface golden in the light of the two lanterns, one on the table and one on the counter. Outside in the fresh air of late evening, she lovingly watered the garden, admiring her sister's deliberate rows, straight and weed-free. Cully came out with a basin of water as she was emptying her bucket. Stella noticed in the dusk heavy as sorrow, the puffiness around his eyes and the swelling that had increased on his face over the course of the evening.

"You all set up in the barn?" Stella asked Cully as she walked across the lawn toward him.

He answered with a grin, "Sure am. I'll be fine out there, but I don't think Maurice and Bossie like having to share their place. How about you? You gonna be all right in there?" Cully wanted to ask her if she was scared to be alone with Ellie.

Stella smiled in her broad, easy way. "Cully Jullsen, if I get the least bit worried about Ellie or anything else, I'll be out to that barn so quick you'll think I'd just appeared out of nowhere like one of Dickens' ghosts." Her brother-in-law laughed. He knew she meant it and thought for a moment that he'd like her company in that barn. Suddenly, his face flooded with heat. If Stella noticed, she didn't let on. "For now," she kept on talking, "Let's just worry about getting this tub drained and this garden taken care of. Nice garden, by the way. I didn't much notice it till now. Nicer than Mom's—but don't tell her I said so." Stella shrugged. "Maybe it's nicer because I still do a lot of the work in Mom's and Lord knows I'm not the gardener either of those two are." Stella raised her voice as she disappeared into the porch so that Cully could hear her finish this last thought. He chuckled and shook his head, dumped a bucket of water on two potato hills and went back in for more.

When Stella came back into the house, she heard Kristoffer let out a hungry wail. "Hang on, little man!" she called out to him. "Auntie will be right with you!" And in that moment Stella thought *Sheesh, my sister's got her hands full here.*

Later that night, stretched out on the chesterfield covered with the smooth sheet she'd brought from home, Stella stared at the ceiling thinking that it could use some paint. Then, she whispered to herself in the dark, "Oh gosh! I'm starting to think like her! Maybe I'm starting to think *for* her!" Instantly, the idea seemed comical and another instant later, it made bumps stand out on her flesh. As if wanting to make his own contribution to the state of her nerves, a coyote howled his hysterical loneliness from the nearby hills.

All of a sudden, Stella wished badly that Cully had stayed in the house. She sat up and swung her feet to the braided rug. In the kitchen, she relit the smaller lantern and brought it into the living room along with Ellie's Eaton's catalogue borrowed from the Pedersen household.

There she fell asleep sitting up, the catalogue open in her lap. This is how Cully found her in the morning.

When Cully'd seen the way she'd fallen asleep, he left Stella there, returning to the kitchen to put the coffee on. She woke up and came into the kitchen where Cully was standing in front of the stove frying bacon and eggs in the same pan at the same time, a way she'd never seen it done before. She held Kristoffer against her side, cradled in one arm, and although he was quiet for now, Stella knew that he'd be demanding his bottle any minute.

In her nightgown, long like the one she'd given Ellie only shabbier, and sleepy-eyed, Stella complimented Cully, "Nice to see a man who knows how to cook and isn't afraid to cook for women." With her free hand, she picked up the greasy spatula he'd just set down and playfully, silently threatened him with it and set it back down. "Did you check on Ellie-Bellie yet?"

"Yeah. I went upstairs soon as I came in. She's still sleeping. I think she looks better today." Ellie's husband smiled. "Thanks for giving her a bath, washing her hair. It seems like she might be thanking you herself soon enough."

"I think so, too. I'm gonna head out to the loo." Stella giggled. "I'm rhyming this morning. That rotten sleep brought out a hidden talent. I'll set this little guy back down in his cradle for now. He won't like it," she predicted and then spoke to Kristoffer, "Will you, little one? But first things first."

"Breakfast is almost ready," Cully told her.

"Great," she said. "Then I'll help you eat it and wash up after."

"That sounds fine to me, sister-in-law."

By the end of that week, Friday it was, Ellie was still sleeping a lot but without medication, and Muriel Pedersen came to stay for the weekend. She helped Ellie take another bath, weeded the garden, pickled a dozen jars of dilled carrots and stayed home with Ellie, sending her son-in-law off to church on his own.

When she wasn't asleep, Ellie was doing needle point or mending, things that required manual dexterity and concentration. But she wasn't talking much, and the young mother eyed anyone who spoke to her with unmasked suspicion. It bothered Ellie's mother, Muriel. But for two and a half months, on those days she'd committed to coming, Muriel cared for little Kristoffer, soaked his diapers and mixed his formula. She cared for Cully, too, but knew enough not to coddle her daughter's husband. Like her own Benson, he wasn't the kind to stand for it. Cully did the dishes each night, fed and watered both Maurice and the milk cow, and made sure the garden was watered before the sun went down. This meant that some nights during harvest he didn't get home much before the sun kissed the horizon, making it blush red and sudden orange.

It was what happened to Muriel that very Friday that kept them all hanging in and, for the first time since "the Czar Lake incident," believing that Ellie's recovery just had to be inevitable.

Kristoffer was down for his morning nap having just finished eating. The three women caring for the household had taken to leaving Kristoffer's cradle in the living room as that's where each of them took turns sleeping. It gave them all a sense of the child's safety to have him resting within the confines of Cully's old cradle. And so that's where the baby slept while his grandma Pedersen peeled and sliced carrots, and while his mother worked on the needlepoint cat with its pink collar and tongue to match. Muriel had asked Cully to wash most of the soil from the carrots out in the yard the night before. Now, she simply rinsed them in the basin before peeling them.

"Mom," Ellie said her name from where she sat at the table.

Between her own humming, the blackbirds in the willow tree and the steady zip-zip of the paring knife, Muriel wasn't sure at first that she'd heard her name being called. Her hands stopped moving and she stopped humming. Ellie repeated, "Mom," followed by, "That knife's not sharp. At the back of the drawer there's a vegetable peeler." Ellie's eyes never left her needlework and her hands never ceased pulling pink thread.

Muriel, both shocked and pleased, never missed a beat. "Thanks, Ellie. Oh, sure enough. Here it is! This will work much better. You'll have to get that hubby of yours to sharpen your knives." Ellie's mom poured the salt into the water she had waiting there on the stove. Muriel stirred until the salt dissolved then continued peeling carrots using the peeler as her daughter suggested.

Ellie remained seated in her chair at the kitchen table. As easily as she'd brought Muriel in, she seemed at once to lock her out again. Still, her mother thought *It's better than nothing.*

— *Chapter 21* —

STILL IN THERE SOMEWHERE

"I was cutting up carrots, working away, not expecting her to say anything, and then she said it," Muriel shared this with Stella and Cully in the warm kitchen. Stella would take over from her mother that evening.

Stella responded, "It's good to know she's still in there somewhere." The three of them had sat down to supper, Stella arriving at the Hughenden Lake house and Muriel leaving that Sunday after supper. Stella had just fed Kristoffer. She'd rocked and held him until he fell asleep, and marveled at the weight he was gaining day by day as he grew. Moving carefully, Stella made her way to the living room and laid her nephew gently in his cradle.

Muriel Pedersen told Stella and Cully about how, out

of the blue, Ellie talked to her, telling her where to find the vegetable peeler. "I miss her! It's like she's gone in a way. Do you know what I mean?" Stella asked the other two.

Muriel nodded to show Stella she did and passed her daughter a bowl of mashed potatoes. Stella took a little and passed the bowl onto Cully. She liked the way Birdie made her mashed potatoes with cream and butter and, some would say, too much salt. In Stella's opinion, her mom's tasted flat and lumpy. Sitting there, Stella poked at her food and thought about Ellie, wishing she could talk to her sister now, like old times.

She considered how Ellie makes her potatoes somewhere in between the two mothers—not as rich as Cully's mom's, but not as boring as Muriel Pedersen's. Stella thought that, in many respects, Ellie was a good blend of both mothers: perhaps not as cheerful as Birdie and probably not as smart, either. To Cully's sister-in-law, Birdie Jullsen seemed wise, like she knew things because she'd lived them and learned from them. Comparing Muriel to Birdie, Stella gauged that her mother was more practical than Cully's mostly because Muriel didn't seem to think very deeply or to examine things. Unless they were depressing. Like religion. Stella contemplated that Ellie was not as morose as Muriel Pedersen and not as fussy about her house, either. The younger sister understood that while some things bothered Ellie, like the nasty things people said and did, her sister seemed more able to let things go than their mom. In Stella's estimation, Ellie was a nice balance between the two moms.

Cully didn't look at Stella as they ate in silence, each of

the three seeming tired and lost in their own thoughts. To Stella, his cheek looked better tonight. Muriel had told Stella that Cully was sleeping in the barn now every night, watering the garden at the close of the day then cuddling up beside Maurice and the milk cow. Stella wondered if Ellie missed her husband. She imagined that she would under the same circumstances, then she recalculated. These exact same circumstances would be very difficult to duplicate, if not downright impossible. Ellie's sister then considered that maybe being alone in that narrow bed helped Ellie to get a better sleep. Stella wanted so badly to ask her, but she knew Ellie wouldn't answer. The young mother hadn't spoken since Friday, vegetable peeler day. Two days before.

Muriel offered, "Would you like some more chicken, Stella?"

"Please and thanks," her daughter accepted, then Muriel asked her son-in-law, "How about you, Culvar? More chicken?"

"Naw, thanks. Think I'll head outside, if you two don't mind, and get some work done. Early day tomorrow." Cully left the table and quietly pushed in his chair.

When he stood up, both women noticed it but Muriel was the first to say it as soon as the back screen door closed. "He's lost so much weight."

"I know, I know. His pants are hanging off him. I'm sure it's sure got nothing to do with your cooking." Muriel laughed a little at this, and her unexpected laughter gave Stella the courage to ask, "How are you doing, Mom?" Stella felt herself stumble over her own words, "I mean, you've been working so hard here and this is about two people you really love and…" Stella didn't see it coming. If she had, she'd probably have stopped talking or changed the subject.

The emotion burst out of Muriel Pedersen without any warning. She gasped as if very surprised or like she'd been shocked by someone's sudden death. Then, Stella's mother laid her head in her arms on the table and sobbed.

If Ellie had been sitting there instead of passed out in that close room right above them, she'd have probably commented, "Now you've done it, Stella. Couldn't leave well enough alone, could you?" She'd be right. Stella never could.

"Oh, Mom. I'm sorry. I never meant to…" Stella jumped out of her chair and put her arms around Muriel's bow-bent back. She pressed her cheek to her mother's hair. It smelled like lilacs. "Don't cry. It was stupid of me to ask. This has gotta be the hardest thing for you. Here. Here's a hanky." She laid her handkerchief beside Muriel's elbow, the handkerchief Ellie had embroidered with little yellow flowers with delicate green stems. As Stella stared at those bright stitches, they began to waver and blur. She couldn't help it. Stella plunked down into the chair closest to her mom, the one Cully had been sitting in, and started to bawl, too. By the time it was all done, Stella had out-cried her own mom. She felt like a baby again when Muriel ended up comforting her.

The next morning, Stella woke up to the smell of coffee—again. This was supposed to be her job, but Cully had so far beat her to it each time she stayed over. Stella got up, promising herself that, from now on when she spent the night, Cully would come into the house and find his coffee made. It would never happen, but that was her plan.

"Good morning, Cully," Stella greeted him as she walked into the kitchen holding a sleepy-looking Kristoffer.

Ellie's husband smiled and tickled his son under the chin. "Morning, you two. Sleep good?"

"I did, but I think this little one slept better than me, after his middle-of-the-night bottle, that is." Stella then asked Cully, "How about you?"

"Not bad at all." He was lying, and she wanted to tell him she knew it. Cully looked tired, eyes puffy and dark underneath, the lines in their corners deeper. But Stella went along with him, secretly fearing that he'd break down like her own mother had the evening before. The chances were as good with those equally stoic characters.

"Glad you're sleeping all right out there. Does Maurice snore?"

"Less than Ellie," he said and they both laughed. Stella had slept with Ellie for years and knew exactly what Cully was talking about. Ellie slept with her mouth wide open, and almost as soon as she'd drift off, the snoring would commence.

"Do you ever wake her up and tell her?" Stella pried, still giggling.

Cully answered, "Yeah! All the time! And every time she..."

"Gets annoyed and denies it!"

"Says it's my imagination! That's the loudest bloody imagination I've ever heard!" Cully shook his head and chuckled. "Thanks, Stell." He clamped a strong hand on her shoulder. "I needed that."

The gesture made Stella smile. "You're welcome, brother-in-law. Trust me. It was good for me, too."

Cully took a couple slices of Muriel Pedersen's baked bread covered in molasses and was out the door before Stella got dressed for the day. As soon as Stella heard his wagon wheels creaking away from the house, she got that cold feeling in her stomach again. It was fear. Fear at being left alone with Ellie, the sister she loved more than anyone. Stella wouldn't admit that she felt afraid of Ellie. She was scared, of course, that Ellie might bite into her like she did Cully. Stella promised herself that she would never let on.

It surprised Stella when Ellie got up early. Stella had just finished changing Kristoffer's diaper and was making up his bottle when Ellie came down the stairs. Stella turned from the infant, and stood up to greet her.

"Good morning, big sister. You're just in time to see your little man wide awake." Stella said this as casually as she could, as if Ellie were just fine and everything was normal.

Ellie looked over Stella's shoulder at Kristoffer lying there on his quilt, the one Ellie had made, spread out on the kitchen floor, scrubbed to shining by Birdie. The baby was hanging on for dear life to a wooden spoon. Kristoffer's mother glanced down at him and then stepped over him to fetch herself a mug of coffee, adding plenty of cream and sugar. Then, without speaking to Stella or acknowledging her own baby, Ellie headed back upstairs.

"Fine, thank you for asking. Why, yes. We both slept well," Stella muttered sarcastically as soon as she heard Ellie's footsteps in the bedroom above the kitchen. Stella caught herself talking to Ellie's retreating back like this more and more often. Kristoffer tossed the wooden spoon onto the floor and started to cry. Loudly.

"Auntie's coming, little man. Hang on a sec. There you go." Stella picked him up from the middle of the kitchen floor. "Do you miss Mommy, baby boy? Do you? I don't know about you, but I'm sick to death of Mommy." She confided this to him very quietly.

The next time Ellie came downstairs was when she heard Cully come home at suppertime. Stella felt badly about this. She thought perhaps Ellie could somehow tell Stella was annoyed with her. But Stella couldn't help how she felt, and she never treated Ellie unkindly.

Later on that evening, after baby Kristoffer was asleep and Ellie was back in her room, that's what Stella wanted to explain to Cully while they sat there on that bench under the willow tree. Stella longed to tell him that you can't help how you feel. They were shelling peas together. It was hot in the house, and it felt good to be outside getting something done. Both Stella and Cully wondered at how Ellie slept upstairs in that rising heat. As for little Kristoffer, he slept all wrapped up snug beside them in the grass. He'd be awake for another feeding before too long.

Picking up a handful of unshelled peas and dropping them into her lap, Stella asked her brother-in-law, "Cully, can you tell I'm getting owly? I mean, I'm feeling edgy. I try to hide it, but I'm not so sure it works."

Cully looked at Stella and then back to the peapod in his hand. "Maybe you should've let Mom take over tonight."

Stella sighed at this. "It's her Bridge night with the ladies. I couldn't ask her to stay. Besides, you'll bring her over first thing in the morning, right?" He nodded. "Then I'll be fine. I just don't want Ellie to think or feel...well, you know, that it's hard with her sick. I know she can't help it and if she could, she'd choose not to be sick. But it is hard, Cully. I just don't feel like myself."

He kept on shelling while Stella talked, cracking the pods and running his finger down the length of the opened green skin, forcing the peas out into the bowl. Stella stopped shelling while she talked. In the back of her mind, she considered that, of the two of them, Cully was the better pea-sheller, but she was by far the better talker.

When Cully didn't respond to what Stella was saying, she took this as his consent to keep right on talking. She'd been especially lonely during the long day. The baby seemed a little under the weather and was cranky. The last times Stella had come to stay over, Kristoffer was very content, and so she was not used to him whining and fussing for what seemed like no reason. These were the things she talked to Cully about, saying, "I don't know how my sister does it day after day. I gotta admit, it's made me think twice about marrying old Henry, that's for sure, much as I love the big lug." Stella sighed again, heavier this time and continued to share her feelings.

"I think your baby might be getting a bit of a cold. Don't worry, though. It's not bad. He can breathe all right, and I only heard him sneeze once or twice. He's a bit grumpy, though, like me. That's how I can tell he's not feeling very good. He's such a good little guy, usually.

When I was making supper, he lay there and watched me. He's very curious, isn't he? I think that means he's smart. Smart already." And she said, "Cully, today Ellie wet the bed."

Stella didn't mean to tell him. Cully stopped shelling peas but didn't look at her. Stella stammered on, trying to reassure him, "It's no big deal, really. It looked like she just forgot to wake up, you know? Maybe she was really tired and dreaming that she was using the pot, or that she'd gone to the loo. When I was a teenager, that happened to me. I remembered dreaming that I was in the outhouse and let go right there. Poor Ellie! Boy, was she ever disgusted with me! We had to get up and change the sheets in the middle of the night. Later on, we laughed about it." Her voice echoed in her own ears, rattling on, but Stella couldn't staunch the flow of the words. She didn't want silence. No more quiet. She couldn't take it. When Cully still didn't say anything, Stella went on. "Anyhow, the sheets needed washing anyway and so did Ellie. So I got the bed and her cleaned…"

"Do you ever shut up?"

Stella was stunned and then stung by his words. At first she didn't think she'd heard Cully right. She couldn't believe he'd say something like that to her and suddenly, she felt like crying. Her eyes stung and her throat constricted. There was nothing she could say so Stella picked up Kristoffer and went into the dark house alone.

— *Chapter 22* —

HOMECOMING

There was already three inches of snow. It had been on the ground since the onset of October, and it wasn't going anywhere. The Farmer's Almanac for that winter, 1935-36, predicted much snow and bitterly cold temperatures. So far, the book had been right on target. Outside Birdie Jullsen's living room window, snow rested on brown leaves with blackened edges, leaves that had missed the opportunity of September's strong winds to find the ground, remaining instead suspended between heaven and earth. The snow had settled the dust but did little to diminish the winds, winds that started at noon and blew on into the night, driving snow beneath the wooden sidewalks and into banks against house foundations.

But inside, the house was warm and all the drafty windows were clouded with turkey-smelling humidity that got too thick for the windows' smooth surfaces and finally joined forces to slide in plump, satisfied drops down to rest on dusty sills. In the kitchen, Cully sat with his sister Alice, baby Kristoffer content and babbling in her full lap. She had declined to stay overnight with Ellie for the last couple of months because of her job as a switchboard operator. Instead, Cully's sister sent meals and desserts along with Birdie every week out to the Hughenden Lake place. Alice had also baked the pumpkin pie the family would eat that afternoon.

At her stove, Birdie whisked the gravy and tended to the last of the vegetables. The turkey was done and waiting on the counter for Cully to carve it. Ellie sat alone in the living room bent over a round needlepoint featuring three plump holly berries and an equal number of pointed leaves to be stitched in two shades of green.

"Listen to her in there," said Alice. She bounced Kristoffer and he clung to her finger for balance, his eyes riveted the whole time on his grandma working at the stove. Alice leaned in toward Cully, as if she was about to tell him a secret. He held a grey whetting stone in his right hand and Birdie's largest knife in his left. Alice asked him softly, "Does she talk like that—to herself—all the time?"

Cully didn't lift his eyes from his work. "Nope. Just when you're around."

Alice didn't say anything to this. She turned away from Cully and asked, "Mom, do you need a hand?"

"You could put these," she indicated a pint Gem jar of

dilled pickles and another of beets sitting at her elbow, "in bowls and set them on the table, please." Alice stood up and, paying little attention to the knife Cully still held, plopped Kristoffer down on his father's knee. Startled, Cully dropped the stone to the tabletop where it made a hollow thunk as he held the carving knife out from his body and away from his infant son.

Alice told her brother, "Here. You hold him. He's your kid." With her back to them both, Birdie rolled her eyes as she removed the peas and carrots from direct heat.

It took a moment or two for Cully to reload, but when he did, the ammunition was deadly. "Mom?"

"Yes, dear?" Birdie replied over her shoulder.

"Bjorn Olanson still in town or did he move to Killam and marry that schoolteacher—you know, the pretty one, Daniel Anreightt's oldest?"

With a force that should've shattered the base of the beet pickle jar, Alice slammed it down onto the counter, having just removed the metal band and glass lid sealed with a thick red rubber band. A few splotches of fuchsia added a festive look to the kitchen window and to the cupboard fronts. Cully's younger sister ran from the kitchen and past Ellie to her tiny bedroom off the living room, slamming the door behind her.

Birdie sighed. "Why do you torment her so?"

Cully couldn't help it. He laughed and then Birdie couldn't help it, either.

"I can hear you!" Alice shouted from behind her bedroom door. Birdie shook her head at her daughter's expected behaviour and at her own uncontrolled laughter as she wiped beet pickle juice from the counter and off the cupboard doors. "If you don't laugh, you'll cry," Birdie Jullsen chuckled. Cully set Kristoffer gently on the floor and forked pickles from their jars into his mom's pretty glass bowls.

At the loud knock on the door, Cully said, "I'll get it." Birdie was busy scooping cranberry sauce from its pot into a serving dish.

Cully licked pickle juice from the end of his index finger, picked up Kristoffer and walked to the front door. He stopped short when he saw who was standing on the other side of the screen in the snow that drifted across the wooden step. Cully whooped his joy. "Mom! Come here!" He opened the door, and the two men stepped in, rubbing their hands together, their grinning faces burnt red by wind and winter.

Their mother, wiping her hands on a thick tea towel, stared for a second and when Birdie found her voice, she said softly, "My word." And then, "I'd given up hope."

Cully extended his hand to Denby and shook it hard as Birdie embraced Norward as if she'd never let him go. "It seems like a long time, brother," Cully told Denby.

"It's been longer lots of times." Still grasping Cully's hand, Denby nodded at the child his brother held. "He's turnin' out good."

Cully turned to Norward who had just been released from Birdie's grip, and wrapped his free arm around his waist, pulling him close. "It's good to see you brother. So good, so good." He murmured into the ragged man's shoulder. "How've you been?"

"Ain't been better than I am today. How 'bout yourself? I see you're a daddy. Good for you. That's real good." Then to Kristoffer, "Hey, handsome boy. You give your parents a hard time? Do ya?" Norward reached out a hand and tickled the infant's rounded belly with a dirty finger. Kristoffer looked scared. Then Norward asked Cully, "Whaddaya call him?"

"Kristoffer. His name's Kristoffer."

Denby pulled back from his mother's arms and Birdie, without a son to cling to, began weeping grateful tears into her dishtowel. Denby poked his head into the kitchen and asked Cully, "Where's your wife? How about Alice? Is she here?"

"Alice is in her room sulking," Birdie answered.

"What else is new?" Norward asked rhetorically.

Birdie gave him a reprimanding look and told Norward, "She'd come out if she knew it was you."

"Yeah. Right," Norward scoffed.

"Leave your boots on for a minute." Cully started to don his own winter footwear. "Come outside with me. Mom? You wanna put Kristoffer in his cradle and come with us?"

"Why? What's up?" Denby asked, doing up the buttons he'd just unfastened. Birdie placed the infant in his cradle on the kitchen floor and handed him his rattle, blue and shaped like a duck. Back in the porch she slipped on a pair of overshoes overtop her knitted house slippers. The four of them gathered on the north side of the house which sat on the street that ran one over and parallel to Main Street. There they stood huddled together like cattle in the driveway, standing close to ensure the privacy of their conversation and to withstand the cutting wind. Cully and Birdie looked at one another, neither wanting to tell the story yet wanting to allow the other an out, if either needed it. Cully spoke first.

"Ellie's been sick for a bit more than a couple months now," he told his brothers.

"Sick?" Denby pressed, "What do you mean 'sick'?"

Cully looked pleadingly at Birdie, and she picked up his cue. She reached out and laid her hand on the upper arm of Denby's too-thin winter jacket. As she talked, Birdie looked back and forth between her three sons, explaining to two, seeking confirmation from the other. "Ellie had a breakdown, boys. She hasn't been well since late August."

The two men turned to Cully and he nodded. "We were out at Czar Lake—the revival. Got Kristoffer baptized there out in the lake and that's when it set in. All of a sudden, Ellie was sure God was gonna take him—the baby—and she tried to hide him." Cully swallowed. "Now she acts like she doesn't even see him."

"Ellie's in there?" Norward motioned to the house with his thumb.

Cully and Birdie nodded simultaneously, seriously.

"Well," Norward continued, "Better go in and say hello anyway." The other three followed Norward into the house. "And get some of that turkey. I'm pretty damn sick of prison food, you can bet."

Back in the cramped porch, Cully made eye contact with Norward as they were both standing up from removing their boots. Birdie and Denby were already in the kitchen, shrugging off their coats. "So why'd they let you out?" Cully asked his brother.

"That guy from Estevan, he fessed up last week." Norward lifted his shoulders to show it was no big deal, not to him, anyway. "They were gettin' close to figurin' out it wasn't me. Would've on their own if he hadn't turned himself in. This was just easier for 'em—and probably faster for me."

Cully told him, "I prayed for you, prayed in front of two hundred people asking for the Lord to get you out."

Norward smiled his crooked smile. "Thanks, brother. But, like I say, I think it might've happened anyway. I appreciate the thought, though." He stuck his nose out in an exaggerated way and breathed in deep. "God! Smells like heaven in here!"

Cully let his brother know, "I'm gonna thank God for letting you out."

Norward looked at Cully, surprised. From in front of the stove, Birdie listened to their conversation. She heard Norward say, "Thank Him if you want to. It's no skin off my arse."

Denby missed this exchange as he'd already found his way to Ellie, bringing little Kristoffer with him, tucked under his arm like a parcel. He barely recognized the woman sitting there on his mother's brocade chesterfield. For an instant, Denby scanned the room for someone else, anyone else, who looked more like his Ellie. She'd lost a lot of weight. He'd always liked hips on a woman, like she used to have. But now Ellie's legs were thin like boys' legs beneath her shabby housedress. Ellie owned a better dress than that. Denby knew she did so why wasn't Ellie dressed up for Thanksgiving dinner? The Ellie he knew would rather be caught dead than to leave the house with hair uncombed and wearing her house clothes. And he told her so.

"Ellie." She looked up from her needlepoint. No recognition. "What're you wearing? Is that your *housedress*? You didn't have anything else to wear to Thanksgiving dinner? You didn't even try to dress decent, did you?" At the sound of his tone more than Denby's voice, three faces appeared crammed in the archway joining the kitchen and the living room. Across the cluttered space, Alice's bedroom door opened a crack, one wide enough to allow her to spy. With a jolt of joy, Alice realized that Norward had been freed from jail in Edmonton. But for now, she opted to stay in her room and listen to what more Denby had to say to crazy Ellie. He didn't sound angry. Not exactly. Instead, Denby seemed amazed, disbelieving, like he was attempting to convince both Ellie and himself that this couldn't be her. Not really. Not ever.

Ellie blinked at him and said, "The Lord took my baby." She started to return her steady gaze to the needlepoint work she held. Denby snatched the project from her and threw it so that it bounced off the wall near Alice's door. Then he held Kristoffer so close to Ellie's face that she couldn't see anything else.

He told her, his words slow and loud, deliberate, "This is *your baby*, Ellie. He needs you. God gave you this baby and this little baby *needs you*—more than anyone else. Where the hell are you? Huh? Where are you, Ellie?"

Denby thrust Kristoffer at her and this time, her arms came out to hold him, stiff but accepting.

Ellie fixated on Kristoffer's soft pink face, his reddish-blond eyelashes and bluish eyes quickly turning to green. A tear escaped from Ellie's eye and glided down her cheek to land on Kristoffer's sleeper with its bleached sailboats and minute buttons. The infant's eyes widened. "God took my baby," Ellie repeated.

Now Denby was down on his knees in front of her, hands on both her shoulders. "Listen to me, Ellie. *This is your baby*. This baby is Kristoffer!"

"From the lake?" Ellie asked him.

At first, Denby didn't understand and Birdie saw this. "Czar Lake!" she hissed in a harsh whisper from the doorway. "Czar Lake. The baptism."

"Yes! Yes!" Denby shouted at her, almost triumphantly. "This is the baby from the lake—the one you had baptized. Ellie, this is Kristoffer, your baby."

None of them had thought to bring up that late August evening to Ellie. Or, if they had, they'd quickly dismissed it as something too upsetting, something which would inevitably result in disaster. They worried that remembering it may set her off, cause Ellie to hurt herself or them, or maybe even sink her deeper into that dark emotional pit. Her family didn't think it would help. But Denby didn't think at all. He hadn't been at the lake, hadn't been bitten, hadn't washed and wrung Ellie's urine-soaked bed sheets. All Denby saw was that a woman who moved him greatly had somehow disappeared from his life, and now he was desperate to get her back.

Ellie's eyes, ringed with black, grew wide. "My baby?"

Denby hadn't let go of her shoulders, hadn't stood up from where he knelt down in front of her. "Yes. Your baby. Kristoffer," he said.

The figures in the doorway, all of them holding their breath, leaned forward a little, craning to see Ellie's expression, straining to hear her speak.

"Then God didn't take him?" she asked slowly, with wonder.

"No!" Denby shook his head to emphasize the truth. "No. He's been safe and sound all along." Looking into her eyes, Denby told her, "I don't think God ever wanted Kristoffer, Ellie. I just think maybe you went a little cuckoo. It happens." He heard his mother's sharp intake of breath from somewhere behind him. Denby continued on anyway, as if the two of them, he and Ellie, were all alone. "It happens all the time. More than you'd think."

"It does?" she asked him.

He brought his hands down from Ellie's shoulders to rest there in his lap. Before her and in that position, Denby looked like a supplicant child. "Why, sure. I seen it lots. Life is tough. It breaks people, Ellie." He looked suddenly sad. "Sometimes they mend, sometimes they don't."

There was a pause while Ellie thought about this and then said, "Well, when was the last time he was fed? And he feels wet to me." Ellie looked around the room. "Could one of you fetch me his diaper bag? Culvar?"

In the doorway, the three of them stood straight and across the living room, Alice's bedroom door opened wider. Cully seemed frozen for a moment but soon shook himself loose and brought from out behind the chesterfield a bulky bag that Stella had stuffed with diapers and pins, a change of clothes, a bottle.

He handed this to his wife, and Ellie took it from him with a curt, "Thank you."

Birdie took in the scene before her, evaluating it and finally allowed herself to smile. She turned back to the stove, telling Norward, "C'mon. You can wash up and then set the table, please." Then, "Alice! Bring those chairs from out of your room. Your brothers are home!"

Thanksgiving dinner felt surreal to everyone there—except for Ellie, that is. To her the event seemed to be just one more task on her list. After dinner, she checked Kristoffer's diaper, reaching under him where he lay awake and happy in his cradle. Then she, Birdie, Cully and Alice cleaned up that heap of dishes as the warm kitchen cooled, shadowy in the descending evening.

When the dishes were done, in Birdie's bedroom in front of that full-length mirror, Ellie brushed her hair until it shone. She noticed how much of it came out in Birdie's hairbrush, and she also looked with dismay at the dress she wore. To no avail, Ellie tugged at its hem and smoothed the thin fabric over her thighs, slimmer now and that, at least, made her happy. But her bloodshot eyes, pale skin and those extra years that had crept into her face and flesh were obvious. This made her miserable.

Alone with herself and with God no longer in pursuit, Ellie dropped to the edge of Birdie's bed. The soft mattress sank under her weight. Ellie curled up on her side with her back to the door and wept silently until she fell into the easiest, saddest sleep she'd had in a long, long time.

Cully left the kitchen table and his slice of pumpkin pie (which they had saved until after the mess was tidied) to check on Ellie who'd been in Birdie's bedroom awhile. Now he sat back down in his chair next to Norward.

"She all right in there?" Denby asked.

"She's sound asleep," Cully answered.

Norward had a thought and shared it. "What if she wakes up the same as before? Maybe her bein' herself is temporary. What then?"

Alice had an answer. "We ought to wake her, you know, before she has the chance to go crazy again." She'd sprung halfway up out of her chair when Birdie's outstretched hand interrupted her upward motion with enough force to sit her back down. Hard.

"No. Leave her be." Birdie looked at Cully. "If she wakes up fine, that will be good, more than we hoped for. We can thank the Lord and pray that things return to normal. If she doesn't wake up fine, we'll just keep on doing what we've been doing. That's it. It's all we can do." Birdie's tone left no room for discussion.

With Ellie away from the table, Cully had the opportunity to ask Denby, "What made you talk to her like that?"

Denby shrugged and said, "I missed her—and I suppose it made me mad to see her that way. Wished I could've been around to help. You know, if there's more… if she gets sick again or if she's slow gettin' better, I can stay around and lend a hand. I don't mind."

"Thanks for the offer, brother. I know you mean it,"

Cully's words were cautious, rimmed with a little of that old familiar suspicion.

Norward added, "He's good with crazy people, Denby is. That's why him and me's such good pals. Ain't it?" He gently punched Denby's upper arm and grinned. "I don't know what the rest of you is gonna do, but I'm gonna go stretch out on Mom's chesterfield. That's about the best Thanksgiving meal I ever ate." No one said so, but everyone agreed.

— *Chapter 23* —

THE OFFER

Ellie didn't get sick again. Days regained their structure under the command of her lists, and Kristoffer grew plump and curious under her renewed interest, which shone on him like the sun. Stella brought Ellie a dress she'd found at a swap and Birdie brought cinnamon buns and orange peach halves shining in quart sealers. With Ellie better, Muriel Pedersen stayed at home and Cully Jullsen slept on the chesterfield. He told Ellie it was easier with baby Kristoffer there in the bedroom and needing Ellie's attention at all hours, for him to just sleep downstairs, out of the way and uninterrupted. She didn't protest his decision, didn't suggest that their son begin sleeping in the nursery, as planned, only locked her husband in that cold gaze he'd grown used to and told him, "Where you sleep is up to you."

Shortly after Thanksgiving, a letter had arrived at Birdie's from Darlene Sinclair. This letter wasn't kept secret from Ellie. Ellie had made it clear that if Cully was supporting this woman and her child when the two of them—Ellie and Cully—could barely survive, then she wanted to know about it. The letter told Cully that Stan Sinclair's parents had fired Darlene from her job at the hotel restaurant. Did he think there was there any work for her in Hughenden? Was there anywhere to live? Could she and Thomas come live there?

Throughout the rest of October, Cully worked shorter hours at the Whitlocks' but took on extra work at the Swendsens'. Their farm sat on the half-section northeast of the Whitlock place and Cully helped to rebuild the corrals and barn they'd lost to a fire late in September. In the months following his wife's sudden recovery, Cully went to work early and came home late to eat his supper alone by lantern light. And when he had time, Denby came out from Hughenden for coffee on those long cold afternoons when the sun seemed to always be rising or going down, never sitting high in the sky for hours like it did in June. Cully didn't ask about Denby's visits and Ellie never mentioned them.

"Gingersnaps. Look good." Denby took one cookie from the china plate Cully had given Ellie on their first anniversary. He dipped the cookie into his coffee and asked her, "Whatcha been up to today?"

Ellie put the coffee back on the stovetop, bent to retrieve another piece of wood from the box and placed it on that steady-burning fire. Then Ellie pulled out the chair directly across from Denby and sat down with relief. "Laundry day today. I'm glad you came over. It gives me an excuse to take a break."

Denby looked alarmed. "Don't let me interrupt your work. I can help you with it, if you want," he offered quickly.

Ellie laughed as easily as she had before the tent revival at Czar Lake. "No, no. That's fine, brother-in-law. It's good you're here or I wouldn't sit down. You're doing me a favour. Really, you are." Her hand alighted on the back of his wrist, which lay loosely and close to her across the tabletop, like he was reaching for her. Denby turned his wrist and grabbed her hand quickly.

She wore the dress Stella had given her, a gift to celebrate Ellie's returned health. It was brighter than anything she would've picked out for herself, but Stella's taste had always leaned toward brighter fabrics. Red it was, red with little yellow flowers and tied at the waist with a neat bow at the small of her back. She hadn't been wearing this dress while she washed and wrung clothes in the back porch. Instead, she'd changed after she put Kristoffer down for his afternoon nap, thinking that if Denby was going to visit, this would be the time. She'd been right.

Denby stared at Ellie hard, holding her hand. Waiting. When she blushed, he let go and said, "You're looking better. Got your hair cut?"

Ellie touched her hair where it ended in a straight bob. Stella had talked her into this style. "It's a nice change," she said, her hand hot and tingling where Denby had held it. She trusted her sister with scissors and so allowed Stella to cut her hair a little differently this time. Denby told her, "I like it. It suits you." He took another cookie and silence fell between them. It wasn't the usual relaxed silence. This one was full of tension, tight like a wire and hot like fire. Mercifully, it was broken by Kristoffer's insistent cry from upstairs.

Ellie leapt up. "He's had a cold, poor little guy. He always wakes up crying. Want to come see him?"

"Sure." Denby downed the rest of his coffee and followed her.

"Shhh, baby boy. It's all right. Mommy's coming!" Ellie called while ascending the stairs. Denby was close behind, watching the sway of those little yellow flowers before him. He felt the heat in his face, felt the heat in his body. Ellie had gained weight and regained her figure following her illness. She had hips again.

In the bedroom, the baby's howls were deafening. Ellie spoke softly to Kristoffer, taking him in her arms and holding him close. His cheeks were slightly flushed and around his tiny nostrils, there were circles of crust where his nose had run and dried. As she rocked him, her body moving smoothly back and forth, Denby set a large hand on the baby's crown, like a blessing. Kristoffer gasped jaggedly twice and then stopped crying.

"Hey!" Ellie laughed her surprised laugh. It sounded well-oiled and easy. "Whatever you did, it worked. I'm going to feed him. I don't think he'll sleep otherwise."

Denby commented, "It's chilly up here. He's got that nice little quilt, but is he gonna get cold? You want me to bring his cradle down, closer to the stove?"

She said. "That's a good idea."

At the table, Ellie fed Kristoffer his bottle and rocked him gently. Denby poured them more coffee, washed up the few dishes in the basin, sat down and ate two more cookies. With the rubber nipple still in his mouth and a dribble of formula on his cheek, the baby fell asleep in his mother's arms. Carefully, Ellie lifted the bottle from Kristoffer's unconscious grip, set it on the table, shifting her hold on him. Denby got up and moved the cradle closer so that Ellie could lay Kristoffer in his bed without having to stand up.

"He's gonna be too big for that cradle soon. Sure is growin'." Denby stated, standing there with his hand on the back of Ellie's chair, both of them looking at the baby. "Bet he missed you when you were…when you weren't feeling good. You're a good mom to him, Ellie. A real good mom."

Denby moved his hand to rest it on her shoulder. He left it there too long, and Ellie stood up. Denby turned toward the porch. "Well, I oughta hit the road before Cu— before it gets dark. Man, it's getting dark early now. You notice that?"

She answered quickly, the relief in her voice evident, her words coming too close together. "Yes, yes. I really have. Gets darker earlier and earlier these days. It's kind of depressing. But I like Christmas and that's something to look forward to. Will you and Norward be staying in Hughenden until then?"

Denby grinned. "Don't see why not."

She stood in the doorway and waited while he got his boots and coat on, chatting about the weather some more and about the chores that awaited her upon his departure.

"Well, take care, Ellie. I'll see you two later on."

Denby turned to leave, and Ellie grabbed his coat sleeve, pulling him back. It was the invitation he'd been waiting for ever since Thanksgiving Sunday and Ellie's recovery. Denby held her hard, both arms wrapped tightly around her. Ellie tilted her head to look up at him and Denby kissed her very deeply for a very long time.

Cognizant of the fact of Cully's eminent arrival, Denby finally released her and put on his hat, asking Ellie as he did, "What are we gonna do, sweet one?"

Ellie smiled wistfully and shrugged, saying, "I don't know what we can do, Denby."

"Come with me. Marry me," Denby told her his solution.

"It's not that simple," she reminded him, adding, "You know I wish it was."

Denby's suspicion gathered itself up and put on a disguise of truth, of certainty. "It's easy for them," he told Ellie.

"For who?" she wanted to know.

"Your husband and Darlene Sinclair," Denby said, forming his hunch into a solid thing.

"What do you mean?" Ellie pressed for details. She, too, held the same suspicions but, mostly, she trusted Cully. Ellie would have to be given a very good reason not to. Denby wanted so much to give her that reason.

Denby shrugged. "I don't know. I just notice that my

brother hasn't been around a whole lot lately."

"Culvar's working two jobs," Ellie heard herself defending her husband.

"He's got to, to support two households," Denby stated and touched Ellie's shoulder. She started to cry. "Ellie, please don't. I'm sorry. Please come with me."

"Come with you where, brother?" Cully asked, his voice deep and icy behind Denby. Denby shoved past Cully without looking at him or speaking to him and walked out into the dusk. Cully pulled the door shut behind his brother and glared at Ellie while she swiped at her tears. He didn't ask her what had gone on between the two of them. He didn't want to know. Cully pushed past Ellie, and she heard his footfall on the stairs.

Ellie sniffled and began stirring around the clothes she'd left soaking in the washtub while she and Denby had visited. A few moments later, when she knew Denby would be striding down that long driveway, she ran to the living room window, pushed the lace curtain aside and peered out. Cully's wife lifted her hand to touch the cold glass that lay between her and Denby's retreating figure, dark against the white of winter.

Later that evening, when Ellie had finished up the laundry, she sat by the stove cradling Kristoffer while he finished his bottle. Cully came downstairs, poured himself a cup of coffee and sat down beside her at the table. The air between them was taut with friction and neither of them, husband nor wife, said anything. It seemed there was nothing to say. When he'd finished his coffee and a gingersnap, Cully put his mug in the basin, put on his coat and hat. He walked out the back door, telling Ellie, "I'm going to stay in town tonight. I'll be back tomorrow for supper."

* * *

It had been a cold journey from the house on Hughenden Lake. The wind had switched directions since the afternoon and cut viciously into him as he made his way into town. Now as he knocked softly on her door, his hands were numb with cold. It wasn't very late; still he hoped he wouldn't wake the child if he were already in bed. Darlene Sinclair opened the flimsy screen door to him, pausing a moment, a shadow of surprise moving across her features, and stepped aside so that he could come in. "Hello stranger," she said, her voice guarded. "I thought we were through. What are you doing here?"

He pulled off his boots and set them by the door. Inside, he slung his coat over a chair and sat down at the tiny table she'd pushed right up against the wall, centred under the uncurtained window.

"Thomas asleep?" he asked her, looking around the little house as if trying to spot the boy.

She smiled and told him, "I hope so. He's been in the bedroom for almost half an hour, and I haven't heard a peep." The young brunette, looking older than her years these days, moved to the low kitchen counter and filled the dented coffeepot with water and ground coffee, setting it on the wood burning range. Leaving him sitting at her table, Darlene went to the back door and brought in two logs from the pile by the door—the wood he'd bought for her last week—even though they were through. With a creak and a crackle, she opened the stove door and placed the firewood inside to rest on the glowing hot embers.

"Come sit down," he told her. "You're making me nervous with all your pacing."

She laughed lightly. "I'm coming. Just didn't want us to freeze to death in here. I swear, these walls are made of paper." She reached out and knocked on the wall, right beneath the window, for emphasis. "How've you been? You look rough."

He sighed and confessed, "It's been a tough day. Saw my brother and it didn't go well."

"Where'd you see him? Here in town?"

"No, back at the house," he told her, then said, "That coffee smells like it's getting close to ready."

Darlene got up and brought two chipped mugs down from where they hung on a couple of hooks mounted crookedly over the sink. "How's Ellie?" Gone was her light tone, replaced by something heavier now. She brought the coffee over and he thanked her. No gingersnaps here. Nothing sweet at all.

* * *

"Hello! Mom? Alice? Anybody home?" he called from the tiny entry at the front of the house. He was glad to be there after finding his way into Hughenden in the dark with that unrelenting wind tearing at him every step of the way.

"Hi! Come on in," Birdie said, coming down the flight

of stairs into her living room and on into the kitchen. "Cold out tonight. You'd better get in here and warm up."

"I'll do that." He'd already hung his coat up in the porch, slapping his hat overtop of it.

"Have you eaten? There's some supper left on the counter. I haven't even put it away yet. I think it's still fairly warm," Birdie invited her son to help himself.

"Where's Alice? Not working, is she?" Alice didn't usually work evening shifts, although sometimes she covered for others.

Birdie sat herself down heavily at her round kitchen table while her son heaped his plate with carrots, boiled potatoes and pork sausages.

"No," she told him. "She's babysitting for Glenda and Ellis again tonight." Birdie shrugged. "She seems to like their children, and I know for certain your sister likes the extra little bit of money she earns."

"You heard from Norward lately?" He talked with his mouth full, but instead of scolding him, Birdie merely appreciated his robust appetite.

Birdie nodded and toyed with a paper serviette as she spoke, "He popped in the other day on his way to start work in Hardisty."

"It's good to have him back—out of jail, especially," he chuckled and shook his head. "That was a close one."

His mother had to shake her head, too, and agree, "Yes, that was close." She reached out and patted his arm. "It's good to have all my boys around, safe and sound.

— *Chapter 24* —

MAKING ENDS MEET

Darlene Sinclair sat in the dimly lit two room shack located directly behind the blacksmith shop one street east of Hughenden's main street. Its interior walls were drab and streaked with grease. A single forty watt bulb hung from a wire in the ceiling in the centre of the room, illuminating the shabby furnishings that had come with the place. An old chesterfield was positioned close to the little wood burning stove, McClary's cheapest model, and a wooden crate sat at its other end. A place to set your coffee cup.

* * *

The tiny kitchen table sat right under this room's only window, and it was here that Darlene felt the night wind come right into the house. The filthy window might have been open for the amount of freezing air it let in. The sink had running water and crooked privy leaned out in the backyard, close enough to the house to be convenient.

The second room adjoined this one. It was the bedroom she shared with Thomas, her blue-eyed son. He would be two next month. They shared the three quarter bed, and Darlene hoped that by the New Year they would have some sort of mattress for it. For now, though, they made due with the bare steel frame. They used blankets that Birdie had brought them from the United Church's basement to lay overtop the cold metal springs. Thomas slept in the bedroom now, and as his mother sat in the next room, she considered how this was one of the best homes she'd ever had. Darlene had the Jullsens to thank for that.

Occasionally, she still caught herself missing Stan. His absence left a hollow space. Sometimes that emptiness felt like relief, and sometimes it felt like loneliness. Sometimes it was a confused combination of the two. For all her life, he'd been the only love Darlene had ever known—until Cully Jullsen, that is. When she met Cully in that northern Alberta tie camp, there was a kindness about him that she had never experienced. There was the respect he showed her, as if just because she was a human being, Darlene deserved it. Respect was one thing Stan had withheld from her. With Stan Sinclair gone, Darlene didn't miss that about him.

Darlene had been waiting for his knock on her door again this evening. Although they hadn't planned it, he'd stayed at her house the night before, both of them curled around each other on the chesterfield. He'd pulled it out from the wall to place it directly in front of the stove so that they could be warmer. Darlene didn't want to get too used to his warmth. His heart belonged to another. At least Stan had been hers and hers alone. And that, at least, was something.

Finally, Darlene heard his footfall on the back step, heard his hand turn the rusted latch on the screen door. He gave a short rap on the exterior door then opened it up. He knew that Darlene would be expecting him.

"Hello!" he called, and she came to the door to greet him with a quick, hesitant kiss on the cheek. Gently, he returned her kiss, kissing her softly on the mouth. "I brought you a little more wood," he murmured into her hair.

Darlene pulled back from him and gave him a smile. "What would I do without you?"

They came into the main room of the shack, and Darlene fetched the coffeepot from the stovetop and filled their mugs at the table. The two of them sat under that drafty window and sipped their coffee.

"You work at the school today?" he wanted to know. He had left his coat on, and she wore a heavy cardigan, worn and two sizes too large for her.

She nodded and told him, "I did. Your sister looked after Thomas while I cleaned. I picked him up around suppertime."

"Are you liking the work all right?"

"I suppose," Darlene shrugged. "I mean, yes, it's good. It's just different, is all, and I'm still learning my way around it." She laughed that laugh, the one he loved, like frost glittering in the air, reflected in the rays of the bright sun. "I really have to get faster at it. The mopping takes me forever, and I know there's a better way to clean those blackboards. I'll get it figured out, though." She paused and studied his face a moment before asking, "How 'bout you, Mr. Jullsen? What kind of a day did you have?"

He shrugged and drank deeply from his coffee mug. "Had words with my brother."

"Words about what?" Darlene knew, but she wanted to hear it and so she pressed.

"About you, about Ellie, about everything," He set his empty cup back down on the table. "I don't really want to talk about it." He placed his cool hands on either side of her face and said, "I just want to be here and look at you."

Darlene smiled. "That's just fine, Mr. Jullsen. That's just fine by me."

The couple moved to the chesterfield and hastily made love there by the wood burning stove. When it was over, he sat up. Even with the fire in the stove snapping away, it was chilly. Darlene pulled her cardigan from the floor, put it on and laid her head in his bare lap. He still wore his work shirt, but the top three buttons were undone. As she lay there, he ran his fingers through her wavy hair and spoke gently, saying, "You know I can't do this anymore."

"I know," she told him. "I understand."

After he left, she walked out into the stinging snow and darkness to the privy. On her way back inside, Darlene scooped up an armload of firewood and dropped the logs by the stove. She turned then and locked the door on the night outside. Neither of them had seen the man at the window, the one who waited for his opportunity to enact revenge.

Softly, she opened the door to the bedroom where Thomas lay sleeping, his breathing deep and steady. Carefully, quietly she found her nightgown and brought it out to the other room so she could change in front of the stove for bed. She left her socks on and wore her cardigan over her night clothes. Darlene flicked the light switch off, and in the bedroom crawled in beside Thomas who slept closest to the wall and under a mountain of quilts.

— *Chapter 25* —

TRAGEDY

Birdie opened the door to Stewart Ames, letting him into her cozy house, ice crystals drifting on the air behind him. At the look on the RCMP officer's face, something inside Birdie, something like fear froze solid and then instantly shattered at Stewart Ames's news. "I'm sorry to tell you, ma'am. Denby is dead." He had more news, and so before Birdie could collapse and while she was still standing, Constable Ames asked,

The RCMP officer should have instructed Birdie to sit down, should have guided her into a chair, but he hadn't had much experience announcing violent death. She fainted immediately, and before Constable Ames could catch her, Birdie struck her head on the shiny linoleum floor.

— *Chapter 26* —

STAN'S PLAN

"It's time you did something more to help support this family," Stan yelled the words at his daughter, not because he was angry but because he was drunk. Darlene was unpacking the crates of supplies her father had brought with him from Meadowlake. As he yelled, she placed all the provisions she would need on the shelves and in the cupboards of the stark shack. There were enough supplies here to feed the CNR tie gang for a couple of months at least. Darlene could stretch them out longer, if she had to.

Stan, wanting more of his daughter's attention, grabbed her by the shoulder and spun her around. Startled, she dropped the can of baking powder she was hold-

hit the floor with a loud thunk. The can rolled uneven floor of the cook shack and stopped at Thomas who was sitting on the floor playing with a bowl. He started to wail which did nothing to ease the tension.

"Can you shut that fuckin' kid of yours up!" Stan fairly screamed.

"Not if you're scaring him," Darlene told him, and she picked Thomas up, hushing him gently. She turned to her father and told him, "I'll put him in the cabin, and then you can yell all you want."

When Darlene returned, Stan was seated on the chair in the corner by the large grill. He seemed calmer and so she hopped up on the counter across from him, ready to hear him out. "Say what you have to say, but make it quick," Darlene said. "Thomas is in there alone." She meant in her sleeping quarters, the smallest cabin on the property, the space Darlene shared with her son and, often, but not always, her father. Already, she had constructed wooden railings around the perimeter of one of the low built-in wooden beds. This made the cot into a crib for Thomas. A safe, confining space.

His features slightly softened, Stan continued to share his plan. "Since you got this kid anyway and it's likely Jullsen's, you might as well get some benefit from the situation."

"How do you mean?" Darlene eyed him skeptically, thinking that the low lighting in the cook shack along with his reddish beard made Stan look like the scheming fox he was.

"I mean, *financially*." The word was emphasized by irritation. So much for Stan's calm. It was long gone. Darlene didn't respond, just kept watching him and listening. What else was there to do? "I want you to go to Hughenden. Take the train there and look up any Jullsens you can find. Forsbie told me they're all livin' around there."

"And tell them what?" she wanted to know.

"Tell 'em I'm dead and you're destitute. Give 'em some sob story and tell 'em you need money." Stan scoffed and said, "That bastard'll give it to you—if he feels as guilty as he should."

"So you want me to lie to them?" Darlene clarified. "To get their money?"

Stan stood up directly in front of his daughter, a threatening stance, one with which she was well-acquainted. "That's exactly what I want you to do. You got a problem with it?"

* * *

At Birdie's kitchen table, Cully set his fork down on his plate, his breakfast half-eaten and cold. Without emotion he said, "I'm sorry for your troubles, Darlene, and sorry I couldn't have been there for you. I didn't know." Then he said, "I thought the boy might have your dad's eyes."

Denby had fetched Cully and brought him back to that tiny house west of Main Street. His brother had wanted to run and, really, Denby didn't blame him. He would've wanted to run, too, the difference being that Denby would've run faster. Denby asked Darlene Sinclair, "Where are you living now?" He knew from what Cully had told him that he and Darlene had met in northern Alberta, but he didn't know if that was still where the young woman was working.

"No, I'm in Meadowlake now cooking at the hotel there," she told him, while Cully and Birdie listened. Birdie smiled encouragingly, and Cully avoided making eye contact with Darlene. Fortunately, Denby kept the conversation light and easy. He was eating a second helping of bacon and eggs.

"How do you like that—cooking in a hotel instead of a tie camp?" Denby asked amiably, shoving another strip of bacon into his mouth.

"Oh, I like it better," Darlene admitted. "It's warmer and cleaner, and the people I cook for are a lot nicer." Tentatively, she smiled at Denby, big, blonde, beautiful Denby. "It's good work and I'm glad to have it."

Denby liked the way this girl smiled at him. It warmed him through and through. He could definitely see what had drawn Cully to Darlene. It was no mystery. She was good looking, with a fair complexion offset by dark hair and to Denby, at least, she seemed accessible. He could sense that Darlene would do what you wanted her to do and be what you needed her to be. To some men, Denby included, this was a very attractive feature. When she left that afternoon, Denby arranged to ride with her.

By the time that train rumbled into Saskatoon, Denby felt like he knew Darlene Sinclair like the back of his own hand. On that long ride through the moon-illuminated prairie landscape, Darlene described her relationship with her father, talked about her love for Thomas, and her fear of Stan. She told Denby, "Now that he's dead, I feel free for the first time in my life."

Darlene felt so free, in fact, that when Denby invited her to stay with him for one night in Saskatoon, she stayed for two.

* * *

When the train pulled into the Meadowlake station, Stan Sinclair was there to meet his daughter. "Where the fuck have you been? I was expectin' you yesterday. Old Mrs. Fallswent agreed to look after your kid for one more day, and it's a good thing, too, because I didn't know where the hell his mother was."

"How is Thomas? Is he all right? Does he like Mrs. Fallswent?" Darlene asked, sounding exhausted and anxious because she was both of these things.

Stan scoffed at her questions, "Like you fuckin' care." He grabbed Darlene's little suitcase from her grasp and commanded her, "Just get in the wagon. We'll go pick him up and get you back to work. The guys are gettin' sick of the leftover stew and biscuits you made for them. You can make something fresh today, give the guys something to look forward to." As Stan clucked to his horse, and the wagon began to roll in the direction of the thick forest and the desolate tie camp buried deep within it, Darlene Sinclair wondered just what it was that she had to look forward to.

Later that day, long after the sun had gone down and after she'd cooked supper and fed the crew, Darlene was doing the dishes and waiting for the bread dough to rise where it sat on a shelf over the still-warm grill. She had made the gang sausages and boiled potatoes along with white cake and strong coffee for dessert. Stan entered the cook shack and took his place on the only chair in the building. He braced his elbows on his knees and interlaced his fingers, looking at Darlene the way he did when he wanted something from her.

"So," Stan began, "Your story. D'you think the hicks bought it?"

Darlene wiped her hands on her heavy apron, picked up a clean tea towel and started to dry a large bowl. She nodded at her father, "They believed me."

Stan pressed, "You're sure?"

Darlene smiled sadly. "Yes, I'm sure."

* * *

For nearly a full year, money came from Cully Jullsen every month and at first, Stan Sinclair was gleeful. "Money for nothin'," he'd trumpet and hold up the envelope, telling Darlene, "This is good business. We should get you knocked up again." The amounts varied, depending on what Cully and Ellie could afford each month. Stan was happiest with the larger payments and seemed to be satisfied even with the smallest; he seemed to understand the sacrifices that the Jullsens would make to keep this money coming, the money he would drink away in the Meadowlake Hotel tavern. He had planned to make Cully Jullsen's life more difficult and the plan worked. This fact alone was almost enough to keep Stan happy. At first. But as time wore on and the novelty of "money for nothing" wore off, Stan no longer took any joy from the child support payments Cully sent.

Darlene didn't think much about leaving. She didn't have time. Her long days were filled with the steady routine of preparing food and caring for Thomas. Two or three times a week, mostly after he'd been drinking, Darlene was awakened by her father's insistently groping hands. She let him do what he was inclined to so that she could get back to sleep, sleep she needed to allow her to keep up with the demands that each new sunrise brought with it.

Sometimes after he'd been drinking, Stan would beat her up instead. The beatings were quick, and although they happened regularly, Darlene never learned to expect them nor did she grow accustomed to the violence. She hoped her body would adjust, would adapt to the pain. It didn't and each time, although this now seemed redundant, new bruises would form and fresh blood would stain her clothes, her pillow, the cabin floor. If any of the men suspected her abuse, none mentioned it. None of them approached Darlene, either, although she was a beautiful girl, friendly and easy to talk to. They just left her alone.

Stan had never laid a hand on Thomas—until that night, the night before the morning during which Darlene wrote that pleading letter she sent to be mailed the same day: *Was there any work for her in Hughenden? Was there anywhere to live? Could she and Thomas come live there?* The child had awoken during one of Stan's late night visits. That night, Stan was enraged, all fists and fury, accusations and acid. Darlene was already on the hard floor doubled over and clutching her stomach where Stan had kicked her. Terrified, Thomas stood up in his enclosed bed, gripped the wooden rails that held him in and screamed a blood-curdling scream.

Often when Stan was drinking, he would begin to slowly stir his anger toward Darlene as he sipped. Then, as his belly filled with liquor, he'd add more malice and a touch more resentment to his anger and let it simmer. Then, when Stan got back to camp and had his daughter alone, it would boil over. There was some relief in this for him. Remorse, too, certainly, but the beatings soothed him more than pained him. And so they continued.

He had never planned to strike the child. In fact, as time passed, Stan had begun to feel an unexpected love for the boy. The child's actions, his expressions, the set of his eyes and the shape of his nose caused Stan to feel a connection, a bond that in his heart, he couldn't deny to himself. But to the world, deny it he did. Vehemently so.

Without thinking and before he was aware, Stan's open palm connected with Thomas's head with enough force to send the boy's body over the side of his homemade crib. He screeched his pain and alarm. The sheer volume of the scream caused Stan to reach down, pick the boy up by his hair and slap him again. Thomas stilled in his grandfather's grip and gently now, ever so gently, Stan picked Thomas up and eased his bleeding, unconscious form back into bed while Darlene watched in horrified silence from where she lay on the floor. Stan walked out of the cabin and closed the door softly behind him.

— *Chapter 27* —

ESCAPE

Stan was gone from camp the following day. Before Thomas was awake, Darlene hastily wrote the letter in the cabin, the early morning light watery through the dirty little window. She planned to send the letter to town with Leif. He'd be leaving right away. Darlene walked down the snowy path and caught him saddling one of the camp's horses. He was speaking softly to the gelding and didn't hear Darlene's approach. When she touched him on the shoulder, Leif gave a little jump, nearly imperceptible.

"Morning," she greeted him. She'd pulled her hat down low and her scarf up high. "Can you post this when you get to town?" Darlene paused before adding, "It's urgent."

Avoiding her blackened eyes that confirmed the letter's urgency, Leif promised he'd post it as his first errand when he arrived in Meadowlake.

In the morning before she sent the letter with Leif, Darlene cleaned and bandaged the cut on Thomas's head and gave him a spoonful of aspirin mixed with sugar and water for the pain. She brought some of their bedding into the cook shack, and in a corner under a counter, she made a bed for Thomas. Other times when he had been ill, she'd done this same thing so that she could be close to her son in case he needed her. Now it was she who was sick, the deep burning hatred in her stomach making her want to vomit. Instead, Darlene cooked and baked all day and into the night, swallowing her own pain along with a couple shots of whiskey to help ease it. It was hard to take a deep breath, and it just about killed her to cough. Still, Darlene moved about the camp kitchen gingerly but efficiently. She would make enough food to see the gang through a couple days the same as she'd done before she'd gone to Hughenden.

Shortly before supper time, Leif stuck his head in the cook shack doorway and told Darlene, "I posted your letter soon as I got to town, miss." She thanked the wiry young man, and he touched the brim of his hat, letting the door slam shut as he left. He wouldn't even set foot in the little building where Stan Sinclair's daughter prepared the meals for the camp workers.

Darlene knew where Stan kept his money, knew where he had it hidden behind that loose board above the window frame in his own sleeping cabin. One night, Stan was lovey-dovey, drunk as a skunk and telling her, "Look, sweetie, if anything ever happens to me, I need you to know that I got some money stashed away." He burped close to her face and it stunk, but this was useful information and Darlene listened carefully. She remembered exactly what he had told her.

By the time the men were finished eating, the dishes were long done and Thomas was tucked into bed, Stan hadn't yet returned to camp. Darlene wasn't surprised. She didn't expect him back for a day or two yet. By then, she and Thomas would be long gone. Under the cover of the coal black forest night, Darlene found her way to Stan's cabin. The door was padlocked. That's why she brought along the axe. From a nearby cabin, Darlene heard the distinct and familiar voices of several of the workers. One of them was strumming his guitar while the others played cards.

Stan's daughter winced has she gripped the wooden axe handle and swung it at the door, aiming for a spot right by the padlock. Through the night air, the sound of the axe's contact with the door and the splintering of wood was sharp, piercing. Darlene stood in the snow before Stan's cabin and listened. Both the men's voices and the guitar had fallen silent. She heard the door of the cardplayers' cabin creak open and heard footsteps squeak in the snow. The inky figure of a man rounded the building and stopped to look at her, this bruised apparition staring wildly and holding an axe across her chest.

The figure lifted a hand in greeting. "Oh, hey Darlene." She didn't answer, and the man turned and walked back the way he'd come. Darlene heard the door close and immediately, the music and card-playing resumed. Trying to ignore the fire in her ribs, she kicked in Stan's door and the shattered wood barely holding it shut fell away. The money was right where Stan said it would be. There wasn't much. Not enough to start a new life but enough to get she and her son on a train and put them up in a hotel for a few nights. Enough to escape. Right now, that was all she needed.

* * *

Cully was able to rent the little house—no more than a shack, really— behind the blacksmith's east of Main Street. The old bachelor who had lived alone there for years and years finally died that fall. With no family to claim the old man's earthly possessions, the place came furnished and in need of a good cleaning. But Darlene Sinclair wasn't afraid of work, and Cully knew that she would have that place dunged-out in no time. The wind blew right through that dingy structure—four walls and a breeze—and he didn't like the idea of a child living there. Cully told himself that the house behind the blacksmith shop was a temporary home for Darlene and the boy, shelter until they could get established and find something better. Darlene could move in at the beginning of the month.

On their way to Hughenden, Darlene and Thomas stayed one night in The Battlefords and another in Saskatoon. They came around the longer way to avoid lengthy waits in either station. It was best to stick to the main lines and ride during the day, spending the nights in soft beds where their bodies could heal. Upon arriving in Hughenden, Darlene and Thomas stayed four days and nights at the Hughenden Hotel across from the train station. Birdie would have taken them in, but Denby was sleeping on her chesterfield these days again, as his work had run dry for now. But jobs always came up, here and there, that Denby would do. Then, he'd rent a room at the boarding house at the top of Main Street. For the time being, though, he was on his mother's chesterfield.

In the past, Denby would often stay out at the Hughenden Lake house when work was spotty. He'd lend a capable hand to Ellie and Cully, and they liked his company. Until now, it seemed. Birdie tried to get to the bottom of the apparent "falling out" between the two brothers, but neither of them was talking about it. Birdie was a patient woman. These things happened in families. She decided to stop asking and, eventually, they would tell her what conspired between them—or not. She would deal with it either way.

Darlene was touched by Birdie's kind invitation and assured her, "Thomas and I'll be fine in the hotel. We'll see it as a little vacation, won't we?" She smiled down at Thomas, whose hand she held tightly. He wore a big cap pulled down low and from under it, young Thomas looked unsure of this vacation idea.

Cully and Birdie were there in the cold morning air to meet them. Immediately as Darlene stepped off the train with Thomas in tow, she delved right into the self-recriminating story she'd prepared to explain the cuts and bruises that were still very evident. Cully and Birdie met them on the platform and listened as Cully carried the Sinclair's luggage. Darlene told them that she had tripped and fallen down half a flight of stairs in the Meadowlake Hotel with Thomas asleep in her arms.

"I feel so foolish," she went on. "I knew the carpet was loose on those steep stairs, and I just wasn't paying enough attention. I'd had a big fight with Stan's folks and was upset. Thank goodness that same carpet I tripped on was there to cushion our fall!"

"And that neither of you were killed," Cully added with a wry grin as he hauled the battered suitcases across Railway Avenue to the hotel. Darlene carried that same small case that she'd brought with her to Hughenden a year ago. Cully asked Darlene, surveying her belongings. "This all you got?"

Birdie noted with some alarm, "It isn't much." Then, turning to her son, asked, "Are there linens over there at the little house?"

He shook his head. "If there are they should be taken out back and burnt. I don't think the old guy's bedding had been washed for at least a decade."

Birdie laid a reassuring hand on Darlene's shoulder and informed her, "There are lots of extra blankets and towels in the church basement for those who need them. Nothing fancy, but we'll get you some of those for now. I've got a neighbour girl who can patch them up new as can be, if they need it." Wisely, Birdie didn't offer either Ellie's or Stella's help with this venture. The sisters sat together that morning out at the Hughenden Lake place, drinking coffee and dunking cookies and feeling both annoyed by Cully's sense of responsibility and yet proud of him, as well.

Upstairs in the hotel, Cully set Darlene's suitcases down just inside the door. Birdie and Cully offered to buy the weary travelers something to eat in the restaurant downstairs, but Darlene told them, "Thank you, but we're both exhausted. I think Thomas and me will have a little nap and go downstairs for lunch a bit later." In an easy gesture, one born of habit, Darlene pulled off Thomas's hat and Birdie gasped. She was shocked at the size of the fresh-looking bloodstain on the bandage around his head, but more than that, she was shocked by Thomas's unfamiliar features. From his turned-up pug nose to his mass of wavy dark hair, he didn't resemble any Jullsen she'd ever seen.

"But you'll come for supper?" Birdie asked.

Darlene smiled. "Of course, Mrs. Jullsen. That'd be swell."

— *Chapter 28* —

STAN SINCLAIR

He was wild with rage when Leif confessed, "They left yesterday, both her and the kid." The young man steeled himself against Stan's reaction. Stan raised his fist and Leif flinched, but the boss man stopped himself, bringing his hands down by his sides and clenching his fists until his knuckles turned white.

"Who let them go?" Stan bellowed inches from Leif's face.

Leif loathed the trembling he heard in his own voice when he replied, "No one let them, boss. They must've left late in the night or real early in the morning. No one saw them go."

Stan whirled around, away from Leif and back to his

own cabin. He flung aside what wood was left hanging from the hinges and barged into the dim room, his boots echoing on the cold planks. The big man roared when he saw the two by four—the one from above the window frame—lying on the floor by his bed, the hollow space above the window empty. Stan snatched up that piece of wood from the cold cabin floor and gave it a mighty throw through the window. Shards of glass flew outward and left their shattered impressions in the snow.

On the edge of his narrow cot, Stan sat down slowly and cradled his head in his massive hands. Darlene's father calmed himself and soothed his anger by promising in a low, sure voice, "I'm gonna kill that little bitch."

Stan still had a bit of money left from the stash he taken when he took off to Saskatoon for a couple of days. After one of those violent incidents during which she made him so angry, it always helped Stan to get away from Darlene. He couldn't think clearly when she was around. Something about her mere presence just set him off. She knew it, too. He could tell by her cheeky backtalk and the way his daughter always looked at him as if he were stupid or like she felt sorry for him. It made him so mad that he wanted to tear Darlene's head off.

Stan Sinclair felt around under his plaid jacket until he found his shirt pocket. From there he extracted a few crumpled bills and some change. This he laid on the red wool blanket beside him where he counted it out. The total wasn't enough to get him on a train and buy him a night's lodging. He figured he'd need at least that much, and a bit more for meals, too. Darlene's dad would have to wait until the Canadian National Railway came through with his pay. That was all right, he decided. A little time to plan his strategy would be good. With more time between then and now, Stan reckoned that he would also have the element of surprise on his side. *Let her get snuggled in safe and sound in Hughenden with some guy. The cow won't know what hit her.*

With the matter settled in his mind, Stan buttoned his coat and went to find a board to nail over that busted window.

— *Chapter 29* —

DENBY AND DARLENE

"You're back," Denby said, standing at Darlene's back door, the wind blowing the snowflakes straight across behind him through the cold night yard. From where she stood on the threshold, he grabbed Darlene and pulled her close, kissing her hard. When the kiss was over, she told him, "I missed you."

"In that case, can I come in out of the cold?" he asked, grinning. Then she laughed that laugh, the one that was like balm to his burn.

Darlene stepped back into the house, telling him, "Come in, Mr. Jullsen." She gave a playful little bow. "You're always real welcome here."

"How welcome is that?" he teased and kissed her

again. Denby removed his hat, and she took it from him and hung it from a good-sized nail hammered into the wall near the back door. He glanced quickly around the room, taking it in, the dinginess, the grease-streaked walls, the odor hiding under the scent of bleach.

When Denby didn't comment on her home, Darlene touched her hair and quickly said, "I know it's not much, this place, but it's just temporary, I'm sure." She wasn't sure, not at all.

"Aw, it'll do for now, all right," Denby said. "A resourceful gal like you will have this house real livable in no time. And then," he shrugged, "Who knows? Probably something better." But probably not. Denby sat down at the table, and she sat across from him. In the darkness at the back door he hadn't noticed, but now in the shadowy light cast by the single bulb, Denby could see the yellow remains of dark circles around Darlene's eyes. He recognized these as bruises from a hard hit across the bridge of her nose.

When Denby winced with empathy, she realized he'd already spotted her fading injuries. Darlene started spilling the same fiction to him as she had to his mother and brother—the Meadowlake Hotel, the stairs, the carpet, the fall—but Denby stared at her disbelievingly. Still, he let Darlene finish spinning her yarn, and when she was done he asked, "Who beat you? Was it those folks of Stan's? The ones you worked for? A customer? Who was it, Darlene?" he pressed her and she began to cry.

Denby reached out and gave her forearm a reassuring squeeze. "You're right," Darlene confessed through her tears. "When they fired me, I demanded my pay. Stan's father, well, he stepped right up to me, but I looked him square in the eye and said 'You owe me that money and now you refuse to pay me? You want me to leave here penniless?'"

Denby wanted to know, "What did he say to that, Stan's father?"

"He said 'That's exactly what I want you to do. You got a problem with it?' And then he hit me." Darlene, resting her elbows on the table, sobbed into her hands. After a few moments, Denby reached out and took a piece of Darlene's hair between his fingertips. He told her, "I'm sorry that happened to you," adding, "Did you ever get your money?"

Darlene brought her hands down from over her face and said, "Yes. After he beat me, Stan's father paid me, a little more than what I was owed, actually."

"The bastard felt guilty," Denby deduced.

"He should," Darlene said and smiled weakly, her eyes, besides being bruised, were now red and puffy. "Here," she offered, "I'll make us some coffee." While Darlene fetched the battered pot down from the shelf over the counter, Denby walked over to the stove, opened it up and put in the one piece of wood lying there on the floor.

"Got more wood?" he asked.

She looked over her shoulder and answered, "There might be a couple more logs under the snow outside by the back door. But I think that's it."

Denby moved across the cramped room and wrapped his arms around Darlene's waist while she scooped coffee directly into the old pot. He buried his face in her hair, saying, "I'll round up some more wood for you tomorrow. For tonight, I'll just keep you warm myself. How does that sound?"

Darlene laughed that honey-coated laugh. "That sounds sweet, Mr. Jullsen. Very sweet." She moved out of his embrace and pulled her old brown cardigan closer around her body against the chill. "I'm gonna check on Thomas, and I'll bring us some blankets from in there." Darlene indicated the chesterfield and told him, "We'll sleep there by the stove tonight."

For Darlene Sinclair, the days in Hughenden fell into an easy rhythm. Working here was certainly no harder than working in the tie camps. She had started out cleaning the school every late afternoon and on into the evening. Her work was thorough and she did it quickly, and so the principal, Mr. Stein, informed Darlene that the bank was looking for a janitor, as well. He smiled and looked at her over his wire framed glasses. "I could put in a good word for you, if you like, Mrs. Sinclair." One time, during her first week of work at the school, he had brushed up against her in a doorway, grazing her breast with his hand as he did. From that time on, Darlene kept her distance from Mr. Stein, but she would accept his reference.

Since she came to the village, Darlene Sinclair had begun wearing a thin gold band on her left hand. If the ring or the young mother's single status came up in conversation, Stan's daughter simply explained that she'd been widowed for a year now and was trying to make it on her own the best she could. It was actually Birdie's idea to tell the story about the dead husband, the tragic accident. "People will talk no matter what, dear," Denby's mother counseled her. "But the less ammunition you give them to shoot you down, the better." Years and years ago, the ring had belonged to Birdie's aunt.

When Denby wasn't sleeping on Birdie's chesterfield, he was sleeping on Darlene's. Around a sleeping Thomas, Darlene would wrap the warmest blankets Birdie had retrieved from the donation pile in the United Church basement. Under the rest of those blankets, she would lie with Denby until early morning. He was careful to be gone by the time Thomas woke. One night, though, Darlene's son had a nightmare that sent him howling out into the other room to find his mother partly dressed and asleep in Denby's arms. Thomas's mother scooped him up and slept the rest of the night in their drafty bedroom, cradling his solid little body. Thomas never asked about Denby and so Darlene never felt the need to explain.

This casual routine with Denby continued night after night for a few weeks after Darlene arrived in Hughenden. Darlene was satisfied with the warmth of Denby's smile and the warmth of his body on those cold early winter nights. And Darlene served as Denby's best distraction from his attraction to Ellie.

On the train to Saskatoon a year or more before, Denby had told Stan's daughter about his love for Cully's wife. So it seemed, in that way, that Darlene Sinclair and Denby Jullsen were in the same boat. It seemed that they were each in love—one with a husband and the other with a wife—who were married to each other. This love was pointless. Futile. And so was the fleeting affection Darlene and Denby currently shared. She understood that Denby wouldn't share her chesterfield by the McClary for very much longer. Each evening he came around, she felt that the distance between them had increased. Drifting apart. She liked that analogy because it laid blame on no one but the tide or the current, and who could control those?

That night, Denby added two more logs to the firebox and poked at the cinders to reawaken the flame. They'd pulled the chesterfield out from the wall, each lifting an end, and placed it directly in front of the wood burning stove. Darlene waited for him under the quilts and blankets, wearing nothing but her old cardigan. He laughed kindly when he crawled in beside her, awkward on the narrow frame of this well-used piece of furniture. Denby asked her, "Why are you still wearing this?" He toyed with one of the fasteners on her sweater.

Darlene swatted his shoulder and said, "To keep my shoulders warm!" She summoned a slight shudder to emphasize her point. "It's freezing in here!"

"Isn't it itchy?"

"It's warm—that's all I care about," Darlene stated and laid her head on his bare chest.

Denby gently cupped her head with his hand, ruffling her hair a little, and said, "I'm warm. Do you care about me?"

From where she lay, Darlene smiled up at him. "You know I do."

They made love, and Darlene couldn't help but think

how quickly such a tender, intimate act had become so familiar and comforting, like supper cooking or the smell of coffee in the morning. Darlene understood that for her, there would be more fried potatoes on the stovetop and more coffee to greet her nostrils, but there would be no more Denby after this. After this, the comfort he gave would be gone.

When it was over, they held onto each other and each knew it was goodbye, but it was Denby who said it: "You know I can't do this anymore."

* * *

It wasn't difficult to find out where she lived and worked. It was a small town and if you engaged folks in conversation and listened hard enough to what they had to say, the information you needed would come to you. Stan knew this, and so he hung around the hotel restaurant for a bit after breakfast, chatting with the locals. He broached the subject of single mothers and how there seemed to be more women raising kids on their own than when he was a boy. "Sure is a hard thing," he said, shaking his head, still holding his empty coffee cup, noticing a chip on its rim. This imperfection annoyed him as he waited for the response he wanted.

The man across the table from him had invited Stan to join him for breakfast. "Horace Williamson," he'd introduced himself. He was due to start work at one of the lumberyards in town, but he had half an hour or so to kill before then.

"Richard Redenberg. Good to meet you." The men had shaken hands and then talked about the weather and the economy. It was mostly what everyone talked about—that and other people, of course.

Now Horace Williamson also shook his head and made a tsk-tsk sound with his tongue against his teeth, indicating his agreement with Richard Redenberg. "Yep," he said. "It's sad all right. Children need a father."

Stan tried harder to pry this clam open, asking, "You got kids of yer own?" And then falsely divulged to Horace, "The wife and I, we got two, a girl and a boy. Can't imagine them with just one of us, 'specially the missus." He kept pressing down this path, his patience already waning. "Awful hard for a woman to support a family." To speed the process, Stan took a risk and added, "Anyone around here like that?" To Stan's ears, the direct question seemed conspicuous, but if Horace thought so, he never let on.

A man unaccustomed to the delicious taste of gossip, Horace straightened his posture and glanced to his left and to his right, before leaning forward to share with the man he knew as Richard Redenberg, "Yeah. A woman came to town a few weeks back." Horace paused here to let out a whistle, soft and low. "Man, is she a looker. Got a kid, little curly haired one. Real cute."

Stan's heart started to pound, but over his emotion, he managed to keep his voice even. "You gotta wonder how she can afford to live on her own. Is she in a boarding house, or does she have a place of her own for her and the boy?"

Horace Williamson, enjoying the coffee and the conversation, missed the fact that he hadn't mentioned a son, only a child. If he'd caught that detail, the tiny slip that Stan made, Horace might have shut up and gone to work a little earlier that day. If only he'd known.

"Yeah, it's gotta be tough," Horace agreed. "She's living in a house—not much more than a shed—behind the blacksmith's. She found a job right away, so that's something."

Stan struggled to control his rising rage, the bile he tasted in his throat, when he asked, "Oh yeah. Where'd she find work around here?"

"Over at the school. She's the new janitor."

Richard Redenberg thanked Horace for his fine company and bought him breakfast. It was the least he could do.

— *Chapter 30* —

MURDER

After breakfast with Horace, Stan Sinclair had lain in his room at the Hughenden Hotel all day, sleeping on and off, and drinking from the bottle of whiskey he'd brought with him from Meadowlake. The train's whistle and his own thoughts were company enough. When nightfall finally descended, Darlene's father put on his belt and before securing the buckle, slid the loop of the stiff hide knife sheath over top. He'd taken care to sharpen the bone handle knife before boarding the train at the Meadowlake station and now it lay on the edge of the washstand, its blade gleaming and ready. Stan picked up the weapon, felt its heft in his palm, and put it in its sheath.

Under the cover of darkness provided by an overcast

night sky, Stan Sinclair headed east along Railway Avenue. There was no one on the street, yet he pulled his hat down low and stayed close to the buildings along the boardwalk. Although he had polished off half the bottle of whiskey that day, his senses were heightened tonight and he felt sharp as a tack. Or a knife blade. This is what Stan had come here to do; killing his daughter had been his primary focus for the last long weeks. What happened after didn't matter much.

Stan smelled the coal fire of the blacksmith shop before he spotted the building itself. He followed the familiar, acrid scent and made tracks toward it. Alongside the building ran a narrow laneway into which Stan ducked quickly. At the end of the laneway was the house, almost right in front of him, just as Horace Williamson had described it.

A window—Stan assumed it was the kitchen window—glowed amber, barely piercing the drapery of the cloudy night. Stan used that pale light as his guide and didn't stop until he stood right beside it, his burly frame pressed up against the tarpaper exterior of Darlene's home. From outside, he could barely make out soft conversation taking place inside. He couldn't be seen. The element of surprise was the main thing Stan had on his side. Slowly, cautiously, Stan turned his head and peered into the starkly furnished house.

A burst of fire shot through him, radiating its rageful heat throughout his body. There, in that room, were two figures lying close together, obviously embracing. Only their heads and shoulders were visible to Stan over the chesterfield's low back. Stan couldn't stop himself from uttering, "That fuckin' little whore." He yearned to burst through that door and slit them open right now, right where they lay. However, Darlene's father realized that patience—not haste—would see him reach his goal. He would wait until he had each one alone. This night, Stan broadened his ambitions and decided that under the circumstances, he would derive twice the satisfaction from killing two.

Snow crunched softly beneath his heavy boots and down the street, a dog barked. As Stan waited, a man called out in the distance and a woman answered. A horse whinnied in the street somewhere, the clip-clop of its hooves sounding loud and seeming close to Stan's ear. After a short while, Stan heard more motion from inside the house and heard the back door open. He darted around to the front of the shack, the side that faced the rear of the blacksmith shop and listened for Denby's steps in the snow. Denby was heading east, making his way toward Railway Avenue from the back of Darlene's rented house. Stan peeked around the corner just in time to see Denby's retreating shadow disappear behind a building as he turned sharply right. Stealthily, Stan Sinclair followed.

* * *

Denby walked along Railway Avenue, the night like a cloak around him, Darlene weighing heavy on his heart. He would miss her, but how could he keep on like this when she'd cared so deeply for Cully? It just wasn't right, and neither was this rift that had formed between he and his brother. As much as he'd miss Darlene, her wavy hair and soft skin, he missed his brother more. And, of course, he missed Ellie. Tonight, before it got too late and before he lost his nerve, Denby would head out to the house on Hughenden Lake and do his best to make amends with the both of them. It was about time.

As he left the smattering of lights that dotted the town behind him, Denby was aware of the frozen road under his boots and of the icy air that pierced his clothing. He was not aware, however, of the man that followed in the shadows, intentionally matching the pace of his steps to Denby's, speeding up only along the grassy roadside where the sound of his footfall was muted.

It was a long walk, and Denby walked quickly, keeping to the middle of the road and away from the ditches on either side. Even though his pace was fast and his stride was long and his intentions were good as he walked out to the Hughenden Lake house, Stan Sinclair easily caught up to Denby and slit his throat from behind. The last thing Denby heard was the sudden scrabble of dirt and gravel as Stan moved in quick and close.

Realizing that it would be in his future best interests to hide Denby's body as quickly as possible, Stan Sinclair turned a slow circle in the centre of the wide gravel road, looking all around him, searching amid the thick shadows for a solution. Then, it caught his eye. A ways off the road and near a stand of trees, Stan could barely make out a darker, deeper shadow in the shape of an old car body. He placed his hands under Denby's armpits and dragged his lifeless form from the road in the direction of the abandoned car. As he pulled Denby along, Stan Sinclair wondered vaguely why dead bodies seemed to weigh so much more than live ones. When he finally reached the car, Stan dropped Denby for a moment while he wrenched a back door, stiff with rust, open. Then, in a motion that took a lot of strength, Stan heaved Denby Jullsen into the back of the vehicle, leaving him sit there as if he were a passenger content to ride along.

Stan turned to leave but then remembered to search Denby's pockets. What good was money to a dead man? Money that would help Stan find his way back to Meadowlake in the morning, after he'd finished with Darlene. Stan felt around each pocket and removed Denby's wallet. It held some change and bills. Not bad. In another pocket, he found a scrap of paper. Holding it up, Stan tried to read the words through the gloom. Eventually, he made them out: Denby Jullsen, Hughenden. Stan tucked the paper back into Denby's jacket pocket, slammed the car door shut and walked back to the road, not giving Denby another thought. He didn't know that the paper was left there after Denby had picked his jacket up from the tailor's on Main Street last week. He didn't know, either, that Denby was going to ease the hearts and minds of both Ellie and Cully, if only he'd made it to their home on Hughenden Lake. If Stan Sinclair had known any of this, he surely would have killed Denby anyway.

* * *

Back outside of Darlene's ramshackle dwelling, Stan tried the back door. He expected it would be locked and it was, so he moved around to the kitchen window beneath which he'd hidden no more than a couple of hours earlier. He placed his big hands at the base of the frame and, although it was slightly frozen to the sill, Stan managed to raise the window. After his success in opening it, Stan lowered the window again, slowly and softly. From by the back door, he retrieved a piece of firewood that he used to prop open Darlene's kitchen window, allowing him to pull himself up and into the window frame. Once there, he carefully removed the log and tossed it out into the snow behind him in one fluid motion.

The window was a tight squeeze, but Stan took his time and held his breath, drawing it inward and holding it there until he was through. He ended up lying on his belly on his daughter's wobbly table which trembled under his weight. Darlene's father sat up on top of the tiny table, turned around and gently, silently, lowered the window pane. As he lowered himself from tabletop to floor, Stan noted that it was barely warmer inside the house than it had been outside.

In preparation, he pulled open his coat and removed the bone handle knife from its sheath. It wasn't any warmer but it sure was darker in Darlene's house than it had been outside. As Stan took a tentative step, his boot's cold sole echoed on the floor. He sat down on the closest of the two kitchen chairs and pulled off his boots. In his stocking feet, he found Darlene sleeping deeply in the next room, the only other room in the house. With precision, he placed his knife under her chin and with one swift stroke, he let his daughter's blood run free. Stan then listened for the boy and peered through the gloom to see if he, too, was in the bed. There was no sound of breathing and no sign of the child. Having done what he'd come to do, Stan left the house and headed back the way he came, back toward the Hughenden Hotel.

* * *

The Hughenden Record, November 27, 1935— Hardisty RCMP reported that the body of Denby Jullsen of Hughenden was discovered late on the afternoon of Sunday, November 24, in an abandoned vehicle south of Hughenden. The non-operational vehicle was located in a field off of Highway 13. The body was discovered by James W. Nillsen who had been hunting in the area. Mr. Nillsen became suspicious when he spotted several magpies flying in and out of the open windows of an abandoned car near where he was tracking deer.

Mr. Nillsen told *The Record*, "The birds caught my attention. When I walked toward the old car, I right away saw someone propped up in the backseat." The body of Denby Jullsen was identified by a slip of paper in his jacket pocket that read *Denby Jullsen, Hughenden*. There was no other identification found on the body.

The Record also reports that in the late morning hours of Tuesday, November 26, the body of 25-year-old Darlene Sinclair of Meadowlake, Saskatchewan was found in her Hughenden home by local RCMP. Hughenden Central

School Principal, Mr. Stein, reported Mrs. Sinclair missing when she failed to complete her duties as janitor the Monday prior to the gruesome discovery. Constable Stewart Ames accompanied Principal Stein to the residence of Mrs. Sinclair. There, the two men entered the house by force and found Mrs. Sinclair's murdered body in her bed. Mrs. Sinclair's son was discovered hiding in the bed beside his mother's body. The boy was dehydrated and hungry but otherwise unharmed.

— *Chapter 31* —

HOME

Ellie started at one end of the row and Stella at the other. When they met in the middle, Ellie would empty her apron full of pods into the basin that Stella threw her peas into. This year, for a change, the peapods were nice and fat. The rain they'd got in mid-July had quenched the soil and coaxed the vegetables along. On that day, as soon as the rain had begun, Cully suggested they listen to it fall in the barn where each drop would sound staccato as it pelted the tin roof and leapt back up again. Ellie and Cully each scooped up one of their boys and off they sprinted, laughing through the welcome rain, the boys thrilled to be bouncing along in their parents' arms. Really, they were too big to be carried and they knew it. That's why they loved it so much.

This early August afternoon, while the women tended the garden, Cully and Henry sat on a bench in the shade cast by the house. In a tangle at their feet lay the harnesses they were supposed to be mending. Instead, though, Henry held baby Rosa—named after Henry's grandmother—cooing to her and watching her smile. Her Uncle Cully commented, "She's getting big, that one."

Henry replied, more to Rosa than to his bother-in-law, "Yes, she is, isn't she? Sweet little baby girl." He tickled her tummy and at this, Rosa laughed.

Cully leaned against the house wall, sipping lemonade from a jar and keeping an eye on his own two boys as they ran around the yard between the willow tree and the garden plot.

"Thomas!" Cully called. "Slow down, let Kristoffer catch you before he topples over." Then as a reminder, "You're twice his size."

Thomas didn't argue and slowed down at the sound of his father's voice. "Sorry, Pa." Three-year-old Kristoffer wrapped his chubby arms around his brother's thighs and cried jubilantly, "I got you, Tom! I got you!"

The older boy ruffled the younger one's hair, an imitation of how Cully playfully ruffled Thomas's. He told his little brother, "You sure do, Kris. Why, you're pretty fast."

"I know," Kristoffer admitted proudly before demanding, "Now you catch me!"

"Girls!" Cully called to Ellie and Stella in the garden. They both looked up from their work. "Want some lemonade?"

Ellie called back, "If you're bringing it out, then yes."

"Yes, please!" Stella sang out.

Ellie told Stella, "Let's just finish up this row and be done with it for today."

"Let's have the boys do the shelling. What do you think?" Stella meant the grown boys, not the little ones, and her sister understood this.

Ellie laughed and wiped the sweat from her brow with the front of her apron. "I think it's an excellent idea."

In the shade of the willow tree, Cully had spread that old wool blanket out on the ground and had brought from the house the pitcher of lemonade and some more jars. The sisters came across the lawn from the garden, Thomas and Kristoffer running circles around them like puppies. Stella set the enamel basin, full to the brim with peas, in the grass next to the bench on which her husband sat, telling him, "Here you go, honey. This'll keep you busy and out of trouble."

Henry smiled at Stella and grabbed her hand, swinging it back and forth slowly. A tender gesture. "I thought it was *your* job to keep me out of trouble." At the nearness of her mother, Rosa lifted her arms to Stella and Stella picked her up off Henry's lap.

"Hello, baby girl," Stella cooed to her. "Would you like to sit in the shade with Auntie and me?" Stella strode to the blanket under the full spreading branches that held the red birdhouse Ellie loved. Ellie, propped up against the rough tree trunk, was already sipping her lemonade. Stella plopped Rosa down and sat cross-legged across from her sister.

"Here," Cully said, handing Stella a jelly jar of lemonade.

"I think we oughta leave for Mom's in half an hour or so. What do you think, El?"

"What time is Alice's mystery fiancé supposed to arrive?" she asked. Alice had recently gotten engaged, but only Birdie had met the fellow. Tonight, everyone else would meet him—even Norward would be there, home from working. Maybe home for good this time, maybe not. Who could tell with Norward?

Cully replied, "Around six."

This from Stella: "I think we should all get there a bit early so that when Alice's sweetheart walks in, he feels really intimidated." Ellie swatted her arm and laughed, telling her sister, "You're terrible, you know that, don't you?"

Stella shrugged and said simply, "I do."

Although it had been their original plan to have the men shell the peas, all four adults, along with Thomas eating more peas than he put in his bowl, worked to get the chore done before leaving for Birdie's house in Hughenden. Even before the shelling was complete, Cully was already harnessing Maurice to the wagon and Ellie was scrubbing her sons' faces and hands clean at the washbasin she'd set out by the back door.

"We should bring these peas over to Birdie's, to have with supper." Stella mentioned this to her sister as she brought Ellie's largest bowl to her, the one she usually mixed bread dough in, now brimming with peas.

Ellie agreed, "At least half of them, for certain."

The summer sun was still high in the sky as the wagon lumbered down the deeply rutted path that led out to the road from the house on Hughenden Lake. An August breeze blew across the sweltering parkland, almost taking Thomas's cap with it, on its never-ending trek into the future. All around the family, birds flew through the sky and perched in trees and on low bushes along the roadside. Far beneath the wagon's slowly turning wheels, worms and insects tunneled their way through the soil, and slowly, ever so slowly, taking longer than the length of human lives, the rocks and shells in the soil eroded, finally generating more soil. And under some of this soil covered now by concrete on the other side of Hughenden Lake, lay the remains of Denby Jullsen. Long before those rocks and shells far beneath Cully's wagon wheels had dissolved into dirt, everyone headed to Birdie's that sunny summer afternoon, would eventually join him.

ABOUT THE AUTHOR

Lori Knutson is the author of three previous books. When she's not writing, Lori teaches elementary school. She lives in Hughenden with her husband, Doug.

CPSIA information can be obtained at www.ICGtesting.com
Printed in the USA
LVOW10s0235250614

391502LV00004B/16/P